THE JOKER

By the same author

A Sisters' Tale
The Last Honeymoon

THE JOKER

Shelley Weiner

Constable · London

First published in Great Britain 1993
by Constable and Company Ltd,
3, The Lanchesters, 162 Fulham Palace Road,
London W6 9ER
Copyright © 1993 Shelley Weiner
ISBN 0 09 4719705
Set in Linotron 11pt Sabon by
CentraCet Limited, Cambridge
Printed in Great Britain by
St Edmundsbury Press Limited
Bury St Edumunds, Suffolk

A CIP catalogue record for this book
is available from the British Library

For Nicole and Stephen

1

When I came into the world, they counted my fingers and they counted my toes. But no one could tot up my hidden asset: a built-in compendium of jokes. After they'd smacked my bottom, I looked around and screwed up my eyes and then, instead of screaming, I laughed and laughed and laughed.

A born comic, that's me. Hardly in the silver spoon league, I admit. Not even fun, a lot of the time. Not nearly as exciting as being endowed with sex appeal like Cousin Lou-Anne, or a mathematical mind like Cousin Norman. But, unfortunately, I didn't have a choice. It happened like this:

You know the old Jewish belief that babes in the womb possess knowledge of the entire Torah and all its teachings? It is said that God (in his infinite wisdom) saves us from boring one another to death by sending down an angel to slap us on the mouth as we take our first breath. Thanks to him, we forget the lot. Most of us do, anyway.

What occurred in my case, you see, was that some clown had replaced the holy books with *A Million and One of the World's Funniest Quips* and then failed to deliver the heavenly knock-out blow. Which was how I emerged as the only neonate ever to include a *bon mot* with her first guffaw. My delivery, I must say, had room for improvement. But my timing, even then, was excellent.

It was almost as good as it would be a few decades later when I came to the punchline of my life's biggest joke: the one about the woman whose husband died laughing. I'll bet you haven't heard that one. Talk about tall stories and enormous protagonists . . .

There he was, poor old Geoffrey, sitting quietly with a gun in his hand. A gun with a bullet that was meant for me, his wife. His larger-than-life wife. Yes – the bullet was mine as surely as if it had been inscribed with my name. If it were possible to fit 'Doreen Bartholomew-Cooper' on to a single bullet.

Probably not. Which is why I'm still around to tell a tale that started – well, with Adam and Eve really. But I'll spare you the first few thousand years and skip the generational vicissitudes that followed all the enthusiastic begettings of the Bible. And the scattering of seed and the ceding of land and age-old questions, like who was chosen and who was saved and who died on the cross and who was burnt in the ovens and what the hell it meant anyway.

Instead, I'll keep it simple and begin in a small thoroughfare in Cape Town called Gladys Street. My first gurgles of mirth had been thoroughly burped away and, after that, the first sound I remember was their voices. Those miserable bloody voices.

To think that some babies are received with gleeful adoration and Mother Goose rhymes. I was swaddled with anxiety, almost smothered with gloom. Quite honestly, if I hadn't been able to see the funny side, I might well have succumbed to the first ever case of terminal reactive postnatal depression. Being me, however, I found it hard to keep a straight face.

'Is she smiling, Molly?' he would ask, frowning worriedly. 'Do you think she could possibly be smiling?'

'Neh. Go on with you, Sam.'

Her dismissive scorn made my stomach turn, even then.

'You don't know what you're talking about. Babies don't smile until they're five, six weeks old, and Doreen's been with us only ten days. It's wind, Sam. That's what everyone says. From too much milk. Believe you me, the child doesn't stop drinking from morning till night. I'm warning you, Sam, she's draining me dry. Honestly and truly. Soon there won't be anything left of me . . .'

'But Molly – she *is* smiling. I'm almost sure she is.'

He knew. I knew he knew. Sam Markowitz suspected right from the start that his daughter expressed far more than the pain of acid indigestion with her twitching mouth and the intermittent grimaces that puckered her already plump cheeks. He would probably have recognized most of my unfunnier lines from his own store of well-worn quips. The ones he would recount compulsively at any opportunity, irritating everyone – except me. Even then, if the motor co-ordination had been up to it, I'd have liked to have given him a reassuring wink. Instead, I had to satisfy myself with yet another fierce drag on my mother's weary nipple. The left one this time. Different tit, same flavour. It was getting boring.

'I don't know what they want from me, Sam,' Molly would say in her highest, most plaintive voice. 'Your family. Ada and Joe. Aunty Naomi. Reuven and Mathilda. Mathilda especially. As if we haven't suffered enough already . . .'

'Shh. Don't upset yourself, Molly.'

He made his usual soothing sounds as I tightened my gums round her nipple. A tried and tested device to distract. Along the lines of 'If you've gone and bumped your head, get someone to step on your toe.' It usually worked.

'Oi! The child is killing me!' Temporary distraction – until, after a moment, Molly sighed deeply with the pain of remembered humiliation. 'Do you know what your cousin Mathilda said to me today, Sam? Have you any idea?'

'No . . .?'

'She saw me at the butcher's. Buying a couple of chops for our supper. Only a couple, Sam. Just for a change. "Molly!" she says in a shocked voice, looking from me to the chops and back. "I'm surprised at you. With the price of lamb being what it is, not even Reuven and I are *indulging* these days. Are you sure you ought to . . .?" Tell me, Sam, what was I to say? Especially when we have to be grateful to them for supporting us. Go on – tell me what you'd have said?'

'I'm – not sure.'

I would gladly have come up with a suggestion if I'd been able to. Sucking and slurping with unrelenting intensity, I regretted deeply that my verbal skills were so normal. There was this great old joke that had come to mind. The one about the beggar who's been given a small hand-out by a rich man and is later seen by his benefactor to be scoffing smoked salmon.

'Is that what you took my money for?' demands the rich man. 'Surely you shouldn't be spending it on such a luxury?'

'And why not?' asks the beggar, smacking his lips and wiping his mouth. 'When I haven't any money, then naturally I *can't* eat smoked salmon. Now, when I have a bit of money, you're telling me I *mustn't* eat smoked salmon. So tell me when you think a poor man will get to eat smoked salmon?'

When indeed? I took a large swig of milk and wondered whether I'd ever get to eat smoked salmon. And Molly's left nipple slipped out of my mouth as I hiccuped and gurgled my amusement. Right from the start, I took immoderate pleasure in my own jokes. Which was quite fortunate, really. It didn't take long to discover that life would provide me with few other sources of enjoyment.

'Look, Sam – she's got wind again. Really and truly, Doreen, you'll have to stop eating so much. She'll get fat, Sam. I'll soon shrink to nothing before your very eyes, but the child will get fat. You mark my words.'

Psychic powers were not generally attributed to Molly Markowitz. At times she swore she had *feelings* about things. These were generally gloomy premonitions about such matters as the weather and Sam's health and the probable ill-effects of a rather dubious-smelling piece of fish. Nothing very demanding in the way of fortune-telling. Her prediction about the future obesity of her only daughter, however, turned out to be remarkably perspicacious. By the time I was four years old, I was already visibly overweight.

'Doreen loves her food,' observed my first kindergarten teacher astutely as she watched me tucking into someone else's peanut butter sandwich, having demolished my own cream cheese roll. Someone else was screaming blue murder. 'It's mine,' she was yelling. 'Make her give me my sandwich back.'

But I held firm. I had never tasted peanut butter before. It was delicious. It coated my mouth with a sludgy warmth that made me think of mud pies and melting chocolate and the trusting eyes of puppy-dogs with soft brown coats. Forbidden. All strictly forbidden. As unattainable as this peanut butter that was lining my mouth with so much longing that I wanted to burst. Reminding me . . . of something. A story? A joke? How come I was forgetting all my jokes?

'No,' they kept saying. 'No, Doreen, no. Don't touch. Don't make a noise. Be careful, darling. Watch out. If you don't take care, my *bubele*, something terrible is going to happen.'

The vast twin shadows of two dark forms seemed to grow as I grew, spreading their chilly greyness to cover my entire world. Keeping me safe. Shielding me from the sun, from evil-doing strangers, from the dangers that lurked in unfamiliar foods.

'No, Doreen, no.'

With each fearful admonition, I felt a 'pop' inside me. The death of a joke. One by one, like row upon row of rapidly fusing light bulbs, they were being obliterated. Pop. Pop. Pop. Until, by the time I was big and clever enough to start communicating my comic birthright, there was little left to say. At least four-fifths of my built-in treasury of humour had been extinguished. The survivors – a mere few thousand quips, including some of the smuttier items of X-rated material – were tucked away. Rescued from oblivion and carefully concealed in the most secret corners of my being. They had been camouflaged in places that I sealed with false

11

doors and blind alleys and hidden annexes and made so safe from discovery that, more often than not, I failed to find them again myself. Most of the time I even forgot they were there. This squidgy peanut butter, though. There was something about it . . .

'*Please* can't we have peanut butter?' I asked Sam and Molly again that night.

They didn't hear. They seldom heard. They had never (even remotely) considered that listening to their daughter should merit inclusion in their comprehensive list of the duties of proper parenthood. Not that they didn't want the best for me. Naturally they did. A pair of more conscientious parents than Sam and Molly Markowitz would have been hard to find anywhere. But listening? Neh. On the contrary, they'd always been convinced that if only little Dorinke would listen properly to *them*, she'd learn everything.

I listened. How I listened. Like a small secret agent, stolidly seated at the dining-room table on a cushion that spread lumpily beneath my burgeoning weight, I spooned potatoes and meat and pickled cabbage into my mouth, all the while cunningly intercepting each word as it flew from parent to parent. I caught hold of the conversation and swallowed it with the same neat and noiseless thoroughness as I devoured my square meals.

'Good girl. Look, Molly – she's cleaned her plate.'

'I can see. Please God she should do everything as well as she eats. Please God she should grow up to be a *mensch*.'

A *mensch*? I frowned. What was that? Hadn't they once called Mrs Venter next door a *mensch*? It was after we had moved in and she had come knocking at the door with a large pink iced cake. 'Welcome to Gladys Street,' she had said. 'If you need anything, anything at all, don't feel shy to ask.' She's a real *mensch*, they had announced after she had gone. Mrs Venter was fat with a pinched mouth and grey hair and a large alsation dog called Rommel and a small meek husband called Rex. Did they want me to turn out like Mrs Venter? What exactly was it that had earned our neighbour the accolade? Her husband? Her hair? Her size?

One thing I knew for certain was that it hadn't been the cake. Molly had placed it high up on the sideboard and said something scornful about 'people like them' having no clue, no idea at *all* about baking. The next day she gave the cake away. It was all a real puzzle.

'What's a *mensch* . . .?' I tried.

But they were already speaking of something else. Into the dank dining-room air, thick with supper smells, had been released another strange-familiar word. This one was mouthed with a caressing kind of reverence. '*Der-Heim.*' They almost sang it out. 'Remember how it was back there – *Der-Heim*? The cherries, Sam? Remember the cherries?' 'Ayaya! The cherries. Could anyone forget those cherries? And the apples, Molly? The sweetness of those apples . . .'

I tried to say the word. '*Der-Heimmm.*' It slipped out lubriciously, for the gustatory references had, as usual, made my mouth water. I wondered if, in addition to its other delights, *Der-Heim* provided ice-lollies and chocolate Smarties and sugary biscuits. And *peanut butter* . . .

'Can we go there?' I asked enthusiastically.

There was a long, heavy silence. I attended to my food. Even if I hadn't been endowed with a highly advanced sense of social embarrassment (among my earliest words had been 'excuse me' after being burped), I'd have been conscious of a gaffe.

'Dorinke,' Sam said mournfully, having exchanging soulful looks with Molly and pushed aside his empty plate. The stale smell in the room seemed to have intensified. I suddenly felt sick. 'Dorinke, no. Nobody can go there any more. Nobody . . .'

'Doesn't matter,' I said, quickly dismissing an impulse to produce an apt little quip. Something diverting. A limerick perhaps. There was a young dame from *Der-Heim* . . . No, I had an instinct that this might make things worse and in those days I still trusted my instincts. 'Please may I leave the table now?' I asked. My manners were always to remain reliable. 'Please?'

But again Molly and Sam – and this time who could blame

them? – hadn't heard. They were thousands of miles away. In Eden. Never mind Eden – it was a slum in comparison. They were in paradise. Elysium. *Der-Heim*. Back up the coast of Africa they'd sailed, away from the glare and strangeness of Cape Town. They had swallowed their seasickness and, drawing deep breaths, had reversed, shut-eyed, through the nightmare that had stripped them of their home and were back in the place where they'd been people. People who had counted. *Menschen* . . .

'On the other hand,' said Sam inconsequentially, as though midway through a dialectical discourse.

Molly raised her eyebrows, a signal for him to go on. She had followed her husband's unspoken discourse perfectly, for after the enormous distances they'd travelled together and the unspeakable things they had seen, they didn't have much need for verbal communication. This, understandably, made my early detective work all that harder. If I hadn't been equipped with tenacity, in addition to my comic potential and innate politeness, I might well have given up. (I might even, theoretically, have stopped listening for clues and started living my own life and been happy. Moderately happy. My story, however, would have been pretty damn uninteresting.)

'On the other hand,' Sam repeated. He was a man of few words but used them often. Same with his jokes. Same with his suits. Same with Molly's dinner menus. 'We should be thankful for what we have – eh, Molly?'

She shrugged, clearly unconvinced. I'd already come to dread that gesture. It expressed all the cynical pessimism with which my mother would greet anything that smacked of good news. An upturn in the household economy. A promising school report. Her daughter's oft-repeated declaration that she was to embark on a diet. Each time the corners of Molly's mouth drooped towards her raised shoulders with her head listing to one side as it swayed wearily, I felt the rat-a-tat-tat of at least twenty jokes being felled by a maternal firing squad. I was fortunate indeed to have been so amply provided.

'Look here, Molly,' Sam was continuing determinedly, one index finger placed above the other, about to count his blessings (which, luckily, never amounted to more than five). 'We have a nice home – short of nothing – and family who will always see to it that we'll never starve. Didn't Joe pay for us to come here, after all? And Reuven? Didn't he set me up in the shop?'

'Set you up . . .' she repeated contemptuously. 'Set you up. And now? Now that you have a hole in the wall with *S. Markowitz, Tailor* written on the front, how much money does it bring in? Tell me, Sam, who can make a living as a tailor these days? It's old-fashioned. Out of date. Kaput.'

'Just you wait, Molly. There's nothing like a well-cut, handmade garment. People will come back to it. Give them a chance. And anyway, I'm not out of date. Do you think a perfectionist like Samuel Markowitz wouldn't make sure to keep up with the latest styles? Huh?'

'Well, it's difficult . . .'

'Let me tell you a story. It's about a poor tailor – maybe you heard it? – who decided there was nothing for it but to wait for the Messiah to bring better days. The Messiah? And how would that help, you're asking? Well, you know that when he finally comes the dead will arise – and, naturally, they'll all need new suits. Yes, yes, I know. The tailors will also come back to life. But what will *they* know about the latest styles? Eh? Eh?'

'Oh, Sam – you're impossible.'

Molly pulled the emptied plates towards her with an impatient clatter while I, almost falling off my cushion with suppressed mirth, was conscious of a warm internal bubbling which I put down to post-prandial satisfaction but which was in fact the revival of several jokes that had not quite succumbed to my mother's last massacre. A whiff of paternal humour (after all, I had to inherit the comic side of my nature from someone) had been enough to bring them back to life. Inexplicably, I thought of peanut butter again as an unguarded giggle escaped in the guise of a choking snort.

'Doreen! Sit still! Sam – I keep telling you the child should *not* be on such a high chair. She'll fall. Mark my words. She'll break something and then we'll have trouble. As it is, the teacher, that Miss Williams, told me last week she was too heavy for her – '

'And of course there's Dorinke.' Sam, unperturbed, was still counting his blessings. He had reached number five. 'What wouldn't you have gone through for the – *joy* – of our own little girl? Answer me that, Molly.'

Personally, I had a strong suspicion that the sort of clumsy, greedy offspring I was turning out to be was doubtful compensation for the deprivations my parents had clearly suffered. I myself would have been more than a little disappointed. But if Sam was satisfied, who was I to argue? I dimpled at him as appealingly as I could. Perhaps now would be a good time to make a repeat bid for peanut butter.

Molly, however, had begun ringing the dinner bell with the thin-lipped demeanour of someone tolling the passing of a soul. She discharged most of the wifely and motherly duties pertaining to the ingestion, absorption and evacuation of food with the same grim-faced solemnity.

'If we've all finished eating,' she announced, her words synchronizing with the clanging gong so as to brook no contradiction, 'the *shikse* can clear the table.'

The *shikse*. Another sociological classification which had already caused Doreen Markowitz, Junior Super-Sleuth, the utmost perplexity. My earliest investigations had revealed that, while the term *mensch* could be used to refer to persons of either sex and was usually uttered in a tone of approbation, *shikse* was limited to someone dark-skinned and female who ate in the kitchen. I'd also noted that, while such a dark-skinned female was clearly a most valuable and useful part of someone's household (in terms of cooking and cleaning and washing the clothes), nobody, as far as I'd been aware, had ever expressed the hope that one day, please God, Dorinke would grow up to be a *shikse*.

And if it were a matter of choosing to be like Mabel (whom I'd heard described as 'honest and willing' and who hugged me and gave me biscuits) or Mrs Venter-next-door

16

(who was beaten by Rex and barked at by Rommel and swore shrilly at her own *shikse*), then I was sure I'd have few problems deciding. In fact, my main reservations about a future as a *shikse* would be to do with food rationing. Sugar, especially, of which I was particularly fond.

'You have no *idea* how many spoons Iris puts into a cup of tea,' I had heard Aunty Mathilda complaining to Molly on several occasions. 'In all fairness, Molly – I have absolutely no choice but to lock the sugar away. You should do the same.'

Molly had followed her sister-in-law's advice. She usually did.

'Mabel,' she was saying now to the heavy-footed tray-bearing individual who had appeared to deal with our supper debris, 'you can finish the rest of the potatoes. Don't touch the meat, though. I'll use that for the master's sandwiches tomorrow.'

'Yes, madam.'

Madam. Master. By this time, as indefatigable a detective as I was, I'd grown tired of making further deductions about the nature of the names people called each other. There were, however, a few vital question that had suddenly occurred to me. Four questions that all at once seemed even more pressing than putting in a further plea for peanut butter:

'Daddy . . .?'

'What is it, Dorinke?'

'Daddy, is a madam a *mensch*?'

'But of course. Usually. What a thing to ask.'

'And a master? Is he?'

'Oh, Dorinke. You are funny. A good master's a *mensch*. Naturally he is. Now go with your mother to have a bath . . .'

'And Daddy – wait – please tell me. Is a *shikse* a *mensch*?'

'A *shikse*? Now that's a question. Yes – well – I suppose a *shikse* can be a *mensch*. Under certain circumstances. Now enough . . .'

'One more thing, Daddy. Just one more . . .'

'Well?'

'Can a – *shikse* be a madam?'

'Er. Um . . . Now you've got me. Molly, what do you think?'

But Molly was concerned with more practical matters. Which was exactly why I hadn't addressed the questions to her in the first place. 'I think the child should have a bath and go to bed and stop worrying her head about such things. It's not good for her. It's not *normal* at her age.'

Normal. Another frequently used and rather puzzling term.

'Does a – *mensch* have to be – normal . . .?'

'Come, Doreen. It's past your bath time. Enough with your nonsense.'

'But . . .'

'Come.'

I knew it was no good pursuing the interrogation any longer. When my mother had decided on a particular course of action, nothing would deter her. Certainly not speculative conversation. Reluctantly, I slid from my chair and followed her to the bathroom, wishing they'd allow me to take a bath on my own. And regretting I hadn't pushed harder for peanut butter. And aware of an inexplicable gap inside me which felt somewhat like loneliness but was due to the demise of more than a hundred more jokes.

By the time I was seven, I had been granted solo bathing rights and had long since tired of peanut butter, which had eventually found a place in my mother's pantry between the plum jam and the pickled cucumbers, and soon acquired the same muddy blandness of all the other Markowitz condiments. I had also learnt to fill the unsettling gaps left by departed wisecracks and late aphorisms with huge quantities of food and a slow-growing collection of evidence for my comprehensive World View. I had thereby become a tiny bit wiser and more than slightly overweight. In fact – to be honest – I was already clinically obese.

This made me unhappy. It made me particularly sad when my father shook his head disappointedly, wondering why his

Dorinke lacked the will-power to acquire the sylph-like figure of her cousin Lou-Anne. I knew he tried to console himself with the belief that his daughter had sufficient wit and intelligence to compensate for her lack of bodily grace. Fat chance. But who had the heart to disillusion him?

Molly did. She was not about to spare anyone's feelings.

'Sam, we have to do something about her. She's a big lazy lump. I don't know how we could have produced such a child. When I think of what Ada – and she's no picture-book – has managed to make of Lou-Anne. Bright, thin as a stick . . . it's heart-breaking. Call her, Sam. Talk to her at least. She listens to you. Get her to understand . . .'

But it was hopeless. My store of understanding was already fully occupied with the enormous task of digesting and ordering my painstakingly acquired collection of clues. By this time, my investigative efforts had revealed the following:

That Sam and Molly had originated in a far-off place they called *Der-Heim* which was, as far as I could ascertain, also known as Lithuania and looked something like the illustrations of the Garden of Eden in my *Golden Book of Bible Stories*. I was still not too sure whether Sam and Molly were, in fact, Adam and Eve and I intended (some time in the near future) to request a rib-count from my father. If that proved positive, it left the question of an unappealing daughter hanging in the paradisial air. It also begged the question of the whereabouts of Cain and Abel. But that was speculative.

Back to the facts – and the demise of *Der-Heim*. No serpent in the verdant undergrowth had brought about this sad fate. That had been confirmed. Instead, *Der-Heim* had been overrun with bad monsters called Nazis who had since been mostly eradicated but were sometimes to be discovered lurking in the boots of German cars. 'That's why we're not allowed to buy them or ride in them or even go near them,' Cousin Norman had whispered – and was rewarded for the information with a brief inspection beneath my knickers. A fair exchange.

To continue: Molly and Sam, meanwhile, had been clever enough to evade the Nazi monsters and had (despite Grave and Terrible Suffering) made it to South Africa where they'd been welcomed by The Family and become a Master and a Madam and acquired a *Shikse* and met a *Mensch* or two. And thanked God constantly for blessing them with a daughter.

And now this very daughter was causing them extreme despair. 'Dorinke,' they were crying, both together in a mournful duet. 'Dorinke, Dorinke, what are we going to do with you?'

I was more than willing to co-operate. I'd have agreed to anything, anything, to facilitate a happier ending to their story. 'What d'you want?' I asked them fervently. 'Tell me. I'll do it. I swear.'

My mother's reply was measured and deliberate. She knew her own mind, did Molly. Always had. 'Doreen, we want for you to start going to ballet classes. Mathilda swears it will make from you a *mensch*. Yes?'

'OK,' I agreed, as obligingly as I could. 'If you think it will help.'

Somehow, I doubted it. I had already acquired a healthy cynicism about adult wisdom. The claims they made for things. Like fish giving one brains and carrots creating curly hair. And the biggest lie of all: Mrs Feather standing in front of us in assembly every morning and telling us with a straight face that the Good Lord had made all things bright and beautiful for which he required thanks. Me, bright and beautiful? Me, bloody hell.

I sighed. It didn't do to be entirely sceptical. Not at my age. Perhaps I should give them the benefit of the doubt. Maybe ballet classes *would* instil some of the brightness and beauty the Lord had omitted when he'd set about making me. Or perhaps a *mensch* didn't need to be these things. I couldn't help wondering whether Mrs Venter was a product of ballet classes but decided not to ask. Things were complicated enough already.

'When am I to start?' I asked instead.

'Soon,' said Molly. 'As soon as possible.'

2

That was how I arrived at the renowned Limelight Academy
of Dance and Drama which, as my mother had been reliably
informed, was so oversubscribed that I'd have to wait at
least three terms for a place. Molly was impressed. Little did
she know that if there hadn't been a waiting list, Dinkie du
Plessis, the academy's Founder and Principal, would have
found it necessary to invent one.

'I'm full,' she announced on the telephone. 'My classes are
absolutely full. They always are.'

But Molly had made up her mind. She was resolute. Not
for nothing had she survived Nazi monsters. Mathilda had
recommended Dinkie du Plessis and nobody else would do.

'Can't you look at the child at least,' she suggested
hopefully. 'First have a look at her and then decide if you
can manage to fit her in.'

Did she imagine that Madame (as Dinkie liked to be
called) would instantly perceive within her daughter the
skinny beauty struggling to come out? A prima ballerina,
perhaps? A future blushing bride? A – star? Who knew what
hopes filled Molly's heart as she presented the inelegant
product of her womb to the hooded eyes of Cape Town's
top connoisseur of balletic potential.

'Hmmm,' considered Dinkie, squaring my shoulders with
hands like pincers. 'Aha!' she muttered, arranging my feet so
that they pointed at more or less ten-to-two. 'Tsk tsk tsk,'
she frowned, circling round her prospective pupil like a beast
considering its impending meal. 'Well,' she said at last,

retying the chiffon scarf that was knotted artfully round her neck. 'Well, well, well.'

Wasn't it an amazing coincidence that, exactly fifteen years afterwards, a certain promising young gourmet and barrister of renowned good taste was to make similar noises as he came upon the stretch marks on the anatomy of his newly acquired wife? 'Hmmm. Aha! Tsk tsk tsk,' Geoffrey Bartholomew-Cooper was to say. 'Well, well, well . . .'

And (perhaps slightly less coincidentally but equally remarkably) I myself would, several years after that, produce the same sounds over the prostrate body of my late laughing husband. By then my stretched skin had been replumped with cushions of fat and my native cornucopia of jokes had been restored. Give or take a couple. 'Hmmm,' I would say with the mordant wit for which I had become renowned. 'Aha! Tsk tsk tsk. Well, well. Well!'

But that was later. Much, much later. As young Doreen, aged seven-and-a-quarter, I endured the painful, probing inspection of Dinkie du Plessis in stoic silence.

'I don't know what to do, Mrs Markowitz.' I heard the teacher sighing in Molly's direction. 'It would be wicked of me not to accept your daughter. A real sin.' This remark, for some reason, reminded me of the one about the sage who'd been asked about the difference between good and evil. His reply, in the typically pompous manner of sages, was: 'As long as a righteous woman lives, she knows she is sinning. But as long as a wicked woman sins, she knows she's really living.'

I smiled rather sadly for it was a small joke and not even my own. And somehow I had a feeling it would be the last one to pop up for a very long while.

'She took her,' said Molly over the baked fish that night.

'What? Where?' asked Sam, mashing the food with his fork. 'Careful Dorinke. Careful for the bones.'

'Dinkie. The dancing teacher. She says Doreen has good insteps.'

'Oh. And . . .?'

'And? What d'you mean *and*? And she can start going to classes next term and she's lucky, very lucky indeed, to have such a wonderful opportunity. And she must practise every day until the term begins. To catch up, Dinkie says. She explained me the exercises.'

'Ah. Good. And so, Dorinke? What do you think?'

Think? Did he really want to know what I thought? I could, I suppose, have voiced some of my deep apprehension about the prospect of being eaten alive by the witch who had pinched me. I could have laid down tools, refused utterly to go along with it. I could have asked them whether they truly believed that Dinkie du Plessis, veteran of a million ballet classes, was a *mensch* – and enlightened them with the facts (had I been aware of them at the time). That (a) the woman revered as a cultured cosmopolitan was born in Belville and liked brandy and Coke and stale marshmallow fish and had never travelled further afield than the Cape flats. And that (b) by wearing plenty of scarves and calling people 'darling', Dinkie believed she had overcome her past. But that (c) the sharp opposition between nature and nurture tended to invoke more psychic stress than even alcohol could relieve – which was why Dinkie sought relief in the systematic and gloriously sadistic persecution of young girls. This she accomplished with such aplomb, such style, such sheer panache that no one had suspected a thing.

Until, one steamy summer afternoon, the seven-year-old, whom she was to loathe as the most blatantly untalented and physically unsuitable creature she'd ever had the goodness to take on, looked into her eyes and guessed. And feared . . .

'Dorinke, eat your fish. It's good for you. But mind the bones. A person can choke.'

'And sit up straight, Doreen. Remember what Dinkie said about your shoulders.'

No, they didn't want to hear what I thought. Of course not. Methodically, I separated the piscine flesh from its dismembered skeleton. I chewed it every carefully and prayed for it to go straight to my brain. If I wasn't bright or

23

beautiful, at least I might become clever. It was my only hope – so I thought at the time. I hadn't yet discovered that there was another alternative: to be funny.

This apocalyptic finding was made during my inaugural lesson at the Limelight Academy of Dance. And it hurt like hell.

'Gels, gels, gels!' Dinkie du Plessis had clapped her claws and called together the gaggle of white-frocked *ingénues* whom she labelled her Grade Twos. 'Settle down now. Stop chattering. We have a new gel in our class. Her name is Doreen – Doreen, darling, where are you? Say hello and give everyone a deep, deep curtsy. No – not like that. Lower, my darling. Lower. Bend your knees . . .

'Oh dear, oh dear. Help her up, Olivia-dearest. And see that she keeps strictly behind you for the meanwhile so that she can follow the steps.'

Yup. I had landed flat on my bum. This was pure slapstick, which was a great deal less subtle than the sort of humour I was to employ later on. But it certainly raised a laugh. Snorts and shrieks from the little ballerinas and a more restrained ripple from their mums. Only three people failed to be amused by my discomfort that afternoon: my mother, the serene-looking priest who sat alongside her, and the perfectly formed specimen that Dinkie du Plessis had referred to as Olivia-dearest.

Molly didn't find it funny for obvious reasons. Her mouth and eyes had narrowed to slits of disapproval and disappointment, and if there had been any jokes left in her daughter's soul, there'd have been bloodshed that afternoon.

The priest refrained from an overt show of merriment because – well, because priests just didn't. (Laugh at other people's expense, that is. This one was not averse to other things, but we'll come to that later.) This particular priest, by the way, wasn't in attendance at the Limelight Academy to offer spiritual sustenance or last rites – even though I would have quite liked to have died and been decently buried when my butt hit the ground. Father Cook was simply there as a conscientious parent. A regular and unfailingly satisfied observer of the progress of his daughter. And this daughter happened to be the above-mentioned Olivia-dearest, who was far and away Madame's favourite, most promising pupil.

And Oivia herself didn't laugh because, in addition to being beautiful and clever and talented and perfectly behaved, she was genuinely kind. Wasn't it a pity, then, that I couldn't help regarding the limpid brown eyes and pert nose and rosebud mouth and slim figure of this paragon who was called upon to assist me to my feet with such instant and enduring dislike?

'So how did it go, Molly?' Sam wanted to know as, with a wooden pick, he carried out a dental excavation for the remains of the delicious stuffed cabbage. He swallowed the last morsel and heaved the sigh of a contented man. Relatively speaking. 'How was the lesson? Dorinke's ballet class?'

'Not good.'

'Oh? Why? Dorinke – what happened?'

'Well . . .' I hesitated, wondering how to describe to my father the humiliation of being laughed at, the horror of the multitude of wall-mounted mirrors in which, inescapably, I had watched my own grotesque reflection behind the flitting, darting, fairy-like form of Olivia Cook. The mocking voice of Dinkie du Plessis. 'Doreen, my darling, *do* open your eyes. This is ballet – not blindman's buff.' And the laughter. The shrieks of the 'gels' and the amused titters of the 'mummies'. The smug smile on the face of the man everyone stupidly called 'Father' when he was really the father of that goody-goody Olivia and seemed to have something wrong with his neck.

I'd asked Molly about this on the way home and she had tersely explained that he was 'a man of the cloth'. This, as I had worked out after a series of persistent questions in the bus, meant a spiritual leader and not a tailor like Sam. What a pity. Further investigation of this fascinating subject (with particular reference to Father Cook's bandaged throat) had evoked a sharp order to 'sit still and mind your own business' which I had thought it politic to obey. My mother was clearly not pleased with me.

And now Sam was wanting to know what had happened.

'I fell,' I said quickly, hoping they wouldn't dwell on the incident but suspecting they would. 'I slipped and fell and everyone laughed at me.'

'That's not nice,' he said, shaking his head with puzzled indignation. 'Not nice at all. How could they do a thing like that, Molly?'

'Let's rather not talk about it,' she said, her lips assuming their hem-pinning position. Stiff and tight, as though bristling with at least twenty steel spikes to be stabbed into the base of one of my dresses. Molly was a perfectionist when it came to the plumb-lining of hems. Among other things. 'All I can say is that it wasn't pleasant for me to sit and watch Doreen with her miserable face. And such beautiful children there are in the class. That Olivia for instance . . .'

I immediately felt my dislike for Olivia swelling into the first stages of hatred. This was a new sensation for me and I found it distinctly unpleasant. Perhaps another helping of stuffed cabbage would ease it away.

'Can I have some more?' I asked, pushing forward my plate.

'Doreen, what did Dinkie tell you about the size of your tummy? Surely you haven't forgotten already? Sam, the teacher repeated exactly what I've been saying ever since the child was born: "Mrs Markowitz," she told me, "your daughter is *extremely* overweight and unless you take her in hand – firmly in hand – there's nothing I can do with her." She warned me that if we didn't watch things now, Doreen would suffer in years to come.'

Molly reached decisively for the dinner bell while I pondered on the possible forms my future suffering might take. Could it be that the sort of monsters who'd been responsible for the torments of my parents had a particular fondness for fat bellies? That they were lying in ambush in the boots of German cars, licking their lips as they waited for me to become plumper and plumper and . . .?

'The trouble is, Molly,' Sam was saying, patting his own stomach, which was developing a marked rotundity with the passing years, 'your food is simply too good to resist. Your beetroot soup. Your cabbage meat. Your *blintzes*. Let me tell you something, Molly – a man could kill for those *blintzes*.'

This alarmed me even further. It didn't seem to please my mother much either. Molly's mouth remained little more than a horizontal hairline crack.

'Which makes me think,' Sam continued undeterred, 'of the story of the dying pauper who longs to taste *blintzes* just once before the end. Remember it, Molly?'

She shook her head abruptly. 'You can clear up, Mabel. And finish what's left of the food. I don't think I'll need it tomorrow.'

'It's an old one. I'm sure I've told it to you before . . .'

'I'm sure.'

'. . . "Please," the poor man says to his wife, "please, Rachel, can't you make *blintzes* for me? My last request? I once looked through a window into a rich person's house and there they were, sitting at the table – and what do you think they were eating? Oi, Rachel – their faces! The smell! Rachel, I beg of you . . ." "But Izzie, we have no eggs," Rachel points out. "How can we afford eggs in our position?" "So make them without," says Izzie. He's desperate. "But Izzie, there's no cream." "Never mind the cream." "And no sugar." "Who needs sugar? Make the *blintzes*. Please, Rachel, please." And so, what does the woman do? Huh? What *can* she do?'

'Who knows? Doreen, it's bath time . . .'

'She makes the *blintzes* anyway – never mind the eggs, cream and sugar. Does she have a choice? And Izzie sits up in bed – he can't wait – and takes a big bite. Then he lies back and shakes his head, very puzzled indeed. "Rachel," he says, "Rachel, as long as I live, I'll never understand what the rich see in *blintzes*."'

Sam, chuckling wryly, rose from the table. 'Thanks for supper,' he said to Molly, who, despite herself, had listened to the end of his story and allowed the corners of her mouth to twitch. Then she remembered: 'Doreen, how many times do I have to tell you . . .?'

Quickly (well, fairly quickly, since I have never been one of nature's swift movers), I made for the door. I didn't mind bath time, as long as the water was deep and soapy enough for me not to be forced to contemplate the unpleasant mound of flesh surrounding my navel. Anyway, there were other things to consider this evening.

These included further thoughts on the nature of suffering and whether it was possible for any torment to be worse than the prospect of remaining a pupil at the Limelight Academy. There was also some need for additional rumination on the meaning of becoming a *mensch*, with particular reference to Olivia Cook, on whom ballet classes had clearly wrought the necessary improvements. At any rate, her man-of-the-cloth father seemed extraordinarily pleased with things. Molly and Sam always looked worried. I hoped they'd be happier when I started to look like Olivia.

But, having been a realist from a very early age, I knew that this was as likely to happen as . . . well, *blintzes* being produced without eggs, cream or sugar. Even then, I had a strong sense that (never mind culinary technique) it was basic ingredients that counted most towards the success of a dish. I could predict, for instance, that my mother, whose breast milk had always tasted slightly sour, would never rise to contentment. And that my father, whose smile always crumpled when he thought I wasn't looking, would always be more sad than funny. And that, no matter how many decades of ballet classes I endured, I would never remotely resemble Olivia Cook.

I was right. After years of transactional analysis and psychotherapy, several Gestalt workshops and a number of expensive primal screams, my early insights into my mother's discontent and my father's deep-seated sadness were finally confirmed. It took only four terms under Dinkie du Plessis, however, to prove I'd been perfectly correct about the uselessness of ballet lessons.

*

'Jump, Doreen. Jump!'

Dinkie was clearly struggling to prevent her voice from slipping into a vulgar treble. I'm sure that never, in all her years of teaching, had her gentility been so tried.

'Bend your knees, darling – eyes up, keep your back straight – watch Olivia – and elevate, elevate, elevate!'

I had forced my feet into first position and launched myself into the series of vertical springs which were a compulsory part of each lesson. 'A dancer has to learn to float,' Dinkie had decreed, making lyrical movements with her hands. 'To be light – as light as thistle-down.' It was hell. Most of the time my body stubbornly refused to defy gravity and, when I managed minor lift-offs, my descents were noisy thuds. And they hurt. Never mind sore pride. I was used to that. A million times more painful were the effects of those landings on the newly acquired swellings around my nipples.

'Doreen, darling,' said Dinkie, when the last of the thirty-two springs had been sprung and, gasping and sweating, I stood cradling my aching chest, 'Doreen, my darling, I think we'll have to ask Mummy to buy you a brassière. Won't we, gels?'

There was a titter through the ranks and a rustling from the row of chairs on which seven mummies and a daddy (Father Cook, as serene as ever) were seated. Molly's mouth stiffened and I thought what rotten luck I'd always had in the manifestations of my precocity. If only I had grown early teeth, like Lou-Anne, or uttered a few cute first words, like Cousin Norman. If only I'd been visibly advanced in motor co-ordination or toilet training or anything else that would have made Molly proud. Who needed an over-developed sense of the ridiculous – and now boobs, of all things? As though I didn't have a superfluity of flesh already.

Before the next lesson, the protuberances in question were swiftly brought into line by Mrs Flora Van Rensburg, doyenne of the Stuttafords lingerie department. Recommended by Mathilda, naturally. Nothing less than a properly certified corsetière for me.

'We'll need to exercise strict control over those boosums,' advocated Mrs Van Rensburg after a full structural survey. 'When they start as early as this, there's always the danger that they'll grow out under the arms.'

With clenched fists and stiffened shoulders, I was averting my nose from the corsetière's cologne-scented cleavage. My eyes were fixed on Flora Van Rensburg's ornately lettered diploma on the wall and, beneath it, a stern order for customers to retain their own panties when trying on swim-wear. I read it through several times as a distraction from the unsettling prospect of my breasts spreading like rampant weeds in the least appropriate places. It didn't bear thinking about.

'Bend over, my dear,' Mrs Van Rensburg was saying. 'Here. Like this. Now, shake them well into the cups. So. And tighten the straps. So. And there we are – a perfect fit. We call this a Stage Three Stretch 'n' Grow Bra – you're already way past stages one and two. But with a little bit of luck, this should do you for a while.'

She turned to my mother, who looked glum. Molly was, quite understandably, rather put out by the implication that she had ignored two of the most vital phases in her daughter's bust development.

'Mind you, madam,' said Mrs Van Rensburg in the specially intimate whisper she'd practised at Corsetry School, 'with her rate of growth, I'd bring her back in a month or so. One can't be too careful. And make sure she *wears* her little brassière. How many times have I come across cases where the mother hasn't – '

'Would you say,' interrupted Molly, eager to make amends for her early neglect, 'would you say that, in your opinion, she should keep it on all the time? Maybe at night as well?'

'Not a bad idea. Not bad at all, under the circumstances. If I were you, madam, I'd try anything.'

And so began my lifelong dependence on round-the-clock boob support. An open-ended sentence of bondage in nylon elastic. Long after I had pared from my body all signs of visible fat, I would never dare unleash my bosom. After that day, no one – not even Geoffrey with his trained legal mind – was able to dissuade me that, if they weren't kept in constant check, my breasts would expand to fill my armpits. Flora Van Rensburg had presented me with a possibility even more frightening than the threat of Nazi monsters.

While that first encounter with corsetry had done little for my peace of mind, it did at least have one immediate benefit. My new Stage Three Stretch 'n' Grow made jumping up and down in first position, if not much easier on the eye of the beholder, at least perceptibly less painful.

'Bounce, Doreen. Bounce!' urged Dinkie gleefully the following lesson. She had noted with some satisfaction that Molly had taken her advice. Dinkie liked her mummies to be suggestible. 'No more excuses now, Doreen darling. You're going to have to stand behind Olivia and see that you jump as high as she does.'

I bounced with obedience but little hope. By now it was patently clear that I'd never reach the heights attained by the lovely Olivia. It was in the nature of things. I had resigned myself to the hierarchical structure of ballet classes. Same with primary school, Gladys Street and Life. There was a fixed place for everyone. An immutable pecking order, with Doreen Markowitz, weighed down by dullness and fatness and bewilderment, firmly on the lowest rank. Clumsy clod of the Limelight Academy, duffer of the playing fields, loner of the street, disappointment to my parents. There was only one place where I didn't feel quite at the bottom of the heap. In the kitchen, in the company of the various holders of the title, 'the *shikse*'.

There had been Mabel, who had admired my drawings. Followed by Posy, who arrived soon after Mabel had disappeared with advanced tuberculosis. Posy had waxed lyrical over the plumpness of my bottom and the curliness of my hair and left hurriedly to have a baby and was immediately supplanted by Patricia. Patricia laughed.

'Oh, Miss Doreen,' she would gasp, supporting her huge quivering stomach with one hand and wiping her tears with the other. 'Miss Doreen, you're so funny.'

'Wait. Wait, Patricia. Don't go. Let me tell you another one.'

It was intoxicating. A revelation. A discovery that I had the power to create the respiratory convulsions for which my audiences would, years afterwards, pay so dearly. (Passing mention of Geoffrey at this point would be tasteless and cruel.)

'Miss Doreen, I can't laugh any more. You make my tummy ache. Tell me your joke tomorrow.'

'But it'll be Sunday. There won't be a chance.'

Sunday was Patricia's Day Off. Or, to be accurate, her Half-Day Off. After lunch, which comprised several courses to sustain ménage Markowitz through the rest of the servant-less day, Patricia was Off Duty. And Sunday mornings, unsurprisingly, were rather hectic in order to make way for this weekly quota of liberation.

'You're right. I'll be too busy for jokes tomorrow,' agreed Patricia. 'I want to finish as quickly as possible. Guess who's coming to take me out?'

'Robert,' I said immediately. He was Patricia's boyfriend. A porter in a beach-front hotel. A jazz trumpeter. A church-goer. A real catch. I had been told about Robert's accomplishments and seen him smiling, all teeth, in a grainy black and white photograph.

'Yes – Robert!' Patricia laughed happily. 'You must say hello to him when he comes to collect me. And, I promise you, Miss Doreen, on Monday you can tell me jokes. Many, many jokes.'

'OK.' I felt suddenly hungry. As though a gap had appeared inside me. An emptiness demanding to be filled with – something.

'Doreen,' my mother called. 'What are you doing? I told

you not to spend so much time in the kitchen. That's all you seem to be interested in these days. Fatter and fatter you're getting. I don't know where it will end. Haven't you got homework?'

'Yes. Coming.' I turned to Patricia. 'All right – on Monday, then. Wait for it, Patricia. On Monday, I'll make you laugh and laugh . . .'

But Monday never happened.

Sunday happened first.

3

Sunday lunch *chez* Markowitz was everything that a midday meal in a February heat-wave shouldn't be. Long and heavy and dry.

'Delicious,' said Sam, wiping beads of sweat from his forehead. 'There's nothing to beat a well-done weekend roast.' He placed his knife and fork carefully on his plate which contained four surplus peas and a gravy-slick. Enough was enough.

'I don't know,' worried Molly. 'I've told Patricia again and again not to overcook the meat. She doesn't seem to understand. I must admit, though, her potatoes are improving. Even if I say it myself, I do seem to have a knack when it comes to teaching them to roast potatoes. With soup, on the other hand, I wouldn't trust another soul. Making good, thick soup is an art . . . Doreen, *can't* you brighten your face a little and sit up a bit straighter? It makes me miserable to look at you.'

I tried unsuccessfully to force my features into the required expression of convivial alertness. But I was melting. There was no doubt about it. My thighs had turned to puddles of grease that dribbled down my legs, and beneath my Stretch 'n' Grow (which felt as though it had Shrivelled 'n' Shrunk) were two sticky, weeping creme caramels that were trickling towards my waist. Such as it was. Perhaps there'd be ice-cream for afters instead of the usual baked apples . . .

'I'm hot,' I complained.

The dining-room was duller and more airless than ever. Molly had a theory that the higher the outdoor temperature,

34

the tighter all windows should be shut. 'To keep in the cool,' she'd explain, drawing the curtains as well for good measure. 'And to keep out the flies. And the noise from the neighbours. If only they weren't always in the streets at this time of year. Honestly, all that shouting and screaming can give a person a permanent headache.'

My glance settled on a shaft of sunlight that had forced its way through the sealed window. It illuminated several million flecks of dust, and I marvelled at how they managed to defy death by Molly's voracious vacuum cleaner. It gave one hope somehow. From the other side of the glass, I could hear muffled shrieks and splashes, balls thudding against bats and intermittent barking. The Venters and their visitors. Probably Rex's policeman brother, Frikkie, and his family. Frikkie was large and bald and wore khaki shorts. He had a small blonde wife called Babs and a big blonde baby called Bee. Babs laughed when Frikkie pinched her bottom and Bee laughed when Papa tossed her in the air. They all laughed hysterically when Rommel bit someone. The Venters seemed to laugh a lot. I could never quite understand what they found so funny.

'I'm very hot,' I repeated, remembering my discomfort. 'I think I may be melting.'

'Please God,' said Molly. 'You can do with a little melting. I'll call Patricia to bring the dessert. That will put you right. All I can say is that I hope you manage to look a bit more cheerful later on when the family arrives for tea. You know how critical Mathilda always is.'

I knew all right. Mathilda and Ada would mutter to one another and shake their heads sadly in my direction and smile fondly at Lou-Anne. Lou-Anne, in her smocked sundress, would preen herself and giggle. The men would talk gloomily about money and the state of the world and I would strain to look cheerful and suppress angry tears and comfort myself with chocolate cake and strudel and almond tart and maybe another slice of chocolate cake. And a couple of biscuits, why not? And then a long, cool drink . . .

'I'm thirsty,' I said.

'How many times do I have to tell you how unhealthy it is

35

for you to drink water with your meals? Eat your baked apple, Doreen, and stop whining. One day you'll realize what a lucky girl you are.'

From the kitchen there came bustling sounds and the ululating voice of Patricia. She sounded happy. I remembered about Robert and wished that I, too, had a smiley jazz-man collecting me for the afternoon. Now *that* was lucky. I was about to say something of the sort to my parents when Sam, with several deep and satiated groans, rose to his feet and announced he was ready, more than ready as it happened, for his afternoon nap.

'I wouldn't mind a little sleep myself,' confessed Molly. A regular siesta was, as far as I was ever aware, my mother's only self-indulgence. She protected it fiercely. 'I'll ask Patricia to give me a hand with the tea tray so that I can fit in maybe an hour or so before they all arrive.'

The sounds from outside had abated. Sam retired to bed and Molly made for the kitchen while I, bored and listless, ambled to the window and tried to peer through a crack in the curtain. The sunlight dazzled me. The glare and heat and sultry silence almost took my breath away. Then Rommel barked.

'Go on, Rex. Don't be an old meanie,' I heard in a wheedling high voice. 'Give him a stukkie boerewors. You know how he loves it.'

So the Venters were eating. A braaivleis. I moved to another window where I'd have a better view of the proceedings (what else was there to do?), and settled on the sill to observe their meal. A curl of smoke hovered above the brick barbecue.

'More, anyone?' offered Mrs Venter. 'A chop? Some sausage? Rex? Frikkie? What's the matter with you boys?'

Babs and Bee were sucking on cigarette and bottle (respectively) and Rommel was salivating. They all seemed to be wilting in the heat. Even the Venters.

'Can I go now, madam?' I heard Patricia ask.

'I suppose so,' answered Molly. 'I'd have liked a bit more

help with the tea, but it doesn't matter. I can see you're on edge.'

'Miss Doreen,' Patricia called after a moment. 'Miss Doreen – where are you?'

'Here. At the window. Behind the curtain.'

'I'm off now, Miss Doreen. I'm going to my room to make myself look beautiful. Today's the big day, remember?'

'Of course. Tell you what – shall I be the sentry and let you know when Robert arrives? This is a really good look-out point, Patricia. I can see everything from here. I'll warn you when he comes.'

Patricia laughed, agreeing, and I settled down to my vigil. After a while, though, it became boring. The Venters had retreated indoors and a dense, hot haze seemed to hang over the stillness of Gladys Street. A fly hesitated above Rommel's sleeping snout. He didn't stir. Half dozing, I decided that spying wasn't much fun after all. My lids had dropped and I dreamt I was dancing in a desert in nothing but my Stretch 'n' Grow bra. 'Lightly, Doreen – try, for God's sake, to keep it light,' Dinkie was saying. But I was hot and heavy and heard myself landing. Thump . . . thump . . .

I opened my eyes with a start and saw that the sound came from Rex and Frikkie, who had reappeared in the garden armed with beach bats. They were hitting a ball to one another. Aggressively, back and forth. Thump . . . thump . . . thump.

'Women!' snarled Rex. 'They don't know when to shut up, do they?'

'You can say that again. Stupid bitches.'

Things had clearly hotted up with the Venters. This, I thought, could get interesting. I sat up and listened intently, hoping to hear more. But the brothers were speechless, venting their rage on the ball. Thump . . . thump . . . with furious monotony. It was hypnotic. Maddening. I wished they'd shut up and let me sleep.

Just then I heard whistling. Joyful whistling. The celebratory sort of sound that's expelled through the teeth of a man with a satisfied soul. A vaguely familiar tune. It was coming from the mouth of an advancing stranger in a jaunty straw boater and a crisp white suit.

'Patricia,' I called excitedly. 'Patricia, it's Rob – '

Then I froze. The Venter brothers had stopped playing. Robert's song had suddenly ceased. Rommel began to growl.

'Hey, kaffir,' said Frikkie. The brothers dropped their bats and took menacing steps towards the stranger. 'What you got to be so happy about, kaffir? I'd wipe that smile off my face if I were you.'

'Yes, baas. I mean – no baas. I mean . . .' Robert had taken his hat off. He looked scared.

'What do you mean, you cheeky bastard?' demanded Rex, joining in. Rommel growled louder. 'Rommel! Come here! See this dog, kaffir? He's been trained to give a lesson to cocky buggers like you.'

'Yes, baas. Can I go now, baas?'

'Go? What d'you mean, go? You can go when we decide. Eh, Frikkie? What do you think?'

'The kaffir deserves a good hiding. That's what I think. Coming here and making a racket on a peaceful Sunday afternoon. Christians *rest* on a Sunday, kaffir. But how would you know what Christians do? A damn heathen like you . . . hey, Rex?'

'I'm a Christian, baas . . .'

'Shut your bek! You're right, Frikkie. He needs the dog set on him, the bleddy cheeky sod. *Rommel!*'

It was over in less than thirty seconds. I heard a yelp and a howl and several mighty snaps as Rommel wrapped his jaw round his prey. Then laughter. Great cathartic gusts. The Venter brothers slapped one another on the back and laughed till tears came. 'Come,' said Frikkie. 'It's enough. Let's go in.' 'Ja. Kom, Rommel. Rommel! Enough! Let's go see what the girls are doing.'

Robert lay bleeding on the pavement. His hat was on the far side of the street. His suit was no longer either crisp or white.

'Patricia!' I had recovered my voice. I sobbed the name. 'Patricia!' Louder. A petrified cry!' I was shivering. The

38

temperature was in the high nineties, yet I was shaking with cold. 'Patricia ... somebody ... please come and help. A terrible thing has happened.'

Terrible: causing terror, fit to cause terror, awful, dreadful, formidable (OED). The worst.

I couldn't sleep that night. My father sat beside my bed with his hand on my shoulder. I shivered in uncontrollable spasms. 'Why do people do things like this?' I demanded again and again. 'Please – tell me why?'

'Why?' Sam echoed, shaking his head hopelessly. 'Who knows why.'

He said it was like the story about the German Jew who'd been walking along the pavement, minding his own business, when he was accosted by a disgruntled and drunken Nazi. 'Who caused the war?' demanded the Nazi. *Terribly.* 'The Jews ...' was the prompt reply. Old Jews didn't get to be old Jews for nothing. Not then. 'The Jews – and the pretzel bakers.' 'Pretzel bakers! Why the pretzel bakers?' puzzled the Nazi, taken aback. The old man shrugged. 'And why the Jews?' he asked.

'Why Robert?' I persisted. I had to know.

'Because he was there,' Sam said finally. There was silence.

'But, Dorinke, he'll be all right. I promise you. The dog didn't do much damage at all. Robert was lucky.'

Lucky: constantly attended by good luck, enjoying it on a particular occasion, having as much success or happiness as one deserves and more (ibid). The best.

'Was that – *lucky*, Daddy?

'He could easily have been killed, Dorinke. That Rommel's

39

a monster. Believe me, it looked much worse than it really was.'

'But – Patricia . . .?'

'Dorinke, it was no good. We had to sack her. Rex Venter's been complaining for weeks about her boyfriends loitering in the yard. There was bound to be trouble. You heard the way she was carrying on after – the thing happened? The noise was shocking. Crying. Screaming. The brother – Venter's brother – said she'd been drinking and he was going to have her arrested for disturbing the peace. What could we do? Eh? We did manage to keep her out of jail . . .'

'Daddy, they *made* the dog bite Robert. I saw them. I promise. He didn't provoke Rommel. He did nothing. Daddy, I'm telling you the truth. They were lying . . .'

He sighed and squeezed my hand. He looked hopeless. Hopeless. He probably knew that one day soon I would learn for myself that truth was as illusive as luck and that the only certainty was terror. It was a damn depressing prospect.

'At least that Mrs Venter came out with bandages for the boy,' he said after a while. 'The others did nothng . . .'

Of course. I remembered. Mrs Venter was a *mensch*, after all. She had bandaged Robert's wounds and Patricia, her noisy outrage muted by fear, had been sent to pack her bags. And, huddling in my window perch, too shocked to cry or protest or even say goodbye, I had watched them leave. Robert, limping ever so slightly, had been carrying an old brown suitcase while Patricia had marched ahead with an overflowing plastic bag in each hand. I had noticed that her dress was the same shade of red as the bloodstains on Robert's rumpled suit. Neither of them had glanced back. Not once.

After they had gone, Gladys Street had seemed to hold its breath for a moment. Nothing had moved. It was as though the street had paused for its shame to branded on it by the scorching sun. Then, shattering the silence, had come a screech of high laughter from next door and, with my eyes squeezed shut and hands pressed over my ears, I had tried to make myself as small as I could. I had prayed for obliteration.

'So there you are!'

Molly had discovered me before long, and ordered me to get a move on and fix myself up. Quickly, quickly, because 'they' would be coming soon and she was dreadfully behind with her tea preparations. It had been *such* a bad start to the afternoon . . . And after a while, the family had arrived with wet kisses and weather-complaints and disaster stories from the week before.

'Doreen's looking well, a nice healthy girl, touch wood,' Ada had said, pushing forward for general approval the simpering Lou-Anne.

'What a lovely child you have, Ada,' Molly had murmured, and moved almost immediately to her news – a detailed description of the day's domestic drama.

'Honestly,' Mathilda had tutted, 'sometimes I think having a *shikse* is more trouble than it's worth. When they start with their boyfriends. Honestly! Do you know that ever since we had those problems with Annie – remember her? – we decided . . .'

Eventually, they had exhausted their tales of misdemeanours in the servants' quarters and their appetite for cakes and tarts and pinwheel sandwiches. They had yawned and stretched dyspeptically and begun, in slow stages, to leave. Their departure had coincided with that of Frikkie and Babs and Bee from next door and, for a while, Gladys Street had rung with fond farewells. By then, the temperature had dropped and a gentle fanning breeze had risen. I had sedated myself with quantities of carbohydrates that would have caused coma in a lesser being and tried to pretend that it had been a Sunday like any other. Same as usual. Nothing different. And until late in the night, I had almost believed it.

'Why don't you try and fall asleep now, Dorinke?' suggested Sam. Having exhausted logic and wisdom as tools to comfort his distressed daughter, all he had left to offer was oblivion. 'You think too much about everything. Far too much. It's not good for you.'

Oh well. If he couldn't give me answers and there wasn't any more food, oblivion would simply have to do. I offered a damp cheek for his kiss.

'good-night, Daddy,' I said, pulling the blankets over my head and shutting my eyes.

Seraphina arrived two days later. 'Miss Mathilda says you are needing a new girl,' she announced to Molly at the door. 'I have a good reference, madam. I can start straight away.'

'I'll give you a try,' said Molly sceptically.

When I returned from school that afternoon, Patricia's space in the kitchen had been filled. Half-filled, to be more accurate. Seraphina was a fraction of the size of her predecessor, with sunken cheeks and calculating eyes. Patricia's pink overall and white apron hung loosely round her middle.

'Hello,' I ventured.

'Afternoon, madam.'

Madam? What had brought about this elevation in status? Surely not the bra? I was about to point out that I was an early developer who had not yet turned twelve. That I was three sizes too large for my age. 'I'm not a madam. Not for a long while yet,' I wanted to protest. 'Just call me Doreen and admire me and – tell you what – I'll make you laugh. They say I'm quite funny, believe it or not.'

But what was the use? A comedian without jokes was like a baker without flour, a tailor without thread, a rich man . . . without. And my repertoire, every last quip, had been mortally wounded on Sunday and died that night in my sleep. Passed away peacefully. 'The best way to go,' as Sam would have said. And in a way it was a mercy or relief or deliverance or whatever other lies are told to comfort the bereaved. You see, each one of those last surviving jokes had been afflicted with a wasting disease and been suffering for years.

The last to snuff it was – as these things tend to happen – the sickest joke by far. A shaggy dog story, I suppose you could call it. About this guy. This black guy, whistling along the road on his way to collect his girl for an afternoon of fun. He's happy, this fella, d'you get it? Loudly, offensively happy. The sort of happy that makes some geezers –

42

especially those who're feeling especially put-upon and mean and miserable – want to kill. Or, if they happen to have a blood-thirsty mongrel conveniently at hand . . .

The hell with it. Seraphina wouldn't have appreciated the joke anyway. Neither that one nor any of the others. She didn't look the laughing sort.

'She's got a long face, the new *shikse*,' said Molly over supper. 'I can't stand it when I have to look at a long face in the kitchen.'

'Nice rice,' remarked Sam.

'Ye-es,' Molly agreed grudgingly. 'She says she learnt to make rice at her last family. English. They liked curries and that sort of thing. And steamed puddings. But as far as I'm concerned, I'm going to have to teach her to cook from scratch. In all honesty, Sam, I don't know if I have the strength . . .'

I wasn't listening. I had given up. Resigned from my self-appointed position as family spy. 'No job satisfaction,' as I was later to explain it. 'Opportunities for advancement – nil. Financial rewards – nil. Social status – nil. A dead end.' One can rationalize anything. In truth, the job had possibilities. It was me who'd been dead-ended. My sense of justice had been defeated by Sam's defeat and my curiosity dulled by the acid of Molly's disappointment and, in the end, I hadn't the heart to be a dishonest or indifferent dick. Despite my faults, I always had high standards.

'I'll never take another order from old Finkelstein again,' Sam was grumbling. 'Five times I had to alter the trousers – too long, too short, too tight, too loose. And the collar. Tell me, Molly, have you ever known me to turn out a collar that didn't fit? Eh?'

'You're too soft, Sam. That's your trouble. Talking about Finkelstein – have you heard about his wife . . .?'

Apart from anything else, the job had grown boring. Dead boring and, when you got down to it, quite inconsequential. I was amused by my naïvety in having believed there was a

43

code to be broken, a logical structure to reveal. A universal Tournament of Truth: the goodies on one side (mainly madams and masters and select others who'd made it to *mensch*) against the baddies on the other (Nazi monsters and those with foul habits), with a few *shikses* etc. on the sidelines to serve refreshments (to the victorious goodies, naturally). Now I knew – being almost thirteen and fully conversant with life's little ironies – that labels were meaningless, that a goody could be a *mensch* but a *mensch* didn't need to be good, and one man's luck was another man's adversity. And that enlightenment made me miserable and food made me fat. And there wasn't a single joke left inside me to lighten the burden. Not bloody one.

'Doreen,' my mother was saying. 'Doreen, you're slouching again. Really, I'd have thought that *by now* your posture would have been better. Four years of ballet clases. Honestly! To think of the amount of money we've paid out . . .'

Ah yes. Ballet classes. Perhaps one joke had remained after all. The hilariously stubborn tenacity of Molly's belief that one day her ugly duckling would – by the grace of God and the magical ministrations of Dinkie du Plessis – be transformed into a swan. A dying swan, if all else failed. Even a dead one, if necessary. Very funny indeed – unless you happened to be the duck or the poor deceased swan.

'. . . the bottom line is,' Molly was concluding with her hand extended towards the dinner bell, 'that if I were you, Doreen, I'd get into my room and practise some barre-work. Now. Otherwise tomorrow Dinkie will have something to say.'

4

Dinkie had plenty to say the following day, but not about the state of my barre-work. It was the first lesson of the spring term. An important one. The lesson during which parts were allocated for the school's famous Summer Concert. 'My annual show-case,' as she liked to put it. 'A chance to dazzle all of Cape Town with what the Limelight Studio can do. An opportunity for you, gels, to *shine*.'

I had, on successive years, played a pumpkin, a weasel, the rock at the entrance to Aladdin's cave and the North Wind. In my last great role I had been stationed in a back corner of the stage and had blown with such ardour that I had almost fainted. But, however hard I tried (for my mother's sake, if nothing else), I had so far failed to sparkle.

Olivia, on the other hand, positively coruscated. Year after year. It helped, of course, when one got to play most of the crowned heads of fairyland. Cinderella, Aurora, Rose Red, Snow White, the lot. Molly, with the usual reproach in her voice, made regular references to Olivia's unparalleled loveliness and regal bearing. And I, nodding in agreement, meanwhile compiled a series of secret contingency plans for the assassination of whichever member of royalty Olivia was currently pretending to be. My dislike for Miss Perfection had ceased to disturb me down the years. In fact, the feeling had fired me through enough rounds of first-position springs and fuelled sufficient salvoes of *changements* to be seen as rather a useful tool.

'Gels – welcome back from the holidays.'

Dinkie, clapping her hands, was calling the class to attention. Her gels, who had mostly reached pubescent surliness, were no longer the compliant *ingénues* who had simpered through Grade Two. Most of them (Olivia, naturally, was one of the exceptions) had acquired body-odour and breasts and premenstrual tension and flatly refused to curtsy to *Madame* or kiss her cheek or perform any other of those little acts of balletic homage traditionally due to a mentor. They were there under sufferance.

'Gels,' repeated Dinkie warningly. 'Stop chattering.' She had an intense dislike of puberty. It was bad for discipline, disturbed concentration and adversely affected the sleek line of an *arabesque*. Dinkie, who had long before forsaken the joys of sex, could find nothing in its favour at all.

'Gather round now. Quickly. As you're probably aware, I've been having thoughts about – our Summer Concert.'

There was a bustle then a hush, for the concert had retained its power to capture their attention, hormones or no hormones. Everyone, deep down, still longed for a chance to shine. The girls eagerly surrounded Dinkie, standing as prettily as possible, and nobody but me seemed to observe that there was a newcomer in our midst.

I saw her first. A beauty. So pretty that even Olivia, alongside her, paled into plainness – and that was saying something. The stranger had long golden hair, exquisitely slanting green eyes, a peachy complexion and a perfect figure. Interesting, I thought, waiting with relish for the moment when Olivia finally took in her new rival. I noticed her brief sideways glance and the fleeting frown that creased her forehead and couldn't help smiling. Interesting indeed.

'First of all,' Dinkie was saying in her most ingratiating voice, 'we must welcome our new pupil. Wendy, darling, would you like to curtsy for the class?'

Would she just! Wendy dipped into the most heart-stoppingly graceful salutation that the Limelight Studio had ever seen. I watched Olivia's face and wanted to burst into applause.

'Wendy Watson and her mummy have come to live here from Johannesburg,' continued Dinkie enthusiastically. 'Her mummy – Minerva, you won't mind my saying this? – her mummy and I are old, old friends. Minerva, you might be interested to know, gels, is a *theatre person*. A real pro. A wardrobe mistress. We're hoping she'll give us a hand with the concert. Aren't we, gels?'

All eyes had moved to the seat alongside that of Father Cook. It was occupied by a tiny woman in black trousers with a deep red turban round her head. Her lipstick was an even brighter shade of crimson than the turban, and her eyes – enormous in her pinched, high-cheeked face – had been boldly outlined in charcoal. Minerva Watson exuded *theatre person* through every pore.

'Of *course* I'll help, Dinkie,' she breathed. 'It will be a *pleasure*.'

There was a slight ripple through the row of watching parents. It was the sort of premonitory discomfort that drifts through crowds before a storm. An uneasy shuffling and clearing of throats that spread from Molly (whose lips were pursed more tightly than ever) at one end, all the way along to Father Cook at the other. The clergyman was flushed and had his eyes raised heaven-ward. His mouth was set in its usual beatific smile, and I might have imagined it, but I'm almost sure he licked his lips.

'And now,' said Dinkie, clapping again, '*now* – we must talk about our concert. This year, we're going to be terribly ambitious. The Academy is to present its very own version of Hansel and Gretel, choreographed by – ahem – me. And, gels, I shall be watching you all very carefully over the next week or two before I make my final decisions about the leading roles.'

'Doreen's the witch,' Molly announced at supper a fortnight later. 'She's got one of the main parts in Dinkie's show, Sam. What do you think about that?'

'The witch?' Sam looked up from his schnitzel. 'And so – are you happy about it, Dorinke?'

I offered him a weary shrug for, as an up-and-coming starlet, I felt obliged to display a certain ennui. 'I suppose so,' I said, attending with deliberate disdain to my plate. I would probably have managed the air of boredom better if the schnitzel hadn't tasted quite so good.

'It's one of the three leading roles,' continued Molly. I marvelled at her enthusiasm. The wicked witch, after all, wasn't exactly the stuff of which prima ballerinas were made. Could this be a sign of acceptance – an indication that my mother was coming to terms with reality at last? I somehow doubted it. Even at thirteen, my understanding of human behaviour told me that enlightenment wasn't acquired as painlessly as that.

'Doreen's the witch and Olivia – you know, the beauty – is Hansel. And the new child is Gretel. I must say, Sam, that little Wendy is even prettier than Olivia. Isn't she, Doreen?'

'Definitely.'

The eclipse of Olivia was giving me more pleasure than ballet classes had ever before provided. In fact, it was this pleasure that had inspired the gleeful malignancy with which I had landed the part of the witch.

'I've got it!' Dinkie had exclaimed, when the class had dissolved into giggles at the sight of me auditioning for the role. I had been pretending to nibble at a piece of gingerbread roof as I had contemplated (with my customary rapacity) the prospect of consuming two tender young prisoners.

'Hush, gels! I've just had an inspiration. Doreen, darling, you can be our witch. We'll play this for the laughs . . .'

Long, long after I'd forgotten the French terms for the various balletic tortures I had been forced to endure and all the technical faults to which I'd been prone, I was to remember that declaration. It had been a seminal remark. The sort of throwaway statement that inspires youngsters to become engine drivers ('He's certainly got a way with trains!') or cartographers ('She's not too bright but *what* a sense of direction!'). Or comedians. Dinkie's spontaneous utterance was to shape my destiny. Later on, when all else failed, I would play life for the laughs.

*

Hansel and Gretel. What a story. What lives. What laughs . . .

There were these two kids, see. A brother and a sister, who'd somehow escaped the eagle eye of the social services and suffered the most appalling abuse. Poverty, misery, cultural deprivation, the lot. Well, not quite the lot. That came when Pops in a drunken fury one day expelled them from the family home. 'Out, silly buggers,' he snarled. 'You're a drain on our limited resources. Away with you. Get out into the jungle and start bloody fending for yourselves.'

'But, Father, it won't pay you to do this to us,' tried Hansel. He was eventually to become a successful accountant and already had a strong sense of profit and loss. 'You'll lose your low-income supplement, child benefit, not to mention family support. You'll be much worse off. Believe me.'

Gretel, who would one day be a leading relationships counsellor and advice columnist, tried another tack. 'Daddy,' she said earnestly, 'why don't we talk about it. *Properly*. All of us. Perhaps we ought to try and have more *insight* into our behaviour . . .'

'Piss off!'

Pops meant it. The snotty little bastards (for whom one couldn't really feel a great deal of sympathy) beat a hasty retreat and, having travelled for miles and miles on buses and trains and articulated lorries, finally found (or rather lost) themselves in a dark and eerie forest. Things were at their worst. So they thought.

'I'm hungry,' whined Gretel.

'Me too,' snivelled her brother.

'And scared.'

'And broke.'

Neither Hansel's monetary giftedness nor Gretel's superior social skills were of much practical use when it came to survival. All seemed lost until Gretel, blinking excitedly, suddenly exclaimed: 'Look, Hansel – look over there!'

'Where?'

'Over there, idiot. Behind you. A cottage made of After

Eights and chocolate buttons and cream horns and jelly beans and hazel-nut pralines and liquorice allsorts . . .'

'Gretel, didn't I warn you about the hallucinogenic properties of strange mushrooms?'

But she was gone. Between the trees and over the undergrowth and under the overgrowth, in search of her vision of bliss. Gretel already had a tendency towards bingeing on junk food that would ultimately develop into full-blown bulimia. Hansel, on the other hand, didn't care much for sweet things even then, but had a deep-seated (and justifiable) fear of abandonment. He followed close on his sister's heels.

'Look! Here it is! Was I right or wasn't I?' demanded Gretel. Without waiting for a reply, she settled down to the systematic consumption of the front pathway with its caramel camellias and corn-chip crazy-paving. Hansel, more cautiously, followed suit.

'Helloo-oo . . .'

Enter the witch, who was the roundest, most maternal-looking member of a coven you'd find anywhere. This witch wasn't frightening. On the contrary, she was a lost child's image of paradise regained. An Oedipal dream.

'Hello my sweethearts,' she cooed. 'My angels. My darling ones. Goodness gracious me, you're hungry. Why don't you stop eating the flowers and come into my – er – home and I'll feed you properly. How about some barley soup and brisket and potato pudding and indigestion tablets and maybe a cup of tea? Huh? What do you say?'

Who could resist that? Certainly not cruelly orphaned little Hansel who, throwing a half-eaten camellia to the winds, scampered like a puppy to the witch's side. 'Yummy, yummy,' he said, regressing several years.

'Me too, me too,' cried his sister, motivated more by sibling rivalry than enthusiasm for the proferred meal. She was quite happy knocking back dolly-mixture daisies, thank you very much. Inside, however, while they were nibbling on a toffee-table as they waited for their food, she did feel duty-bound to point out to her brother the dangerously high saturated fat content of the forthcoming banquet.

50

'I don't want to spoil your fun, Hansel,' she said primly, 'but you ought to be slightly more cholesterol-conscious. Even at your age. The old woman's kindness could well clog your arteries and kill you. Eventually.'

Eventually? Never mind *eventually*. The said old woman in the kitchen (overhearing Gretel's warning) added several more dollops of chicken fat to the pot, for she was determined to have her two waifs fed, dead and dressed in time for dinner.

You see, this particular witch loved little children more than anything else in the world. For as long as she could remember, she'd had a predilection for pinching small plump cheeks and saying 'Mmmmm – I could eat you up!' Then once, on the spur of the moment, she'd thought, 'What the hell,' and tried it. After that she had never looked back. Not after she had made the discovery that there was nothing in the world to beat the taste of a pair of tender roast children seasoned with love and gratitude.

'Your supper's almost ready, dears,' she called, moistening her lips in anticipation. The oven was ready (Gas Mark 5). The trick – a handy hint she'd once contributed to a specialist publication – was to keep their moods mellow. This, she was convinced, made for melt-in-the-mouth meat.

Hansel and Gretel, having devoured the toffee-table, had then gone on to demolish several scatter cushions on the three-piece sweet. They were a-bubble with marshmallow but, alas, far from mellow. Overdosing on junk food had set their blood sugar levels rising and falling like two drunken yo-yos. They were nauseous and irritable and, oddly enough, wanted to go home. (Enforced exile does strange things to the memory, as we know.)

'It was your fault that we came inside this creepy house,' sniped Gretel. 'I don't trust the old bag. I don't trust anyone who keeps *Cookery for Cannibals* on her shelf between *War and Peace* and the Old Testament.'

'If you hadn't been such a pain in the neck,' sulked Hansel, 'Pops would never have wanted to get rid of us in the first place. I'd have organized our finances, milked the government for all it was worth . . .'

'Let's go then.'

'What d'you mean?'

'Run. Scarper. Return to the family fold.'

'*No, you won't!*'

The witch, who'd been eavesdropping again, was blowed if she would let her main course escape. Mellow or not, she'd have them in the oven. If it killed her.

To cut a long story short, it did. She was about to deliver to her captives a *coup de grâce*, having force-fed them with the desired fatty stuffing, when her heart gave in. Obesity, stress, and an exceedingly unhealthy diet of low-fibre foundlings were thought to be the main contributory factors towards this fatal attack.

Hansel and Gretel, much relieved, disposed of her remains in the oven intended for them. They'd raised the temperature to Gas Mark 9 for the purposes of cremation. Soon afterwards, Hansel applied for a Small Business Loan in order to realize the potential of the witch's house, which was demolished and sold in profitable job lots to various confectioners round the country. Hansel studied accountancy on the proceeds and Gretel entered psychoanalysis. Both remembered their brush with the witch as the most exciting thing that had ever happened to them, for they went on to live rather ordinary and moderately miserable lives. The witch, meanwhile, had (through a clerical error) been misdirected to heaven and died happily ever afterwards.

If you think that was one rum fairy-tale, just wait till you hear this one:

There was once a priest called Prosper who had a beautiful daughter called Olivia. There was also a theatre person called Minerva who had an even more beautiful daughter called Wendy. Now it happened that, while Olivia and Wendy were pretending to be Hansel and Gretel and deeply engrossed in out-charming each other, Prosper and Minerva, who were

52

pretending to be Conscientious Parents, were becoming increasingly engrossed in charming one another. Prosper was struck by her sophistication. Minerva was enchanted by his refreshing awkwardness. Both were convinced it was love.

Olivia and Wendy were quite unaware of developments between their respective parents. There was far too much else to absorb their attention. For instance, the question of which one of them would emerge as the star of Dinkie's show. Would it be handsome Hansel or gorgeous Gretel? Or would the Limelight be captured by a third surprise contender – that ridiculously fat witch-woman as played by one Doreen Markowitz?

So far, the outsider was winning hands down. While Olivia and Wendy danced their little hearts out, prepared to *pirouette* till they dropped to win a round of applause, the witch had only to raise an eyebrow to steal a scene.

'Your daughter's a born comic,' pronounced Dinkie to Molly a few weeks before the show. 'You should be very proud of her. It's a talent like any other.'

'Uh-huh?'

Molly evidently wasn't sure that being the mother of a laughing stock was quite on a par with producing a pianist or a painter or a mathematical genius. On the other hand, it was better than nothing. She supposed.

'Well, thank you,' she said.

And so the weeks passed in a mounting frenzy of practices and costume fittings and final choreographic adjustments. Father Cook and Minerva Watson had kindly volunteered to make the scenery and dedicated many ardourous evenings to the task. At last came the night of the dress rehearsal. Nerves were taut, several tutus were found to be too tight, and the set seemed unstable. 'It'll be all right on the night,' shrilled Dinkie, who had fortified herself with a few large brandies for the ordeal. 'You know what they say about a bad dress rehearsal . . .'

This one couldn't have been worse. Hansel and Gretel were hesitant and lacklustre. 'More *oomph*, gels,' yelled Dinkie. 'Liven up! Liven up!'

At least she didn't have to say that to me. On the contrary, I was putting everything I had into my performance and the invited audience (senior residents of the local Red Cross Home, who were being treated to Dinkie's annual act of charity) was in stitches. However, after a few of the less continent enthusiasts had wet their pants and been forcibly removed, Dinkie was advised to instruct the witch to 'tone things down'.

'Save yourself for the big night, darling,' she told me drunkenly. 'Tomorrow, you can let yourself go. You'll bring the house down.'

I didn't wait for the big night to demolish the house. That happened in Act Three after Hansel and Gretel had made a dispirited lunge for their would-be devourer. Backwards I sprang – with an energetic and most admirable *ballon*. Into the scenery. And my cottage (made of After Eights, chocolate buttons, cream horns, hazel-nut pralines and liquorice all-sorts all imperfectly cemented by a love-struck priest and his irresistible Minerva) came tumbling down.

'Props! Stage-hands! Somebody – help!' screamed Dinkie. 'This isn't supposed to happen. It's Hansel and Gretel, not the bloody Three Little Pigs. Doreen, you clumsy idiot! . . . Father Cook, Minerva darling, where are you?'

There was a minor hubbub of proferred help. Stage-hands stirred. A few props persons came forward and heads were shaken helplessly at the scale of the devastation. The stage was in ruins.

'Father Cook . . . Minerva,' Dinkie called again. There was no response. They were nowhere around.

For it emerged that the passion of Prosper and his new-found beloved had exploded with enough force to propel the couple several hundred miles along the Garden Route to a picturesque and secluded hotel in Plettenberg Bay. Precisely at the moment that the scenery was falling, the priest was on the telephone informing his patient wife, Regina, that he was not coming back.

'Back!' she exploded. 'As though I'd have you back! Don't you ever darken my door again!'

Regina, poor soul, had been longing all her life for a chance to say that line, so at least she got something out of the affair.

The Limelight Academy, however, suffered badly. For the first time in its twenty-two-year history, there was no Summer Concert that year.

'Cancelled due to infirmity,' Dinkie had written in a wavering script above the posters. 'All tickets will be fully refunded.'

The word 'infirmity' had been carefully chosen to cover a multitude of disabilities – from the damaged set to shattered egos and several incapacitating bruises acquired by the witch. Not to mention the abrupt extraction of Hansel from the cast.

Regina had come to collect her daughter soon after the call from the priest. Olivia had quietly gathered her things and departed in silence and, in keeping with the long-established practice of martyrs and saints, immediately embarked on a long-term hunger-strike.

Wendy Watson, meanwhile, had been overcome by such a noisy attack of hysterical sobbing that Dinkie was forced to slap her face. But neither this nor the misdeeds of her mother were to do any lasting damage to Wendy's psyche, which had been thoroughly pre-stressed by early deprivation and was tough enough to withstand anything. She recovered enough to take her place as Dinkie's undisputed star and later went on to become a leading department store cosmetician.

I had been struck on the head (among other places) by falling scenery, and wondered whether the dramatic events that had followed my tumble were a product of concussion but had been too shocked and sore to question my mother, who had hastily taken me home.

The next evening, Molly told Sam she had decided that my dancing lessons should be terminated.

'I'm giving Dinkie notice,' she said.

'I see,' said Sam. The potatoes were half-cooked and the meatballs dry and he was about to suggest that the new *shikse*, Beatrice, be given notice as well. But his wife didn't seem to be in the mood to take domestic advice. Molly looked grim.

'So irresponsible,' she muttered. 'What kind of parents would carry on like that behind the scenes . . .?'

'What? Carry on like what?'

'Nothing, Sam.' She frowned in my direction. 'I'll tell you about it later. Disgusting. I've never come across anything like it in my life.'

Listening intently, I filled my mouth with meat and potatoes and tried not to smile. No more ballet classes! I suspected that the real reason for my abrupt extraction from the Limelight Studio hadn't been moral outrage or falling scenery but the fact that – as Molly saw it – her daughter had made a fool of herself. All that laughter hadn't pleased her one bit.

'Anyway,' Molly was saying, 'I'm not sure whether ballet is the right thing for Doreen's weight problem. Mathilda was telling me just the other day that there's a new diet doctor in town. She says Margot Fleischmann sent her daughter Anita there and now she's got a figure second to none. What do you think about that, Sam?'

He shrugged wearily, shaking his head. I held out my plate for more food. A diet doctor sounded ominous.

5

LOCAL PRIEST UNFROCKED was the way they put it in on page three of the *Cape Times* a few weeks later. I thought it was about the most obscene thing I had ever read. The idea of Father Cook, who had watched so benignly over four years of ballet classes, being stripped down to his bare, pink torso was quite disgusting. Much worse, in a way, than the 'adultery' he'd confessed to.

On the contrary, 'adultery' sounded to me rather grown-up and sophisticated. A bit like tennis and dancing the cha cha cha. Exactly the sort of thing my mother wanted me to do – once I'd been slimmed down and discharged by the famously effective Arnold Gleeson, my new diet doctor. A set on the court, a turn on the floor and a spot of adultery. What a prospect. What fun.

It was all a matter of perspective, I supposed. Anything was probably fun after someone had been in the hands of a diet doctor. Even hands as expertly gentle as those of Dr Gleeson, who had, everyone said, 'worked miracles' on Anita Fleischmann. Would he rise to the challenge of defleshing me?

'Hmm. Aha! Tsk tsk tsk,' Dr Gleeson had muttered as he'd matched my statistics to those on his charts. Balancing on the scales, I had tried to remember where I'd heard those noises before. Several sighs later, the doctor had faced Molly Markowitz across his mahogany desk. The surgery was large and opulent and the smooth-skinned doctor had an air of success. Deservedly. Gleeson had once gambled away a

57

fortune on pork belly futures but, pound for pound, he was making it back on lost fat.

'It's going to be a long hard haul, Mrs Markowitz,' he had finally said. 'My success rate is – er – unparalleled as you've – ahem – no doubt heard. The Gleeson Weight-Loss Method is guaranteed to work as long as you, young lady . . .' He swivelled his chair towards me. I was engrossed in the framed photographs of calorie-counted foods on the wall. '. . . are committed to it. Are you?'

'She is, she is,' Molly said quickly. 'Aren't you committed, Doreen? She's absolutely determined, Dr Gleeson, I can tell you.'

'Doreen?'

'Well – er – yes . . .'

I tried to imagine myself thin. Like Lou-Anne and Olivia and Wendy Watson. Long-legged, lissom and lovable in a 32A bra. Bare-backed and brown in the briefest skirt and bangles. Lots of bangles. As the bikini-belle of the beach, I would saunter down the sands, snapping my fingers for attention and everyone would call me by my surname. I had noticed they did that with the most popular girls. 'Hey, Markowitz,' they'd say, fawning round, vying for my attention. 'D'ya want an ice-cream? A Coke?' 'Perhaps,' I'd reply coolly. 'Why not?' And they would shower me with goodies. My favourites. Double-thick malted milk shakes. Honey-crunch cones. Banana splits. Chocolate dips . . .

'Sweet things are strictly forbidden,' the doctor was saying, as though he'd read my mind as well as my weight. 'You're going to have to be iron-willed about it, Doreen. The only way we're going to get results – *meaningful* results – is to put you on our thousand-calorie-a-day diet and keep you there. And that means cutting back to basics. The minimum. Do you understand?'

'Yes,' I said resignedly. Oh well. That was that. I'd have to make do without life's shakes and cones and splits and dips. It wasn't as though there weren't other pleasures. Like crisps . . . salty buttered popcorn . . . savoury bits. After all, sweet things weren't all *that* important. Not really.

58

'And no fatty foods either,' continued Dr Gleeson. 'You've no idea how many calories there are lurking in each innocent-looking globule of oil. My patients are always dumbfounded by the sheer numbers – which is why I keep these – er – illustrations on my wall. As reminders.'

I squinted to examine the portrait of a rather photogenic beefburger in a bun (350 calories) and a cheese and tomato pizza (580 calories) and, alongside it, a matching pair of sausage rolls (280 calories each). Then my eyes settled on the jar of peanut butter in which a mind-blowing 2,040 calories lurked. No wonder Molly had been reluctant to have it in the house. She probably suspected that the innocent-looking brown sludge harboured legions, battalions, vast fighting forces of the little mites. It was like inviting the enemy army to set up camp on your pantry shelf. Never mind Nazi monsters in the boots of German cars. This was a threat from within. A fifth column. A civil war which Molly and Sam, being true survivors, had come through with hardly a scratch. And look at them – thin as rails.

Now it was my turn to take up arms and vanquish the would-be invaders. I drew a deep breath, girding my substantial loins for the battle to come. For an epic conflict between me and those millions and millions of calories camouflaged within my favourite foods.

Then I slumped. I saw certain defeat. The impossibility of this contest. I pictured the calories, victorious, feasting on my fat. And how, exhausted from the fray, I'd allow them their celebrations but be quite unable to enjoy the delicious things they had brought along for the party. What a waste.

'And go easy on the starches,' the doctor went on. My mother was leaning forward, listening intently. Neither of them had noticed my dismay. 'Bread, potatoes, spaghetti, rice. Plenty of calories there too.'

Suddenly I began to wonder if there wasn't perhaps a way out of this. A deal I could do with the enemy. Something in the way of negotiations. A peace settlement. Maybe the occupying forces could be persuaded to withdraw from certain areas. A couple of chocolate éclairs. A few bags of chips. The odd fizzy drink. That was all. Surely they could be prevailed upon, to save energy if nothing else . . .

'So what,' I asked tentatively, 'am I allowed to eat?'

'Salads, grills, greens. Nothing to beat the old celery stick or the carrot – if you *must* nibble between meals. It's all carefully explained in the Diet Pack I'll give you.'

'Oh.'

This was worse than anything I had imagined. Bouncing through ballet classes had been made bearable – just – by the prospect of the tuck-in at the end of the toil. But this new regime looked like being sheer deprivation. And for what? Were things really better for the thin? As far as I could tell, slimness hadn't done much for the health or happiness of my parents. Or several others I could name – including much-lauded Lou-Anne, who was developing galloping acne. Hee hee.

No. I'd resist. Go underground. Engage in small, secret rendezvous with the opposing forces. Consort with the calories. Did Dr Gleeson honestly think the celery stick or the carrot were enough to subdue the might of the enemy? I knew better. I would engage all my cunning, all that early training in subterfuge. And when victory day came, guess who'd be there trumpeting with the other side? Doreen Markowitz – fatter and fitter than ever. Feasting on cream horns. I smiled at the thought.

'That's my girl,' Dr Gleeson was saying as he noticed my smile. 'The right sort of attitude. I have a feeling about you, Doreen. Plenty of weight to lose – but plenty of grit to go along with it. Here – take a Diet Pack and study it properly. Calorie charts, meal plans, handy hints. All the information you could possibly need. I'll see you next week for a progress check. Any questions, Mrs Markowitz?'

'No. Only – eh – how long will it take? The diet?'

'It depends. It all depends . . . How old is Doreen now?'

'Thirteen. She'll be fourteen in August.'

'That's – um – five months. I'd say that – looking at her and getting such a strong sense of her determination – you could have quite a little birthday celebration there. Quite a party. How does that sound, Doreen?'

'Well – fine, thank you.'

'Good. And now, Mrs Markowitz, if you could speak to my receptionist about your bill. We have an easy payment plan, which she'll explain to you.'

'He took her,' said Molly over the Low-Calorie Creamed Poached Haddock that night. It was a variation on a recipe included in the Gleeson pack. What you might call a collaboration – between the hand of God (who'd made the fish), the inspiration of Thelma Gleeson, the doctor's wife and biggest dieting success story (who'd designed the low-fat sauce), the initiative of Molly Markowitz (who'd substituted hake for haddock, tinned peas for mushrooms and a chicken stock cube for fresh vegetable consommé) and the finishing touches of Beatrice (who slung salt and pepper over everything).

'What? Where?' asked Sam, puzzling over the unfamiliar fare. He didn't like to make a fuss but it somehow didn't taste quite right. Salty and peppery he'd got used to since the advent of Beatrice. But this was somehow different . . .

'Arnold Gleeson. The diet doctor. He says Doreen has a good attitude.'

'Oh. And . . .?'

'And? What d'you mean *and*? And she can start on his programme and she's lucky, very lucky indeed to have such a wonderful opportunity. And she must follow the diet strictly. To the letter. And see him every week for check-ups. Dr Gleeson, I must tell you, is a *lovely* man. He explained me everything.'

'Ah.' Sam put down his knife and fork, overcome with apprehension. He agreed with his wife on most issues but had a sudden feeling that they'd not see eye to eye on the loveliness of Dr Gleeson. Not if it meant having meals like this. On the other hand, if it brought happiness to his daughter, who was he to complain?

61

'Good,' he said resolutely. 'And so, Dorinke? What do you think?'

I stopped eating. Think? Did he *still* believe he wanted to hear what I thought? I might, I supposed, have shared with him my misgivings about a war against such overwhelming numbers of heavily armed calories. I might have shed light on my defence strategy, my brilliant 'if-you-can't-beat-'em-join-'em' plan. I might – if I'd been really daring – have told him of my belief that Dr Gleeson was a quack. A sleazy, sex-crazed charlatan who had touched my left breast in a most suggestive way. I might even have given them strong advice not to waste their hard-earned money. Instead, being easy-going old me, I nodded pleasantly and was about to agree with the sentiment about my good fortune, when my mother butted in. 'And guess how long the doctor said it would take, Sam? Take a guess?'

'One, two years. Maybe three . . .'

'Five months. He thinks that by the time she turns fourteen – please God, all being well – she should be down to the normal weight for a girl her age. What do you say to that?'

'Wonderful.' Sam looked gloomily at the half-eaten plate of food in front of him and wondered how he would survive even a week. But that was selfish. Unworthy. He reached out his hand and squeezed mine. 'I'm pleased for you, Dorinke. But Molly – tell me – do we *all* have to be on this – diet? All three of us?'

'It helps, Sam. Dr Gleeson says it's a great help. Solidarity, he calls it. Family support. Anyway, what's so terrible about eating meals like this? Eh? Fresh fish. A nice sauce. Nothing wrong with it. When I think of the starvation we've gone through, me and you. Your memory is short, Sam. I'm surprised at you.'

'All right, all right.'

'And what's five months in a lifetime? Nothing. It will pass so quickly that, before we know where we are, the birthday will be here and Doreen will be thin like a stick. Which reminds me – Mathilda suggested we let her have ballroom dancing lessons. To help her socially. Lou-Anne has already started going to mixed parties and I'm sure that when Doreen's lost the weight . . . in fact, Sam, it occurs to me that maybe we should do like Dr Gleeson said. Give her a great big birthday party and start her off. Eh? What do you say?'

'I don't mind. As long as it all doesn't cost too much. Things are tight, Molly. MacWilliams cancelled his suit yesterday and for weeks I haven't seen a new customer. Times are not good. You know the old joke about the – '

'Yes, yes. In fact, Sam, what I think I'll do is to call Mathilda right now and ask her for the name of the ballroom dancing school. We haven't got much time. Beatrice! You can clear the table. And put the rest of the fish in the fridge for tomorrow. It's special. For Miss Doreen's diet. She can take it in a box to school.'

And so began the Five Month War. Western military history includes hostilities of far greater duration and at least one other Battle of the Bulge, but this was among the fiercest. It raged on several fronts (including, despite severe restraints, further outbreaks of mammary tissue on my irrepressible chest) and came to a head with the Great Birthday Battle. That was when my mother took to her bed, struck down by her First Terrible Migraine.

'Haven't I always told you that you shouldn't take things so hard, Mollinke?'

Sam had positioned himself at her pillow and was arming her with aspirin and tea. He'd hovered mainly on the sidelines of the struggle, having opted to act as a one-man medical and entertainment corps for the duration. An arsenal of good cheer. Morale-booster for the fighting forces. Tireless provider of jokes and encouragement for Molly and secret calorie-reinforcements for me. It must have been exhausting – especially on restricted war rations. And these seemed to be diminishing day by day.

'It's better you should look on the bright side, Molly,' he tried, hunger putting a severe strain on his optimism. The poor man longed for the days of *blintzes* and *borscht* and glistening piles of golden potato *latkes* and wondered how long he was expected to last on steamed fish and cottage cheese. 'Dorinke's a clever, healthy girl. So what if she's not skin and bone? A little bit of extra fat never hurt anyone.'

'A *little* bit,' moaned Molly. 'If only I could forget . . .' Poor woman. The flashing lights in her hot head were exacerbated by an even more upsetting visual disturbance. It was the memory of me straining, straining at the zip of my party dress. The new one they had bought specially for the occasion. Ordered a few sizes smaller in the anticipation . . . 'He *guaranteed*, Sam. With my own ears I heard him say five months.' She groaned, recalling again – despite all her efforts at obliteration – the sight of yours truly in the purple satin garment that had finally split apart at its major load-bearing seams. Great gaping rifts had revealed volumes of flesh that Molly was sure, she could swear it, were more abundant than ever before.

'Doreen!' she had exclaimed, shocked, acknowledging for the first time what should have been clear for months. 'Look what you've done!' I had bent down to inspect the damage, my shoulders visibly shaking. 'Crying won't help,' Molly had said with some scorn.

Then she'd seen that I wasn't sobbing. Far from it. I'd been laughing in great, quivering waves that had broken in a series of the most ungainly snorts imaginable. That had been more or less when her migraine had struck.

'Sam,' she said now, her voice reverberating painfully in the raw cerebral space that had once been so comfortably cushioned with hope. The diet doctor, the dancing lessons, the expensive eight-session course at the Arlene Carter Charm School. Then the party. The birthday party that was to have been the realization of all her aspirations for me.

'Sam,' she repeated weakly, 'can you see where she is now? What she's doing? We have to do something about the guests. Somebody has to tell them that the party's off . . .'

*

64

And where was I while my mother lay groaning her worry and despair? Where do you think? In the kitchen, naturally. Well, perhaps not so 'naturally'. As Molly would have put it, a *natural* daughter would have been at her mother's bedside mopping her brow. Gentle. Concerned. Thin. Or if not quite thin, at least repentant. Ready to do anything, anything at all, to make up for the way things had turned out.

But since when had I ever behaved in a way she might have expected from a normal child? Would a natural daughter, for instance, have sucked her poor mother dry and eaten herself fat and made a complete mockery of everything her mother had decided was best for her? And would a natural daughter now be celebrating, smacking her lips on the sweet tastes of victory, while Molly suffered in bed?

And, boy, was I celebrating. Perched on my Formica throne, I was contemplating the feast spread before me on the table with immense and joyful relish. Platters of custard kisses. Meringue curls. Butter-cream twists. Sponge fingers. My lush fields of conquest. My captured calories. My prisoners of war. The delectable fruits of my battle-wisdom, my wily strategy. Talk about Napoleon and Good Queen Bess and Winston Churchill rolled into one. Get the idea? That was me, Doreen Markowitz, triumphant.

Slowly, majestically, I settled on a pale pink meringue which I lifted and placed between my lips. It melted against my tongue. Such sweet dissolution. It was like the delicious flavour of subversion I'd first tasted when, after three futile months, I had seen how Dr Gleeson was struggling and falling to contain his irritation. He had weighed me three times over, just to make sure.

'No change,' he said, shaking his head. 'Slightly – er – heavier, if anything. Doreen, are you *sure* you're sticking to my programme? Hmm? Not cheating, are you?'

He directed a searching stare deep into my eyes and I looked straight back, unblinkingly. He saw – what? Earnest effort? Honest intent? Devious malice? Who knew? Who cared? I knew exactly what I could see. Greed. Sheer greed. A greed far greater than my own voracious appetite for things gustatory. I saw that Arnold Gleeson's hunger was for the power to devour the longings of little people like me. He wanted control. He needed money to stay in control. And a never-ending supply of compliant fat females who would pay to be weighed and measured and moulded to his specifications. That was what he wanted and it was mostly what he got. Until I came along.

Not me, you old bugger, I vowed to myself as I met his gaze. (Not in those words, of course. My thoughts were sometimes nasty but my thirteen-year-old vocabulary was still heart-breakingly pure.) You may get the others, but you sure as hell won't get me. I smiled as artlessly as I could.

'Of course she's not cheating!' Molly, who'd been anxiously observing the weekly weigh-in, was appalled at the thought. 'I see to her breakfast. Personally. And I make her packed lunch. With exactly the things you recommend. And the suppers, as my husband would tell you, are absolutely . . .'

'Doreen?'

He looked at me even harder, trying to penetrate beneath my air of bemused candour.

'I'm doing my best,' I said.

'Ah. Well.' He wasn't fooled. Of course not. As though Arnold Gleeson hadn't dealt with a million devious dieters in his career. But he was also quite aware that if he punctured Molly's hopes or shattered her illusions, he risked losing face as well as a rich source of revenue. Pounds and pounds and pounds . . .

'And she's *looking* so much better,' Molly put in with determined good cheer. I kept smiling ingenuously, but detected a shrill edge to my mother's voice. Desperation? A crack in her armour? My nostrils twitched with the first whiff of victory while Molly rushed on breathlessly: 'Do you know, Dr Gleeson, a relation of mine was saying to us only on Sunday how much Doreen had improved. Her figure. Her posture. Her hair. And you should see the encouraging report

Arlene Carter sent in after Doreen had finished the course at her Charm School. Did I mention that we'd sent her there?'

'Er – no. Well. Good. Very good.'

Dr Gleeson, sighing, at last disengaged his eyes from mine. And I, remembering the said 'encouraging report', suppressed an urge to giggle wildly.

Doreen has made a tremendous effort, it read. *She promises to be quite a young lady!*

What a laugh. What a lie. Despite the hard-won expertise and ardent dedication of Miss Arlene Hazel Carter (Dip. Beauty Care, Onderstepoort Technical College), I had cleverly managed to avoid mastery of the entire list of accomplishments specified in the curriculum. These, for the record, were:

1. Basic ramp-modelling skills on medium-high stilettos, including opening and closing a sun parasol while showing, to best advantage, a full-skirted frock. Simple twirls. Elementary glove work. Buttoning and unbuttoning jackets and coats.

2. Light make-up and lessons in complexion care. Lip-enhancement and effective eye-lining. Application of blushers, spot-concealers and other aids to facial attractiveness.

3. Hair management.

4. A foundation course in etiquette. Small talk and the art of listening. Correct manipulation of crockery and cutlery, and other aspects of meal-time manners. Some essential tips for the appreciative guest and the hospitable hostess.

5. Graceful posture. Walking tall and sitting straight. Descending a staircase. Entering and leaving a crowded room. Entering and leaving a car.

Poor Arlene Carter. How she had tried. I felt quite sorry for her, especially during Motor-Car Manoeuvres (Section 5c). These were conducted in the Charm School Mini Minor, which was parked outside the studio.

'Hold your knees *together*, Doreen,' Arlene pleaded, almost in tears. 'Keep both feet on the pavement and lower your bottom on to the seat. With control. Much more control. Good. Very good. Now – swing the legs across. All in one movement . . .'

It was hopeless. By my fifteenth futile attempt, a curious crowd had gathered.

'Right, Doreen. One last try,' Arlene said, determinedly ignoring the spectators. Frustration had unravelled her blonde perm and smudged her lipstick and defeated the efficacy of her underarm anti-perspirant. Since I had perceived neither du Plessis malice nor Gleeson avarice in my unfortunate charm teacher, I wanted to advise her to call a halt to this impossible exercise. To save her from further embarrassment. But Arlene, clearly, was quite determined. And so I explored yet another angle in a final bid for a smooth and unimpeded posterior descent.

'Better, Doreen. Much better. Now the legs. Carefully . . .'

'I – can't.'

'Of course you can. You're doing beautifully.'

'But – I'm stuck. My – um – hips. They seem to be wedged . . .'

Talk about mortification. I thought I'd be trapped there for ever. At last with the help of an obliging male onlooker, I was hoisted out of the upholstery and followed my charm teacher indoors. Arlene was muttering something about how, until that day, she had always considered Motor-Car Manoeuvres to be the glorious climax to a Charm School course. The moment when a pupil, in full possession of skills 1 to 4, would emerge into the street and, like a fair damsel of old, be swept off her feet by a knight on a charger and spirited away. Metaphorically speaking. Imagination, she confessed, had always been her strongest suit, which was why she'd been drawn to Charm School teaching. Then she looked at me accusingly. We both knew that no imagination in the world could override the brutal reality of Doreen Markowitz's failure at her final unlearnt lesson.

'I'm – sorry, Miss Carter,' I said. 'Perhaps if it had been a different car . . .'

'Don't worry. Forget about it.' She sighed. 'Oh dear. I don't know *what* I'm going to say in your report. We don't want to disappoint your poor mother.'

'No.' I shook my head emphatically. 'We don't.'

Arlene Carter, who was nothing if not good-natured, finally assembled her carefully chosen words of encouragement . . . *quite a young lady!* Faint praise indeed. But compared with the verdict of Shawn and Sheena West of the Twinkle-Toes Ballroom Dancing Studio, my Charm School report was a rave review.

The Wests (an amiable brother and sister partnership, who had once reached third place in a world Foxtrot Olympiad) had been proud of their no-nonsense guarantee that a course of ten lessons would bring 'dazzling party-time success to any willing wallflower'. Justifiably proud. In twenty-two years, there hadn't been a single pupil who had failed to respond positively to their renowned rhythm method. Until I bowled along.

They were suspicious from the start. I heard Sheena trying, as tactfully as possible, to persuade my mother that I'd be best suited to private lessons. Strictly private. 'We could do so much more for her if we had her on her own for an hour a week,' she urged.

'Yeah, send her on her own for an hour a week,' Shawn repeated dolefully. He seemed to support his sister with the same stolid reliability on the dance-floor as in real life. I wondered if he knew which was which.

But Molly had made up her mind. 'I believe you run Saturday morning classes for young people. Mixed classes, they tell me. That's exactly what I want for Doreen. To join in with a mixed class. It's what she needs. It's what I'm paying for. It's what I'll get.'

And so, for ten successive Saturdays, I was trundled round the room by either Shawn West or his sister. They took it in turns. I suppose they reckoned it halved the damage that way. Not only the bruises on the insteps and lacerations on the calves, but the embarrassment. Shawn led me through the slow-step and Sheena willed me through the waltz and they pretended not to hear the spasmodic explosions of giggles that spread from one pair of pupils to another like firecrackers.

Clearly they assumed that I was the butt. Who else? After all, a clumsier, more ill-proportioned dancer would have been hard to find anywhere. My attempts at the foxtrot were sheer travesty. At first Shawn and Sheena reacted to the laughter with increasingly dazzling smiles and regarded me quite compassionately. The fat girl no one else wanted to partner.

Then, after about four lessons, they suddenly became aware that I was laughing too. Not aloud. Not in an obvious way. No, I'd contained my amusement in silent shrugs of my shoulders and a sort of gleam in my eyes. The way I'd shuffle past my classmates. The shameless grins with which I would acknowledge their titters.

'Do you *enjoy* being laughed at?' Sheena asked me angrily, clearly beset by an unsettling suspicion that somehow I'd been diverting the amusement of the class from myself to my teachers. 'You're a trouble-maker. I knew from the start you'd be a trouble-maker. I wish we'd never taken you on. I'd like to get rid of you now. Right now.'

But my mother had paid for ten lessons. She had booked them and paid for them and insisted on them.

'They are doing Doreen a lot of good,' she said in a voice that brooked no contradiction. 'The dancing isn't so import-ant. It's the *mixing* I want for her. In fact, it could be that one course won't be enough. Maybe I should speak to my husband about . . .'

'No, no, Mrs Markowitz,' Sheena interrupted quickly. She

70

knew when to cut her losses. 'One set of lessons will be quite sufficient.'

It certainly had been. I picked out a pair of plump butter-cream twists and made them quickstep round the table before stuffing them into my mouth. They squelched satisfyingly on impact with my incisors. Delicious. I giggled to myself and remembered the joke about the fat little funny-girl whose mother desperately wanted her to be thin and charming and socially acceptable. D'you know the one?

The point of it was that the funny-girl had a feeling she had to hang on to her fatness. Something inside her told her she should defy the diet doctors and charm vendors and dance teachers and dressmakers with all the ammunition she could lay her hands on, uisng fair means or foul. It became a life-or-death issue for our funny-girl.

So she went to war. Secret forays into ice-cream parlours. Pâtisserie raids. Invasions of chip shops. She stopped at nothing to preserve the fatness that was hers as surely as her inborn treasury of wit. The poor girl hadn't been able to save the jokes from seeping away. Millions of them had been lost for ever. But she still had her fatness and she vowed to defend it through thick and thin.

And she did. She fought valiantly. She fought with all her might until she finally took occupation of the kitchen. As large as ever. As large as life. The funny-girl, feasting victoriously, was hugely enjoying the last laugh. Wasn't she . . .?

Well, perhaps not as much as I'd anticipated. There was something missing. I stopped eating, wondering exactly what it was that my joke lacked. Timing? Surprise? Coherence? No – none of those things. What it needed, I decided, was an audience. Someone to share my laughter.

Just as I'd reached this conclusion, I heard footsteps approaching the kitchen. The unmistakable footsteps of my father. That was it. I'd tell him. I'd share my joke with him and we'd laugh together and my pleasure would be complete.

71

'Dad,' I began, turning towards him with arms out-stretched. 'Dad, listen. D'you want to hear the funniest thing . . .'

Then I saw his expression. Was that a shadow of disgust passing across his bland features? A shudder of revulsion with which he was retreating from my open hands? Was it nausea with which he was turning away? I was suddenly aware that my face was shiny with excitement and flushed with excess calories and sticky with the vestiges of party fare. My torn satin dress was stained with sugary smudges and damp patches of sweat.

'Dad . . .?'

He composed himself so quickly that I could almost have sworn I had imagined it. Within moments he was regarding me with his usual kindly concern.

'Dorinke,' he was saying, his eyes moistening with tears. 'Dorinke, Dorinke what are we going to do with you?'

'I don't know,' I answered. In a dull voice. A dead voice. My audience had fallen flat. Doreen the funny-girl had died. It was death by distaste. I had always felt fat but never before had I felt unlovable. My victory didn't matter any more.

I heard them discussing me that night. Mumbling, anxious voices.

'What are we going to do with her?' my mother kept asking. My father, in an uncharacteristic display of initiative, had telephoned all the party guests and explained that, owing to his wife's unfortunate ill health, the birthday celebration had been put off. Indefinitely. Then, in silence, we had tidied the kitchen together, me and him. So that Beatrice wouldn't suspect my gluttony. Then I'd taken myself to bed and settled into the darkness and listened to their litany.

'Answer me, Sam, will you? Please. What's to become of her?'

'I don't know, Molly. Honestly, I don't know.'

'One thing I can tell you – oh, my head. My aching head. Sam, she won't get a husband. Not if she carries on this way.

Tell me honestly – do you think any man on earth will want to marry a girl who looks like that? Never. Never in a million years.'

A million years was stretching it. Less than a dozen, as it happened. It might have cheered my mother to know that there was indeed someone out there whose destiny it was to marry me. Someone a few thousand miles away, who would, around that time, have been consoling himself with his favourite fantasy about an adoring and beautiful princess. It was fortunate – or unfortunate – that young Geoffrey Bartholomew-Cooper couldn't see the unappealing heap of misery that was spurting snotty tears in the pretty pink room next door to that of her parents. The course of this story might have run very differently if he had.

But then, aren't most classic tales of true love heavily dependent on Cupid's arrow falling at a particular time and place? For instance, do you imagine that Romeo would have fallen for Juliet if he'd been around to see her toddler tantrums and ignominious early failures at faecal control? Or that Tristan would have been attracted to Isolde if he had first clapped eyes on her when she was bloated and cross with premenstrual tension?

Geoffrey certainly wouldn't have fancied me fat and going-on-fourteen. But then, I wouldn't have been exactly cheered by the prospect of being wedded to a nasty, wimpy Mummy's boy with chicken-pox. I was depressed enough already. A glimpse of spotty Geoffrey in self-pitying isolation in the sanatorium of his fancy boarding-school might easily have pushed me over the edge.

6

No, Geoffrey and I didn't meet till much later. We didn't clap eyes on one another until long after he'd turned into the man who grew out of the boy who had chicken-pox and dreamt of happiness for ever with a fair princess. The man with the gun and the trained legal mind. The man who disapproved of my stretch marks. The man who died laughing.

Laughing?

Quite. That was a shock. Even more of a shock than the dying. You see, I'd never before heard Geoffrey laugh. No one had.

His mother, apparently, made desperate attempts to induce a smile on the face of her infant son.

'Goo, goo, goo,' she would repeat in a mounting frenzy of impatience and manic intensity until, by the time Geoffrey was nine months old and every other kid in the neighbourhood was smiling and gurgling and some were even chuckling out loud, she was getting down on her hands and knees and braying like a donkey and barking like a seal. 'Gullabagoo-oo-oo. Gollyballoo-oo. Goo, Geoffrey. Goo, Geoffrey. Goo, goo, *goo-oo-oo* . . .'

But nothing happened. Geoffrey continued to stare at her with unblinking solemnity.

'Geoffrey, you little prick, will you wipe that accusing look off your face and smile, dammit!' she finally screamed. It was on a Sunday, her worst day of the week. The day of rest. The day when all the niggling little Monday-to-Saturday droplets of discontent found space to coalesce into an oppressive cloud of gloom. The day when Roger and Dick and Martin and John and the others retreated to their families in the suburbs, leaving lovely Lulu Cooper alone in her well-appointed Chelsea flat. With her brat. Her boring and stubbornly unsmiling brat.

'Right. That's it. I've had it. I've bloody had enough,' she said, pulling herself to her feet and steadying herself against a marbled rococo pilaster. The flat was choked with orna-mentation. It was a dizzying cornucopia of neo-this and pseudo-that and in-the-style-of-Louis-the-other which was to exert an unfortunate influence on Geoffrey's later taste in decoration. Lulu's fondness for rum, particularly on a Sunday, would have an equally unfortunate effect on his later taste in drink.

'How much is a person expected to put up with?' she demanded of the rather drunk and dishevelled blonde who confronted her in the brass-framed mirror adjacent to the pilaster. The blonde, she couldn't help noticing, had roots in need of bleaching and puffy red eyes and a sagging jaw-line and a shiny nose. The blonde, she had to admit, looked a mess.

'Beautiful Miss Bubbles. The toast of London. The cham-pagne girl with everything,' muttered Lulu bitterly. 'And what's she got now, huh?'

She swung round and, ignoring all her other (apparently considerable) possessions, addressed a discontented frown to young Geoffrey in his play-pen. He frowned back.

'You. She ends up with you,' Lulu said with some venom. Maternal warmth was not among her endowments, despite misleadingly large breasts. 'And a bloody misery you're turning out to be. A born depressive, just like your father.'

She was referring to an earnest and affluent young medical student called Lionel Bartholomew who had, one mad night when the moon was full and a bottle-and-a-half of superior rum had been emptied, lost his virginity to glamorous and worldly Lulu Cooper. It had been a pleasant, if expensive, experience for Lionel. Lulu had discovered soon afterwards that she was pregnant.

'It's yours,' she had announced to rich, hapless Lionel. 'Unless you do – um – the honourable thing, I'm afraid I'm going to have to . . .'

'No!' Lionel had been horrified. Some of his worst nightmares had featured the accidental death of a patient-to-be. How would he live with the knowledge that he'd been an accessory to the murder of his own unborn child? But marry *Lulu Cooper*? That would be unthinkable. 'Please – don't, Lulu. Surely there must be another way.'

'What? Name it?'

Money. The acceptable alternative had been cold hard cash. Enough to maintain Lulu in a fox-fur and a four-poster, and to feed her sour-faced son the most expensive formulae on the market. A seductive monthly payment that kept Lulu afloat in a tide of tat and turned her from an independent earner into a kept woman. She hated it. She hated the blameless man who had tempted her into this predicament. She grew to hate all men, including the unsmiling speck of testosterone that was eventually to become my husband. Poor Geoffrey. Let's face it. He never had a chance.

'Sulky brat,' Lulu said when, having abandoned her efforts to amuse him, she finally turned away from her son and headed for her bedroom. 'If you think I'm going to stay in all day trying to please you, you have another thought coming. I'm off. Off, d'you understand? And maybe by the time I get back, you'll be happy to see me. You'd better bloody be.'

Geoffrey's eyes followed the figure of his mother as it swept into the adjoining room and divested itself of its daisy-print house-coat and, clad in brief black snippets of satin and lace, settled itself at its dressing-table and started to do its face. He watched with great absorption as the face emerged. The smudges of blue that turned her eyelids the colour of the summer sky. The coral-pink cheeks. The pale puffs of powder. And finally the lips. Shiny plum-red lips that swelled into voluptuous curves and made Geoffrey's little heart stop.

Even then. He always maintained that nothing after that ever quite matched the erotic appeal of his mother's painted lips.

'Right,' she said, standing up and pulling something over her head. The black bits of lace and satin were smothered in a tight (and even blacker) dress and Geoffrey waited for the familiar flowery smell when he saw her squeezing an atomizer to release a mist of scent.

'Right,' she said again, inserting a clutch bag into her left armpit and taking steps towards the door. They were rather faltering steps, for Lulu had, during the course of that unsatisfactory day, consumed more than her customary quantity of rum.

'Right,' she said yet again, with slightly less vigour, as she reached out to steady herself against a plinth supporting a marble bust. The bust (an archaic sort of female with curls and a cleavage) fell heavily against a standard lamp, which wobbled and crashed on to the glass coffee-table. And Lulu, grabbing frantically and ineffectually at the falling sculpture and failing light and the disintegrating table-top, lost her clutch bag and her balance and landed in an indignified position on the deep-pile rug.

'Right.' She was almost in tears but didn't cry, for she wasn't the crying sort. 'Well then, I'll be off . . .'

Then she caught sight of her son in his play-pen. Her wet-blanket baby who'd been watching her stumble with his usual reproving stare. Her misery, her mistake, her millstone – and what was that she saw on his face? A smile? Was that a *smile*? After nine dead-pan months, had his mother's misfortune finally brought about small Geoffrey's first-ever expression of merriment?

Yes indeed. For it seemed that, despite his backwardness in jollity, Geoffrey had emerged as an infant prodigy of *schadenfreude*. This came to be one of his most enduring and least endearing talents. It was probably why he turned out to be so universally disliked at school.

*

77

'Stop smirking, Bartholomew-Cooper,' were the words Geoffrey most frequently heard from his teachers, almost from the start of his educational career. Such a pity. There were so many other more positive aspects of his personality which might have drawn comment. His meticulous neatness, for instance. The exercise books filled with arithmetic all relentlessly correct and compositions without a single unforced error. The shiny shoes and symmetrically combed hair. Geoffrey might have gained a reputation as the boy who never lost a mark. The cleanest boy in every school he attended. A model pupil. Instead he became known as The Smirker. It was a nickname that, once acquired, seemed to stick.

It certainly came with him to Brewers, an austere establishment in the heart of Sussex with an academic reputation that bore no relation to its fees. A hugely expensive parking place for the teenage sons of the idle rich.

'But Lulu,' objected Lionel Bartholomew, now a struggling general practitioner. His night of passion had put paid to any prospect of idleness or wealth. In addition to Geoffrey, he had acquired a thoroughbred wife and two legitimate children and lived carefully in a cul-de-sac in Epsom. 'This school's going to cost me a fortune. Surely there must be another place we could have considered for Geoffrey?'

Lulu, however, had made up her mind. No other school but Brewers would do. For one thing, it was conveniently remote from Chelsea. Far enough to make Geoffrey's home visits satisfactorily infrequent. And, most importantly, it offered to take him *now*. Lulu had found single parenthood neither glamorous nor fulfilling. She couldn't wait to resume being *femme fatale*.

'Lionel,' she said warningly, 'when you undertook to foot the bill for Geoffrey, it was on condition that all the decision-making was left to me. I've had to put up with the kid for thirteen years and I'm warning you now, it's either the school or . . .'

'All right, all right.' Lionel was a soft touch, which was

why Lulu found him so boring. 'If you think it's best, then I'll find the money somehow.'

He did. He always did, no matter how extravagant Lulu's claims. That was how Geoffrey came to be among the seven new boys who were gathered in the gloomy Brewers dining-hall for a welcoming address by their house master. Four of them were tearful, two audibly sniffing, and Geoffrey's mouth twitched. He couldn't help it.

'Is that a smirk I see on your face, Bartholomew-Cooper?' demanded Hans Gelderman, the master, an uncertain homo-sexual with sadistic leanings and various other unsavoury inclinations. His instant dislike for the skinny and bespec-tacled clever-clogs with the sneer was even sharper than his scorn for the homesick snivellers. 'Give me one term, Bartho-lomew-Cooper, and you'll have nothing to smirk about. Nothing.'

But Gelderman, in common with most of Geoffrey's adversaries, completely underestimated the tenacity of this *schadenfreude*. It was anchored deep in the pit of his soul, its roots knotted firmly around all the sadness and unwanted-ness buried there. Through the passing pleasure that he found in the misfortunes of others, Geoffrey had found that he could stifle his longing for the woman at the dressing-table mirror with eyes the colour of the summer sky and delicious plum-red lips. It was his lifeline, his mainstay, his relief. The only way he knew of choking out the taunting images of Roger and Dick and Martin and John and all the other men who took his mother out into the darkness each night. His only means of expelling their voices and keeping his own darkness at bay.

That was why, a term later, despite the most vigorous suppressive efforts of the teachers and the loathing of his peers, Geoffrey's smirk remained intact. He sniggered under his breath when Dent received a caning. His lips curled into a sarcastic leer when Campbell was discovered to have cheated in a test. And his *schadenfreude* reached a peak of derisory relish when brainy, brawny Richard Blott, the only boy in the school who'd proved capable of defeating him at chess, developed chicken-pox. *Chicken-pox.* Of all the unglamorous diseases.

'You look fowl, Richard,' gloated Geoffrey through the sanatorium door. He had recently discovered that puns, scrupulously used, were an effective way of getting the knife in. They also seemed to signify a sense of humour, which suited Geoffrey. He was already beginning to work on his image as a sharp-witted man of the law. 'Blott the blotch. D'you know they've put Spotted Dick on tonight's dinner menu? Eh? Eh?'

Geoffrey chortled and kept chortling until, a fortnight later, he began to itch violently in various unmentionable parts of his anatomy and was banished to a small, single-bedded cell.

'Hard luck, Bartholomew-Cooper, old cock,' called Blott, who had staged an excellent recovery by then.

'Piss off,' said Geoffrey. Under stress, he sometimes found himself reverting to the maternal scatology he'd been weaned on, and all traces of his emergent highbrow poise disappeared. 'Get lost, Blott. Everyone. Leave me alone.'

They did. Entirely. For two miserable weeks Geoffrey itched and scratched in total isolation. Very rarely had the chicken-pox virus invaded a teenage body with such tenacious malice. He scratched and itched and, during brief periods of respite, began to question the meaning of all his suffering. The way one does when things are at their worst. Geoffrey might even have turned to God at this nadir of his young life if his opportunism had developed as early as his *schadenfreude.*

Instead he sought comfort in fantasy. Sentimental and mawkish visions of being cared for by someone tenderly and totally adoring. Someone with soft white hands to wipe his eyes and soothe his spots and cool his forehead. Someone with luscious rum-smelling plum-red lips to shower him with kisses. Hardly someone like me.

*

Not then, anyway. Many years were to pass before the fat girl and the spotty boy would be transformed into the handsome couple who marched with such assurance into the misery of their marriage. Geoffrey, tall and upright, would retain the relic of a single small pock-mark above his left eyebrow. And I, slender and graceful (believe it or not), would delight my man with a liberal application of damson-coloured lipstick. I tried to make sure it was a coating thick enough to obliterate the memory of the custard kisses and other delights that had passed through my lips on the eve of my fourteenth birthday. I couldn't bear to remember the joy of that feast – and the disappointment afterwards. Most of all, I wanted to forget the awfulness of the following day.

'Good morning, Dorinke. Happy birthday.'

Was I in heaven? Or hell? Most likely the latter, I decided. With my luck, I was probably marking the fourteenth anniversary of my birth in the company of the souls of assorted Nazi monsters and Rommel the dog (who had recently come to a gratifyingly unpleasant end in combat with a puff adder). And my father.

My father? Surely, after all his noble trials on earth, he couldn't also have been consigned down here?

I opened my eyes and wondered why hell looked so much like my familiar pink room and noticed the ruins of my purple dress and Sam hovering at the end of a bed that bulged with Himalayan mounds of daughter. Daughter, sighing, tasted sourness. I tried to clear my throat, and a wave of nausea reminded me of the excesses of the night before. I wiggled my foothills and watched them shuddering and then tested several peaks and crests before deciding that the range was undoubtedly alive and would have to face the music. Ah well, I thought resignedly. So much for hell.

'Morning, Dad.'

Rather wistfully, I recalled that today I was supposed to have starred in a dazzling production featuring not only the transformation of the Ugly Duckling and Cinderella's ball,

81

but the highest-kicking and most rousing finale that had ever set fire to a Cape Town stage. And this time I hadn't been cast as the witch. Oh no. Not in the Molly Markowitz Show. I was to have knocked them out as the lovely heroine. And instead, here I was . . .

'Dorinke, I want you should go and say sorry to your mother.'

He had moved closer to the bed and, even in the dim early-morning light, I could see the puffy signs of strain round his eyes. He was dressed in his work suit and a piece of tissue marked a spot on his chin where his razor had slipped.

'She's going to make herself sick from the worry and disappointment. Tell her . . .'

'What?' I interrupted angrily. 'I didn't ask for the party and all that.'

'I know.'

He looked sad, beaten, hopeless. I remembered the way his face had once glowed with nostalgia for *Der-Heim*, the relish with which he'd swallowed Molly's pre-calorie-controlled meals and the hope with which he would count his blessings. All five of them, including the joy of his little girl.

Then I remembered the resignation with which he had faced reduced rations and the mounting pile of bills for the improvements lavished on the same joy-giving little girl. The worry-lines that had deepened as expenses had mounted and demand for his suits had dropped and his little girl's weight had gone up and up, and food-portions had diminished inversely with Molly's growing hysteria. And Sam, with dogged and tiresome persistence, had kept repeating old jokes to break the tense meal-time silences. Jokes about lawyers and beggars and chickens and eggs. About hypochondriacs and used-car salesmen. About tight shoes and loose women and surly waiters and merry thieves.

I'd been the only one to smile at the punchlines. His delivery was dreadful, but I had always seen the point. On the whole, however, Sam's jokes usually fell as flat as I had believed any joke could possibly fall – until the failure of my own big birthday joke. Which reminded me of his expression

82

of disgust the night before, and how I had believed I had died. And how little I cared now, one way or another. But if it helped to cheer him up, to make him less defeated and more hopeful, well then, what the hell, I'd toddle off to Molly and get down on my knees. What did it matter?

'All right. I'll go and apologize.'

He nodded and seemed about to bend down towards me. Then he straightened his back and cleared his throat, absently touching the tissue on his chin.

'She – only wants the best for you, Dorinke. Please try to understand it.'

The tissue had come away. I saw the small red puddle that swelled and burst its banks and started to trickle slowly downwards.

'Dad – you're bleeding.'

He pressed a finger to his face and frowned as he examined it. 'Hmmm. So I am. So I am.' Then he shrugged with his usual resigned smile. 'Oh well. Plenty more where that comes from. Blood, sweat and tears. Your heritage, Dorinke.'

That's great, I thought. Terrific. Some people get oil wells and houses in the country and family jewels. And blonde hair and blue eyes and a portfolio of stocks and shares. Lou-Anne gets glamour. Cousin Norman gets brains. And Doreen Markowitz gets with blessed with blood, sweat and tears.

'Is that all?' I asked. I knew that Molly and Sam had quit Europe in a hurry and had heard about the candlesticks and cloths and silver samovars they'd been forced to leave behind. And the cousins and aunts and the pine forests and hoar frosts and all the wonderful things that South Africa could never, ever provide. But surely, even in their great haste, they might have managed to smuggle out more than the fluids excreted by pain, work and misery?

'All?' He shrugged again. 'Dorinke, believe me, it's plenty. Sometimes I believe it's everything.'

Was he being funny? I searched his face carefully, but his expression hadn't changed. Then he looked at me enquiringly.

'Tell me, Dorinke – what else would you have wanted?'

83

'Um – I don't know. Money, maybe? Yes, lots more money.'

'And then?'

'And then – well – we'd have a big house filled with – things. Books, records, games. An enormous swimming pool.'

'And then?'

'What d'you mean, Dad? Then I'd have loads of friends.'

'Uh-huh. And so?'

'And so – well, eventually I'd find a really handsome man who'd want to marry me. Rich ladies usually do. Even fat ones.'

'And then?'

'Then – then I'd be happy. Wouldn't I?'

'You would?'

There was silence for a moment. We looked at one another and Sam shook his head wryly.

'Happiness,' he said. 'What's happiness? At least with blood, sweat and tears, there's no nonsense. You can count on it. You know exactly where you are. As for money . . . I'll tell you something about money, Dorinke.'

'What?'

'It's what my father used to say to me. "Sam," he'd say, "Sam, we're not rich people and the chances are you will have to make your way through this world a poor man. But Sam – be patient with your poverty. Be patient until you turn fifty."

' "Why fifty, Papa?" I'd ask, imagining God-knows-what. The fortune that awaited me maybe. "What will happen to me when I'm fifty?"

' "By then," he would say, "you'll be used to it." '

Chuckling to himself, Sam started for the door. 'Oh, Dad,' I laughed. I loved him then.

'Just remember, Dorinke,' he said over his shoulder, a smile crinkling the corners of his sad strained eyes. 'Remember that a person can get used to anything.'

*

If that was true, perhaps my mother had finally got used to the idea of an intractably fat daughter? Or had her migraine wiped out her memory?

'Mum – I'm sorry about . . .' I began, having dragged myself out of bed and gathered as much dutiful humility as I could squeeze into my already tight nylon dressing-gown. I had tapped on the door and taken tentative steps into my parents' room and immediately launched into my speech of apology. But the room was empty. Molly wasn't there.'

Then I heard her voice drifting from the kitchen. Her *madam* voice, as imperious as ever.

'Beatrice, I want you to give the kitchen a good scrubbing. The floor, the cupboards, the sink. Everything. And later, when I come back from my shopping, I'll show you how to make cabbage meat. Cabbage meat and potato *kugel* and carrot *tzimmes*. We'll have that for supper . . . no, you can put away the diet book. I told you already – we don't need it any more. We've finished with all that . . .'

I listened, tranfixed. What was I hearing? *Cabbage meat? Potato kugel? Tzimmes?* What had happened to Molly? Surely she wasn't going to set all those hordes of calories free on to the supper table? They'd run riot. There'd be chaos. She must have gone completely mad.

'Mum . . .?' I called out in panic.

'. . . and tomorrow I want you to go through the house, one room at a time, and clean it properly. From top to bottom. You've been slacking lately, Beatrice. I noticed this morning that the taps in the bathroom were dull. From now on, I'm going to have to keep a closer eye on things . . .'

'Mum!'

Why had he lied about her being sick? Sick with worry and disappointment, he'd said. What nonsense. Molly didn't care. Not really. So what if her daughter had let her down? There was always the house and the *shikse* to attend to instead. Much easier to control. Much more amenable to being polished to a state of immaculate perfection. I tried to tell myself that I should be feeling relieved, reprieved. As free as a bird.

A bird? A 200-pound bird with a 38DD bust? Would such a creature ever get off the ground? I was a threatened species, if ever there was one. Never mind threatened. Look what had happened to the dodo.

'Mum,' I cried, bursting into the kitchen. No, I didn't want to be consigned to extinction. Not then. Not yet. 'Oh, Mum, I'm really, really sorry . . .'

'Doreen! Why aren't you dressed for school? Look at the time already?'

'But – didn't you say I could stay home on my birthday? I thought . . .'

'You thought! Don't tell me what you thought. Plenty things were said about your birthday. So many plans. But I think it's better we shouldn't go into it again now. Get dressed and go to school and we'll try to forget about the whole business.'

She spoke in a voice so brittle that I could almost see her words splintering in the air. Her lips were drawn tighter round her mouth than I had ever before seen them and her hair-do, after its night-time restraint in an elasticized net, was still moulded to her head like a helmet. Her eyes were hard and black.

'Mum – I give up,' I wanted to say. What chance did a grounded bird have against the might of this warrior queen? She could easily take it into her head to have me plucked and trussed for dinner. I was frightened. Terrified. 'Mum,' I wanted to plead, 'save me. Please save me.'

I started moving towards my mother and opened my mouth to speak. But Molly had turned away and carried on issuing instructions to the servant:

'So you understand what has to be done, Beatrice? The kitchen first. Properly. From top to toe. Remember – I'll be checking up on it when I get back from town.'

'Yes, madam.'

Slowly, I backed out of the kitchen and made my way to my room and, in a trance, I dressed for school. 'A person can get used to anything,' he'd said. I had almost believed him

86

until I had faced my mother's steely indifference. Could a person ever get used to that?

It proved much easier than I had imagined when I discovered that all I had to do was eat. And eat. And keep eating. How amazing food was. How versatile. How convenient. Once upon a time, it had offered pure sensual delight. Then it had given me the thrill of a fight-to-the-last-laugh battle, with horde upon horde of warring calories. Now it had become a drug that granted oblivion.

'Mollinke, what a meal! How long is it since we've had *tzimmes*? You certainly haven't lost your touch.'

'Oh Sam, the trouble I've been having trying to train Beatrice. Between you and me, I don't know if I have the patience. So clumsy. Such a heavy hand with the salt. I'll have to think about letting her go.'

'So – you'll see what's best. But the food, Molly. Such food! I'd almost forgotten . . .'

With some trepidation, I had raised the first forkful to my mouth. Surely this feast hadn't been intended for me? At any moment Molly would turn disapproving eyes on me. 'Doreen!' she would say. 'A person your size shouldn't be eating such things. Don't you know that by now? Sam, what are we going to do with her?'

But Molly said nothing. Nobody said a word. Not about me, at any rate.

'MacWilliams came in today with another order, thank God. He used to be a good customer in the old days. Maybe it's a sign that things will start picking up now, eh?'

'Who knows, Sam. As long as he pays. By the way, did you ever collect the money from that Max Levine? A *gonif* if ever there was one. How long is it since you gave him his suit?'

'Six months, a year – what's the difference?'

'Really, Sam, you should be more careful. Your biggest problem is that you're too trusting. You let people get away with murder. Here. Have some more meat.'

Quietly and methodically, I emptied my plate and then, with some apprehension, nudged it forward for a refill. 'Doreen!' I expected to hear. 'I can't believe what I'm seeing. Such a huge helping I gave you and you're still asking for more. Sam, I give up.'

But again Molly said nothing. She silently reloaded the plate, and no one seemed to take the slightest notice.

'Molly, this is doing me good. Aah. Mmm. I can feel my strength coming back with every mouthful. It reminds me of the old story about the beggar and the rich woman. D'you know the one?'

'No. Sam, please – nobody's in the mood for your jokes . . .'

'Quickly. Let me tell you. The beggar approaches the woman and tells her how weak he is – how he hasn't eaten a thing for five days. And what do you think she says? Eh? Molly . . .?'

'Sam, listen to me . . .'

'Dorinke?'

'What, Dad? What does she say?' Even when things were at their worst, I could never resist feeding him his lines.

'You're going to have to force yourself. Do you get that, heh heh? You're going to . . .'

'All right. All right.'

Molly frowned. I smiled. I'd been forcing myself without any difficulty. The food was slipping down like foam stuffing into a giant pillow. Soft bubbly mousse that swelled to fill all my hollow spaces, my raw and aching cavities. It smothered my pain and dulled their voices and induced the same sort of light-headed lethargy that I was later to attain with Valium and other related soporifics.

'Oi, I'm so full, Molly. Delicious. Delicious meal,' I heard from far away. From another planet. From an incomprehensible, nightmarish place where people were stripped of homes, dignity and flesh and lay gasping with the corpses of spent calories and dead jokes and defeated hopes. Getting used to it. All their lives trying to get used to it. I had eaten enough to make my ears buzz and my eyes glaze and my throat close. I'd found another way. An easier way.

High above the squalor I'd risen, to a soft and silent otherland. A more gentle place, where I could float like a giant cloud through a warm blanket of mist, resting my cotton wool head on my own duck-down chest. Sleeping and eating. Eating and sleeping. Sleeping. Eating. Sleeping.

And so the days and months and years drifted past in a carbohydrate-induced haze. I ate and studied and slept and ate. I ate and ate incessantly, paying little attention to the out-of-focus world with its pointless conversations and meaningless jokes. The stray words that sometimes trickled through my consciousness like drops of water seeping through a sponge.

At meal-times I seldom spoke and hardly listened. Well-worn phrases and time-tested food went to and fro across the table with the same predictability as the salt, pepper and mustard. Sam sighed and Molly served and I chewed and swallowed. Tirelessly I masticated, pausing only now and again to see who would respond to the strident ringing of Molly's dinner bell. The appearance of a new face above the familiar pink overall and starched white apron had become the only changing feature of family meals.

Beatrice didn't survive Molly's renewed madam-zeal for long. One Monday morning, she failed to appear and for the week that followed the only sign of a *shikse* in the Markowitz kitchen was the half-full bottle of enormous pills labelled *Native Aperients* that she had left behind. Beatrice had a constipation problem and had often sworn by the efficacy of her pills. They didn't, however, help her successor, Sophie, who was found to have a drinking problem. One evening, in an enthusiastic and inebriated effort to clear the table, she caught hold of a corner of the laden cloth and pulled it behind her to the door. It took Molly months to match up the shattered pieces of dinner service.

Sophie was succeeded by Maria, who was regarded as

89

'lacking in intelligence'. She kept responding to the chimes of the dinner bell by answering the front door and then rushing to pick up the telephone before finally arriving at the table in a flurry of breathless confusion. Molly's patience was soon exhausted.

Christina followed. Then Martha. Then Maggie (who pinched) and Angelina (who was haughty) and Thelma (who was sly). Until at last Molly seemed to lose interest. She allowed Olive (who succeeded Thelma and was undoubtedly the greediest, untidiest, clumsiest and cheekiest of all the Markowitz maids) a long and relatively unimpeded reign. Beatrice's aperients somehow remained a fixed feature on the kitchen window-sill, while Olive grew to be as much of an institution in Gladys Street as the hound who succeeded Rommel and became renowned for the abundance of his droppings and the keenness of his teeth. The Venters named him Himmler.

Meanwhile, I was becoming renowned for my size. I was getting fatter and fatter and fatter. By my fifteenth birthday I was tipping the scales at 220 pounds.

That was the year when Lou-Anne had her nose job and Norman entered university and Arnold Gleeson diversified into ready-meals. The year when Mathilda endured a double hysterectomy and Farella Venter had a nervous breakdown and Arlene Carter, in response to the *Zeitgeist*, changed the name of her charm school to 'Finishing Touches'.

Feminism had arrived.

It spread like wildfire and even reached the corsetry department at Stuttafords where, after an especially difficult Saturday, Flora Van Rensburg burned her bra. She burned quite a high percentage of the lingerie assortment at the same time, which gave her much satisfaction as well as an arson conviction and a spell in a mental institution. But you can't have everything.

That's what I told myself on my sixteenth birthday. I had thanked my parents for the new candlewick bedspread and

Mathilda for the dictionary and Aunty Ada for the hankies and the five-rand note. With the last I had taken myself to Dagwood's Snack Bar and indulged in a couple of hot dogs, several servings of chips, a strawberry thick shake and a banana parfait. I had swallowed the lot, but without my usual appetite. The flavour had seemed different. Strange. Sort of like – blood, sweat and tears. I had shuddered.

The food may have tasted like bodily fluid but, unfortunately, it had many more calories. It was the sixteenth birthday binge that finally pushed my weight over the 230-pound mark. By then, Lou-Anne had announced her first engagement and Cousin Norman had smoked his first joint and Arnold Gleeson, responding to another *Zeitgeist*, had abandoned his ready-meal operation and narrowed his area of expertise to the streamlining of hips and thighs.

Specialization had arrived.

It spread like an epidemic, penetrating even the inner sanctum of the Twinkle-Toes Studio where Sheena West (whose response to feminism had been to rid herself of Shawn) decided to focus only on the foxtrot. She went insolvent soon afterwards – but not before she had succeeded in conveying the essence of her art to a painfully thin pupil called Olivia Cook. Her mother, the deserted Regina, desperate to distract her soulful daughter and build up a few of her wasted muscles, had picked out the most genteel physical activity she could find in the local directory of business services.

She had overlooked an even more genteel diversion. Eurhythmics, as offered by elegant Mrs Minerva Cook, who had already grown bored with mundane domesticity in the company of her unfrocked priest. Prosper, meanwhile, sold life insurance and missed his Olivia. He did both things very badly and was sometimes quite depressed.

Dinkie du Plessis, on the other hand, was in wonderful spirits. She had anticipated feminism by founding a Women's Group for her loyal bunch of mummies and discovered that fees and consciousness could be raised simultaneously. Then, almost before the advent of specialization, she had trimmed her operation by cutting out the kiddies and offering a comprehensive range of self-expression to her liberated mummies. For a price. The *Zeitgeist* was always a step or two behind Dinkie du Plessis. In fact, it was highly possible that she was the *Zeitgeist*.

How else could she have known before anyone else that the next thing to hit Cape Town would be the Struggle for Equality?

By the time Cousin Norman, stoned out of his mathematical mind, had joined his first university sit-in and Arlene Carter had again renamed her school (Black is Beautiful) and Robert Nkethlo, victim of the late Rommel, had been found guilty of terrorism and sentenced to life imprisonment on Robben Island, Dinkie was two-thirds of the way up the hierarchy of the Black Sash. Her photograph with a placard bearing the message LET MY PEOPLE GO was printed very large on the front page of the *Cape Times* and came to be a symbol of the Struggle.

Newspapers all round the world paid to use this picture, which was seen as the expression of a new era of confrontation in South Africa. It was applauded in Stockholm and jeered at in Abu Dhabi, and in the sixth-form common room at Brewers (which encouraged regular perusal of the *Daily Telegraph*), the bravely smiling countenance of the plucky protester gained a ballpoint moustache and a pair of enormous, flapping ears.

'Silly old bat,' said Geoffrey Bartholomew-Cooper.

Which was more or less what I remarked when I saw the photo of my old ballet teacher. I observed that Dinkie's face had wrinkled and her feet were badly placed in third position and wondered what the placard was all about. For, although the Struggle for Equality was spreading through Cape Town like ragweed, it still had some way to go before its tentacles reached Gladys Street.

In Gladys Street, while students marched and women picketed and workers sulked, Olive still brought morning tea to her madam in bed and Himmler growled openly at any passing black and Rex Venter drank beer with his brother, Frikkie, and they exchanged racist jokes. You know the kind.

And I, still afloat in my padded other-world, ate and ate. I had chomped through feminism and guzzled past specialization and was steadily munching through the Struggle. I was about to ingest my way to a place in the *Guinness Book of Records* when, three days before my eighteenth birthday, I was struck down by a passing flu virus. My weight, by this time, had reached an all-time high of 269 pounds and my temperature had soared past 104.

'I must confess, I'm worried,' said Max Freedman, the family doctor, who had been woken at 2 a.m. and summoned to my bedside.

'We're worried too,' said Sam, anxiously supporting Molly's arm. Molly's face was grim. 'Such a healthy girl usually. Never sick. Dorinke's as strong as a horse. Look at her!'

'I have, I have,' said the doctor, massaging his eyes. 'That's what worries me. Sam – Molly – you have to realize that her weight is dangerous. Her heart . . . Her chest . . . Already her blood pressure's much higher than it should be. Doreen? Do you understand? As soon as we get you better, we're going to have a good long talk about things.'

But I wouldn't talk. I couldn't. For five days, my weight and temperature hovered around 265 and 105 respectively and I cackled to myself for hours on end about the elephant who crossed the road because it was the chicken's day off.

'I think she's delirious,' said Sam.

'At least she's stopped eating,' said Dr Freedman. 'We can be thankful for that.'

I started again on day six. My temperature dropped and my appetite returned and my weight began to rise. And, between meals, I lay with my face to the wall, utterly refusing to engage in Dr Freedman's exhortations for a 'good, long talk'.

'Doreen,' he pleaded, 'don't you see what you're doing to youself? You could easily *die* . . .'

Die? I shut my eyes tighter and imagined an eternal cushion-land where I could float for ever. No more topping up with food. No more intrusive thoughts. No more uncomfortable questions. God, it was tempting.

'Sam – Molly – I'm afraid I have to admit defeat,' I heard the doctor saying. 'I can't get through to her at all. I'm – er – not sure how to put it to you – but I really do think that we ought to bring in a psychiatrist. It would be in her best interests. Honestly.'

'A *psychiatrist*?' Molly sounded appalled. 'Sam, do you hear what he's saying? Doctor, she's not . . .?'

7

Molly couldn't bring herself to say the word. Mad. *Mad*? As though it weren't unbearable enough that her child, her daughter, her flesh and blood, her hope for the future, her passport to belonging, her entire justification for being had turned out fat and funny. Now, God forbid, he was saying . . .

'Doctor, surely you don't mean she's . . .?'

I opened an eye.

'Knock knock,' I said.

'*What*?' said my mother, clutching hold of my father.

'What?' said my father, supporting my mother.

'Who's there?' said Dr Freedman, who knew his lines, I'll grant him that.

'Doreen,' I said, opening the other eye and engaging his bifocals in a meaningful non-verbal exchange. He turned away.

'Doreen who?' he asked dully, defeatedly, aiming a sad shake of the head in the general direction of my parents. They retreated wide-eyed from my bed, still supporting one another. I sat up. They took another step back and Dr Freedman opened his mouth. He was about to say something else, but I didn't let him.

'That's exactly what I'd like to know,' I yelled as hard as I could. This was brilliant. Amazing. My best performance ever. 'Who the hell am I? Who? Who? Who?'

*

As it happened, I wasn't mad. Never have been, clinically speaking, even though my behaviour at times has bordered on the bizarre. In the end, what I've suffered from have been the most boring manifestations of common or garden neurosis. You know the sort of thing. Identity crises. Episodes of body image distortion. Sporadic outbursts of existential *Angst*. Nothing much.

Geoffrey, on the other hand, was bonkers. Truly. He was barking. Crazy. Out to lunch. Beneath his outward respectability ticked a time bomb of paranoid psychosis.

The interesting thing, however, was that (unlike me) he looked normal. His weight, height and other dimensions were always comfortably within the average parameters set by the rest of the measurable population. He also sounded normal. His quips and puns were uttered with enough self-deprecating irony to win him a reputation of sophisticated intelligence. A reputation somewhat unjustified by his rather modest IQ scores, but that's the way things go.

My IQ rating, by contrast, invariably placed me in the top 0.5 percentile. This variation from the mean was, on its own, enough to invoke a certain amount of suspicion. Added to that was my sense of the ridiculous, which, when it bubbled forth from time to time, was seen as crass and anti-social. Finally and most significantly, there was my atypical appearance. According to the most advanced thinking in Cape Town at the time, a person with a mass almost double the uppermost level of acceptability for her age, race, sex and build couldn't possibly be all there.

Which explains why Geoffrey (having achieved moderate A-levels and a lukewarm school report) proceeded smoothly on to higher education, while I was incarcerated in the psychiatric wing of the local general hospital.

'It's for your own good, Doreen,' said Dr Ludwig Kramer, after he had gravely announced that he saw no option but to admit me as an in-patient.

'Mrs Markowitz, we have here a clear-cut case of – er –

morbid over-eating. Psychological obesity, if you'll forgive the expression. A certain amount of oral fixation and – excuse me – penis envy, acted out in behaviour that I would describe as atavistic. Cannibalistic. There's a lot of anger there, Mrs Markowitz. A *lot* of anger . . .'

'But, doctor . . .'

'Yes, I know. It must be hard for a mother to accept that her child's appetite is fuelled by such hostile emotions. Tell me, as a matter of interest – how would you have categorized Doreen as a breast feeder?'

'Categorized? What do you mean, categorized?'

'You know – eager, reluctant, colicky, compliant . . .?'

'Greedy. Greedy like a little pig. She didn't stop sucking – not for a minute. My poor, poor nipples. I used to say to my husband even then that the child would drink me dry.'

'Ah. I see. Hmm.'

Dr Kramer looked meaningfully at me. I had a sudden urge to wink at him. Surely he wasn't serious about – what was it? Penis envy? Cannibalism? I was about to offer him a conspiratorial giggle when his earnest frown told me that he was serious indeed. So I suppressed my smile and, instead, directed a mean-eyed and ravenous glance towards his nether regions. He cleared his throat and crossed his legs.

'Doreen,' he said in a wobbly voice that was at least a change from the remote 'ahas' and 'a-hems' that had punctuated the half-dozen dismal sessions of psychotherapy and made me want to scream. 'Doreen, this – er – hospitalization is going to be a huge relief for you. At last you'll have the space to explore your feelings away from the – *bosom* of the family. Do you understand?'

I nodded, suspecting that the poor, drained bosom in question was probably far more relieved about the impending separation than I was. In fact, if the authorites had left it to me, I'd have been quite content to hover for ever in my satiated stupor. But it seemed that the decision had been taken out of my hands. 'I understand,' I said resignedly.

'You'll find several – ah – like-minded people amongst your fellow patients,' Dr Kramer continued. He had recovered his composure and uncrossed his legs. 'Apart from a few drug dependencies and the like, the bulk of our cases are eating disorders. Of one sort or another. It's our special field.'

'Oh.'

There was silence. Dr Kramer, bolstered by the apparent compliance of his patient and her mother, uncrossed his legs further.

'Any questions?' he asked.

'Well – um – yes,' I said. I was leaning forward, displaying the first sign of real animation that afternoon. Kramer quickly crossed his legs again.

'What is it, Doreen?' he asked warily.

'This – place. This – wing. Is it a *nuthouse*?'

'God forbid!' exploded Molly.

'Take it easy, Mrs Markowitz,' said the doctor, who quickly rose from his seat and moved to Molly's side. He placed a reassuring hand on her shoulder, which was as rigid as a board. 'Doreen, of *course* it's not a – lunatic asylum,' he said, as though explaining the facts of life to a very dense child. 'You see, the patients in our wing are all neurotics. We don't cater for psychotics at all. You know the difference, of course?'

'I think so.' I remembered something I'd once heard about neurotics building castles in the air, psychotics thinking they lived in them and psychiatrists collecting all the rent. But I doubted whether Dr Kramer would appreciate it. 'D'you mean there'll be no loonies? No strait-jackets? No mad laughter in the night?'

'God forbid!' exclaimed Molly again while Dr Kramer, sighing, sank into his chesterfield. 'No,' he said. 'Nothing like that.'

'Oh,' I said. I couldn't help feeling slightly disappointed.

'He's admitting her,' said Molly over the pickled brisket that night. Olive, after a long period of total ineptitude, was slowly acquiring mastery of some of her madam's simpler cookery techniques. The meat was sheer perfection. Sam savoured it ecstatically.

'Mmm. This is delic . . .' he began.

'Can you hear what I'm saying, Sam? He's admitting her.'

Sam swallowed and raised his eyebrows in enquiry. 'Who? Where?' he asked absently, and was about to submit his plate for replenishment when he saw the fraught expression on his wife's face. Something was seriously wrong. 'What are you talking about, Molly?' he demanded, putting down his knife and fork. The brisket suddenly seemed to have lost its appeal. It had left an unpleasant fatty film on his palate. Sam took a large sip of water and sloshed it round his mouth. 'Who is admitting who?'

'Ludwig Kramer. The psychiatrist. He says Doreen needs to be in – hospital. For her weight.'

'Oh. And . . .?'

'And? What do you mean *and*? Sam – listen to me – your daughter's being sent to hospital. Not just hospital. A special – wing – for . . .'

'What? Dorinke, will you explain to me?'

I stopped eating. My mother, I saw, was almost speechless with anxiety. Not since the heady days of Gleeson and Co. had I observed such evidence of maternal concern. And what was that moistness round her eyes? Surely not – tears? Watching Molly's face with much interest (and some relish), I reported to my father Dr Kramer's conclusions *vis-à-vis* anger, cannibalism and the like. I informed him of the general relief my detention was expected to bring and told him about the predicted like-mindedness of my fellow inmates. 'And Dr Kramer says the place is not *exactly* a loony bin,' I concluded, poised for my mother's response. It came.

'Doreen!' shrieked Molly. 'Stop it!'

The pair of forked rivulets that trickled down her wrinkled cheeks were now unmistakably tears. Beseechingly, she turned to Sam. And when he reached across the table to pat her arm, she broke into convulsive sobs.

'Molly, it's not so terrible,' he soothed. 'This Kramer – I'm sure he must know what he's doing. Freedman recommended him, didn't he? And we all know what a genius Freedman is. With some doctors, you're treated for a broken leg and you die of pneumonia. With Freedman, if he treats you for a broken leg, you die of a broken leg . . .'

'Sam. Please. I beg of you. This is no time – for – jokes.'

'All right. All right. But Molly, why such a tragedy? Look – Doreen's not so upset about it, and she's the one who's going in for treatment. Eh, Dorinke?'

I raised my shoulders carelessly. Upset? Me? Not a chance.

'You see?' Sam handed his wife a clean handkerchief. Still weeping, she accepted it and blew her nose hard.

'She has a bed booked from Sunday. Sunday – afternoon,' Molly managed, after a few hard sniffs.

'And so? We'll take her. What's the problem?'

'Sunday *afternoon*, Sam. Surely after all these years you know what happens on a Sunday afternoon?'

'Of course. The family. And so? We'll take Dorinke to the hospital and settle her in as soon as they've all had their tea.'

At this, her tears resumed flowing and her shoulders began to heave. 'Oh, Sam,' she wailed, 'it's the – disgrace. It's killing me. How I'm going to explain this to Mathilda, God only knows.'

She managed admirably. I'd been confined to my bedroom, but I heard it all. She simply edited her account to exclude any reference to my mental state. You see, physical 'conditions' were acceptable, as far as the family was concerned. Better than acceptable. An obscure and incurable ailment (not catching, of course) aroused interest, compassion and even a certain amount of envy. But any hint of psychological abnormality was taboo.

'Putting her into hospital is the only way we can force Doreen to take it easy,' she announced with a worried shake of her head – a movement designed to imply that her daughter was of an irrepressively active disposition and generally overwhelmed with engagements. 'The doctors are very worried about her – um – kidneys, you see. That's why they're insisting on admitting her. For strict bed-rest. And tests. I can't *tell* you how many tests!'

'Oh dear,' said Mathilda, taking a delicate sip of tea. 'Poor child.'

'Yes, it's hard,' sighed Molly. 'Terribly hard. But have another biscuit, Mathilda. Go on. They're very light. I've been trying to teach Olive to bake them but, honestly, that girl takes ages to learn anything. It's hardly worth the trouble . . .'

'Can we visit her?'

'Who?'

'Doreen. Is she allowed visitors?'

'No. Absolutely not.'

'Oh. And flowers?'

'Um – no. No flowers either. She's not supposed to have any excitement.'

'I see,' said Mathilda in a voice that implied she didn't. Not quite. She dabbed at her mouth with her serviette and, frowning, directed a searching glance at Molly. 'It's unusual to come across such – *rigidity* in hospitals these day. She must be very sick indeed. How worrying for you, Molly. But tell me – which specialist is she under? Maybe you should be looking for another opinion?'

'No. Thank you.'

Molly quickly rose to her feet and started collecting cups. 'More tea, anyone? How about another biscuit, Ada?' she asked loudly, determined to drown Mathilda's nosy speculations with the clatter of crockery and the clamour of politenesses. She succeeded – temporarily.

'Oh, no. Couldn't manage another thing.'

'A lovely tea, Molly. Delicious. I don't know how you manage such a spread every week.'

'Wonderful. We must be off, now, mustn't we, Joe? Molly and Sam are taking Doreen to the hospital – and don't you have a bowls club committee meeting tonight?'

'Thank you, Molly. Thank you, Sam. See you next Sunday, please God.'

And they were off. At last. 'Give Doreen our very best

love,' trilled Mathilda at the door. 'I do hope they get to the bottom of whatever it is that's wrong with her . . .'

'So do we,' said Molly, turning away from her sister-in-law's speculative gaze.

'See?' said Sam a moment later, when my grim-faced mother was restoring the sitting-room to its pre-Sunday tea order before our departure for the hospital. 'Didn't I tell you that you were making too much of this explaining to the family? Look at Mathilda, for instance. She couldn't have been nicer.'

'Hmmph,' sniffed Molly sceptically, as she straightened the antimacassars. 'Such an idiot you are, Sam. Do you think she's going to leave it at that? Do you think she's not going to go snooping round all week till she finds out exactly what Doreen's problem is? Huh?'

Sam shrugged and followed Molly into the kitchen to make another attempt at pacification. 'It's not important what Mathilda thinks, Molly. The main thing is that Dorinke . . .'

'Dorinke!' She turned on him angrily. 'Dorinke, Dorinke. That's all I've been hearing for eighteen years. Sam, have you any idea of the amount we've sacrificed for that child? How much we've worried about her, day and night? I've just about ruined my health to give her a chance to make the most of herself . . .'

Then her anger seemed to dissolve. She slumped into a chair and bowed her head defeatedly. Sam reached out and touched the back of her neck.

'Mollinke . . .' he began.

'Did we deserve this, Sam?' she demanded. 'I'm asking you – didn't we deserve better? After everything we suffered, don't you think God could have given us at least a daughter we didn't have to be ashamed of? If only Doreen had turned out to be like every other child . . .'

She covered her face with her hands and began to cry.

*

102

I suppose it's as well to point out, for the record, that round about the time my mother was bewailing my abnormality, Geoffrey's mum was shedding profuse and noisy tears because her son was turning out to be so normal and boring. In fact, he was as much of a disappointment to her as I was to Molly. Bloody ironic, I tell you.

By this time, Lulu Cooper's Chelsea flat had shed its scrolls and pilasters and sweet cherubim, and become a prototype of monochrome modernity. It had been stripped of its lavish ornamentation and, instead, filled with glass and chrome and the sort of angular black furniture that looked austere and functional but was wildly expensive and ergonomically unsound. Everything should have been gleaming with sophisticated sterility. Instead, it looked a mess.

There were layers of dust and plates of stale food and soiled items of clothing in the most unexpected places. Lulu, bawling her eyes out in the sitting-room, was inelegantly spread-eagled on the once-shiny floor and dressed up as a belly-dancer. She was surrounded by a sordid assortment of empty bottles and full ashtrays and the hovering presence of a disappointed male companion called Jeremy, who had hoped for a different ending to the day.

Lulu Cooper invites you to a surprise party to celebrate the twenty-first birthday of her son, Geoffrey, the invitation had read. *Please come to lunch on Sunday 12th August. Fancy dress optional.*

The response, predictably, had been enthusiastic. Latterly, Lulu had taken to skipping (with amazing agility after forty-eight years of wear and tear) around the fringes of the London literary world. The outermost fringes, where it was more important to look and talk creative than to be creative. The never-never land, where would-be writers and unsuccessful agents, a few desultory publishers and a librettist or two warmed one another with mutual consolation and some nasty denigration and liberal quantities of rum.

The rum had been Lulu's contribution. Her hallmark. Her creative stamp. Lulu came to be defined by her rum – until she established her Sunday lunches as a weekly fixed point

103

for the ever-mutating group. And if the rum had been creative, Lulu's lunches were sheer genius. Dirt cheap and endlessly amusing. Her guests' contributions of edible bits and drinkable bobs had cut down costs to almost nil, and the weekly diversion had almost eliminated her Sunday blues.

Until Geoffrey's surprise party.

'You'd have thought we were having an *orgy*,' sniffed Lulu on the floor. She handed her glass to her male companion, who filled it obligingly and felt stirrings of hope, for he was young and optimistic. But his stirrings dissipated when Lulu, having swallowed deeply, gave a shudder.

'An orgy! As though I'd consider anything like that with stuffed-shirt Geoffrey around. He's always done that to my libido. Killed it stone dead.'

She took another long sip, thinking with maudlin nostalgia of the way she'd looked forward to the ill-fated celebration and how honourable her intentions had been.

'I only wanted to *include* the silly bugger,' she whimpered. 'I wanted to show him there were no hard feelings – you know, sending him away to school and all that. I thought a boy his age would be interested to meet my friends – a bit of glamour after all the miserable libraries he spends his time in. A bit of fun. I don't know why he's such a . . . Jeremy? Jeremy! Where the hell are you?'

But Jeremy, who had given up on a happy ending and was bored with Lulu's keening, had sidled to the door.

'Lulu, I must be off . . .'

'You – *what*? And who's going to help me tidy up this mess, huh? How dare you leave me like this, you little twit! Jeremy. Jeremy . . . Oh, fuck off then. Who needs you?'

As she drew breath for a new round of lamentation, she heard the door clicking shut. Lulu exhaled. It was a long, hopeless sigh.

'Who needs any of you?' she asked forlornly, cradling her bare midriff which suddenly felt cold. And not quite as lean as it had once been, if the truth were to be told.

'Mother, you're disgusting,' Geoffrey had sneered. 'You make me sick.'

Lulu removed her hands from her body in a sudden wave of self-loathing. She shut her eyes, trying to dispel the image of her son at the door, immaculate in his grey suit. His face. His thin, pale, priggishly shocked face when he'd taken in the scene of raucous revelry that confronted him.

'Surprise! Surprise!' Lulu had squealed when she'd opened the door. Not quite soberly, she had to admit. But then, some of the guests had arrived early with an abundance of rum and things had got jolly and – it was a party, after all. One would have thought it was Gomorrah revisited by his horrified expression.

'What – on earth!' he'd expostulated, frozen to the spot.

'Happy birthday, my darling. Come in. Everyone's dying to meet you.' She had reached out to give a welcoming pat to his cheek and he'd winced. Unmistakably. Two vertical lines had creased his forehead and he had winced. Then, just as she'd been about to explain that the gathering was for him, entirely in his honour, silly Jeremy had put his foot in it. His hand, to be more accurate. He had appeared behind Lulu and fondled the tassle that bridged her bare midriff and then, languidly stroking the adjacent right tit, he had drawled: 'So this is Geoffrey . . .?'

Talk about dropping a brick. There'd been a moment of ominous and terrifying silence. Then Geoffrey had exploded with his bitter, self-righteous tirade and turned on his heels and left.

And that had been the end of the party, more or less.

'My son's a prat,' muttered Lulu, pouring herself another drink. 'He's a sanctimonious, pedantic pain in the arse . . .'

And that, to give Lulu her due, was rather an apt description of her offspring. Couldn't have put it better myself. Not that such terms of disparagement ever had much visible effect on dear Geoffrey. Even then.

While his mum sat there, moaning and fuming and weeping, Geoffrey, apparently unperturbed, had returned to his bed-sit and settled down to a 1,500-page exploration of the intricacies of Anglo-Norman law. There was no external

105

evidence of the deeply disturbed mental state in which he had left his mother's flat only hours before.

Inside, however, his madness festered. Doctors were later to confirm that the mixture of shame, shock, awkwardness and the *frisson* he'd felt when that crude young upstart had fondled Lulu's breast had combined to form a particularly volatile compound. Added to that had been an explosive tincture made of envy and confusion and nausea and disgust.

Quite a nasty little package, all in all. Geoffrey, ever discreet, had sealed and concealed it beneath his grey-suited blandness and attended to his books. And if not for the intermittent drawing of his right hand to a point somewhere in the region of his solar plexus – a Napoleonic gesture that would remain with him all his life – no one could possibly have guessed he had an internal time bomb ticking away.

But at least he had *something* inside him. More than I possessed, anyway. Admittedly, Geoffrey's viscera contained an unstable amalgam charged with several deadly sins, which was hardly my idea of a satisfying snack. But I wasn't in a position to be picky. Not then. Medical authority had declared that I was to be stripped of all sources of sustenance and, understandably enough, I was desperate. How I longed to wrap my teeth round – anything. Anything at all.

'Nothing?' I'd been horrified. 'D'you mean I'm not being allowed to eat – not a morsel? Not even – a bite?'

'No. I'm sorry,' said the nurse, sounding not the least bit sorry. She frowned at her clip-board. 'You're Doreen, aren't you? Doreen Markowitz? That's right – it's starvation for you. Nothing but water.'

'Oh. Great . . .'

Helplessly, I glanced around the supper table. It had been set for ten, but only four places seemed to be occupied. There was a large middle-aged man with a mole on his nose, who was zealously scooping scrambled eggs and chips into his mouth. Next to him slouched a sulky teenage girl with greasy black hair and mascara-smudged eyes. She was fiddling with a bowl of salad. Opposite her sat a small sparrow-like being, who was apparently transfixed by a plate heaped with unidentifiable puréed mash. It looked pretty disgusting, but even mystery mush would have been preferable to water.

'Mrs Erikson!' The starched angel of mercy, having delivered to me my aquatic allocation, had turned her grace on the poor immobile sparrow. 'Are we going to have to start force-feeding you *again*? Didn't I warn you yesterday that if you carried on being difficult I'd have to report you to doctor? Here. Open up, open up . . .'

A spoonful of grey matter hovered menacingly above Mrs Erikson's lips. She pursed them tighter. The nurse lunged. Erikson spat. I watched, fascinated. Admittedly, this battle of wills would have been more fun to watch on a full stomach. But even so, it beat Gladys Street. Anything beat Gladys Street.

'*Mrs Erikson!*'

The nurse retreated in defeat. I wanted to cheer. A spidery grey splodge had appeared in the heart of the nurse's snowy bib. Mrs Erikson had scored a bull's-eye.

'Right. That's it,' said the nurse. She crossed her arms assertively, then quickly uncrossed them when she encountered the slime on her chest. She looked furious. 'You'd better come to bed and we'll get doctor to decide what to do with you in the morning.' She sighed heavily. 'Bloody Sundays.'

Mrs Erikson was yanked to her feet and wheeled out of the room. There was silence, apart from the relentless munching of the man shovelling chips. I looked at him questioningly. And hungrily.

'Shock,' he mumbled through a full mouth.

'What?' I asked.

'Shock,' he repeated. 'A few volts will fix her. Usually does.'

'Do you mean . . .?'

'ECT. You know. Wire 'em up, turn 'em on and Bob's your uncle.'

'Oh.' I sipped my water nervously. Hadn't Kramer insisted it wouldn't be that sort of place? 'I thought . . .'

'Works like a charm.' He stopped eating for a moment. 'If I had my way, we'd all be plugged in and bugger the talking.'

'You . . .?'

'What d'you mean – "you"?'

'Do you have any say – I mean, what's your – um – position?'

'Strictly missionary these days. Erf, erf, erf.' Chuckling wheezily, he wiped his mouth and gave me a wink. I was puzzled, but winked back. This seemed to provoke a further spasm of chuckling. 'Yep. Now that I'm supposed to know – erf, erf – who I am, it's the straight and narrow . . .'

'Who *are* you?'

'Me? Jerry Miller, thirty-eight-and-a-half, white, agnostic and heterosexual. Wasn't sure about the last until quite recently, as a matter of fact. Amazing discovery – but hard work, analytically speaking. Made me really hungry. And you?'

'Me too,' I said with feeling.

'What? Heterosexual or hungry?'

'Um – both, I suppose. Mainly hungry.'

I indicated the water. He nodded sympathetically. His sulky neighbour was still brooding over her salad and Jerry, noting my questioning look, set down his fork and drew his right index finger across his left wrist with grave deliberation.

'Carol's tried it seventeen times,' he stage-whispered.

'I'm sorry,' I mumbled, slightly at a loss. Did one say 'Better luck next time' in a case like this? After all, seventeen bungled suicide attempts said as much about Carol's inefficiency as her despair. And a lot about a dismal lack of imagination, if all she had managed to come up with was persistent wrist-slitting. There were so many interesting variations she might have tried. Gas, poison, pills, a hosepipe in the car, hara-kiri, stuffing herself to death. Thinking of which, where were all the like-minded people Dr Kramer had mentioned? Hadn't he implied that the place would be teeming with disordered eaters?

'Are we – the lot?' I asked.

'No, no.' Jerry pushed his plate aside. 'The others are still out. Day off. Sunday, you know. Family day – for those who're able and willing. You too will be encouraged to test the waters at home – so to speak, erf, erf – after you've been here a month or so.'

'A month!' I was horrified. 'Oh, no. Not me. I expect to be out of here in a couple of weeks. Dr Kramer said as soon as I started losing weight . . .'

'That's what they always say. Don't they, Carol? A week, another week, and before you look round, a month's gone by. And another. And another. Until, before you know it, a whole year has . . .'

'Oh God.'

I shut my eyes and rubbed my aching head. I was suddenly tired and scared and miserable. My curiosity had drained away. So had the last drop of the exhilaration I had felt after Molly and Sam had deposited me in the ward and hastily scuttled off.

'Dorinke,' Sam had begun, bending over me and taking my hand. 'Dorinke, remember . . .'

But I'd never learnt what. A joke? A warning? A reminiscence? Molly had grabbed his arm and pulled him towards the door and, muttering their farewells with furtive glances from side to side, they had disappeared into the lift.

'Have a good rest,' had been the second last thing my mother had said, averting her gaze from the sign at the door that said *Psychiatry*. Make sure you get plenty of sleep.'

'I'll try,' I had answered. 'But if I get restless, I'm sure they'll find ways of calming me down. A shot of something soothing. A strait-jacket. At the very worst, a padded cell.'

'Doreen!'

That had been her final word, uttered in a strangulated whisper. Moments later, she and Sam had departed and if I'd weighed a few stones less I would have danced a wild jig. I was free. I was free. I had been banished to an institution and yet, insanely, I'd been freed. Doreen Markowitz had made it to Liberty Hall – which, I was forced to admit, had turned out to be shabby and cramped and somewhat lacking in good company. But my parents had gone and the sun had streamed in, and I'd felt light. Light. Lighter than air.

Not light enough to prevent the nurse who weighed me from emitting a familiar-sounding 'tsk tsk tsk' as she noted the reading on the scale. But who cared? Not me. Not then.

'You'll be meeting your doctor this evening,' the same nurse had announced. 'Why don't you go and relax in the Day Room? I'll find you a couple of magazines. Supper will be in an hour or so.'

I'd reclined on a lumpy purple sofa, lazily learning about A Hundred New Ways with Mince and a few Great Ideas for Family Meals and most of the secrets of Advanced Cake-Baking (part three). And Getting the Best out of Autumn Fruits. I had drooled over the fare provided by Country Kitchens. Visited them and revisited them. With drowsy contentment and an eagerly escalating appetite, I had taken in page after page of recipes and hints and lush illustrations and waited for supper.

Supper. Oh yeah. Water. Boring old water, accompanied by a depressed catatonic and a droop with a death-wish and a joker with a gender problem. And the sudden realization that this was for real. I had been tried and found guilty of inviolate obesity and sentenced to an indefinite period of starvation. Freedom? What freedom? This was a bloody nightmare.

'I'm leaving.'

With a scrape and a clatter and a thud, I rose from the table and turned to the door.

'D'you think I'm stupid enough to stick around and be tortured? Shocked and starved and sedated? Oh no. Not me. I may be fat, but I'm not thick. Cheers, folks. Hope you make it out of here soon.'

'Cheers,' said Jerry Miller absently, beginning on his jelly and custard. Carol said nothing. She was studying her fingernails.

'I'll just get my things and . . . and . . .'

And what? I paused and considered my options. I could either: pack my bag and head for the main road and hitch a ride back to Gladys Street, or: pack my bag and head for the main road and hitch a ride as far away from Gladys Street as it was possible to go.

What a choice. Of the two, the second was more appealing. Marginally. Admittedly, it precluded the delights of my mother's kitchen. But at least it eliminated further contact with miserable Molly herself. And if I grew desperate out there in the wilds of the Great Unknown, I reckoned I could always sustain myself with some well-chosen acts of crime. Nothing major. Merely the selective liberation of a few million calories imprisoned in various burger bars, supermarkets, Chinese takeaway outlets, ice-cream parlours . . .

'Gosh, I'm hungry,' I sighed, sitting down again, suddenly weak from lack of nourishment and hopeless about my criminal potential and pessimistic about my chances of ever reaching satiation again. Things looked bad.

'I'll bet you are,' said Jerry, wiping custard off his chin. 'Most people tend to be *starving* around here, whether they know it or not. Including old Olive Oil, though she'd deny it with her dying breath.'

'Old – who?'

'Olive – ah, here she comes now. Don't turn sideways, Olivia, my love, else Doreen here won't be able to see you. Erf, erf.'

I followed his gaze to the door through which I'd been about to make my exit. And, even sideways, I'd have recognized her anywhere. Same doll-blue eyes. Same rosebud mouth. Same smirk. And – as though to taunt my obesity – the thinnest body I had ever clapped my eyes upon. Olivia bloody Cook.

'What are *you* doing here?' I asked, trying not to sound resentful.

'Oh, good,' said Jerry. 'You're acquainted with our Olive, then. The ward's most intransigent anorexic, erf erf . . . Anyway, I'll leave you two to catch up on things.'

He rose from the table, apparently replete at last, and

111

headed for the Day Room followed by Carol, who was listlessly fingering the bandages round her wrists. I sat stupefied, staring at Olivia Cook. At the hip-bones protruding from her tight cotton skirt. Never, in all my life, had I seen such cantilevered hip-bones.

'Looks like you know a thing or two about starvation,' I conceded, with grudging admiration.

Olivia smiled. It was exactly the same smile she had worn after achieving a faultless double entrechat in Grade Three. The same tilting of the chin and lowering of the eyelids and curving of the lips she had used when I had landed on my bottom in the execution of my memorable inaugural curtsy.

'It seems to me that *you* know a thing or two about . . .' she began in the same high and reedy voice that had once provided all the correct answers to Dinkie's questions. I wanted to smack her face, but held back. Weight for weight, it didn't seem quite fair.

'It's called conspicuous consumption,' I interrupted instead, drawing myself to my full immensity. 'Greed, darling. Pure greed. The witch, remember?'

Olivia's smile faded and she appeared to shrink even further, if possible. The witch. The fall. The father. The fall of the Father . . .

'I remember,' she said very softly, and I was immediately contrite and uncomfortable. This was out of my league. After all, how could I, a fat girl from Gladys Street, a failed foxtrotter and charm-school drop-out, even begin to understand what it had been like to be the daughter of an adulterer? I'd been nothing but dull Dorinke, while Olivia had been caught up in a tale of Cataclysmic Passion, a Romantic Triangle, Disgrace, Dishonour, Shame. The closest I'd ever come to scandal had been on the unforgettable Passover that Molly's matzo-balls had failed to rise. Maria (or could it have been Seraphina or Christina or Martha or Maggie?) had stolen six eggs and the Markowitz marriage and been strained for days afterwards.

I hesitated, searching for words with which to offer Olivia conciliation. A joke – if only I could think up a really funny joke. But before I had a chance to speak, Nurse Peters reappeared.

'Doreen Markowitz,' she announced. 'Dr Morris wants to see you. He's the registrar in charge of your case. Olivia, will you show Doreen to the doctor's office? You know the way, don't you, dear?'

'Of course I do.' There was a proprietory note in her voice. I forgot my brief benevolent impulse and narrowed my eyes on her smugness, her bossiness, her thinness – and hated her again. That felt better. 'Come along, Doreen,' she said. 'Follow me.'

I glowered behind her, resenting her bony little bottom and the unfairness of my incarceration and the unpleasant emptiness of my stomach and vowing to be out of there within the hour. I'd be fat if I wanted to. It was my business. My prerogative. My right to choose. I'd tell this Dr Morris to stuff his diet and his hospital and his dinky Olivia and take myself off. Right then . . .

And so, what happened?

I'll tell you what happened:

Furiously, defiantly, I marched into the doctor's office, determined to assert my freedom to be fat, my freedom to be, my freedom. Nothing would deter me from my decision to stick with my girth and get out of hospital. Fast.

But then, thirty minutes later, I emerged from that office with my head in the clouds and my urge to flee totally forgotten. I'd forgotten everything except a steadfast resolve to win the undying affection of the doctor to whom I was to have declared my rebellion. I'm embarrassed to confess this, but I – the cynical, independent-minded, self-proclaimed celibate – had done a complete about-turn in the space of half an hour.

For Stanley Morris, I was prepared to forget all my principles. I was ready to enchant him and entertain him and, if required, die for him.

For Stanley Morris, I was even prepared to *starve*.

*

It was a climb-down, I know. But think about it. What else could have persuaded me to embark on the road towards slimness? My mother had failed dismally, despite medical, educational and psychiatric support. My father's faltering attempts at emotional blackmail had been in vain. I had been more or less immune to peer pressure, role-model identification or any of the other behavioural levers used by the advertising industry to sell diet foods, tampons and triple-minted breath-fresheners. I'd taken risks with halitosis, triumphed over the discomfort of looped sanitary towels and protective panties. And, in spite of everything, I had managed to stay fat.

So what, at last, had done the trick?

Believe it or not, I'd succumbed to the most banal and crippling condition that can afflict the human psyche. I had – as the songsters were tunelessly crooning up and down the land – fallen deeply, truly, passionately and chest-achingly in love.

8

I once asked my mother what she thought about love. She was shaping bagels in the kitchen on the *shikse*'s day off and seemed unusually content and communicative.

'Love?' She looked sharply at my face to reassure herself that I wasn't perhaps alluding to matters improper. Perhaps secretly hoping that (in the interests of normality) I was. But of course one glance told her that I couldn't have been. Never. Not clod-hopping old me. She formed a sausage of dough into a perfect circle and expelled a heartfelt sigh.

'Between us, Doreen,' she said wearily, 'I'm not a great believer in love. Not that kind.'

What kind? Did she mean the stuff of sonnets and high drama, ecstasy and despair? Or maybe the sort of grappling in the dark that Lou-Anne had once assured me led to sore tits? Was Molly referring to s-e-x? 'What kind d'you mean . . .?' I asked, trying to hide my eagerness.

But Molly wasn't listening. She was rubbing her hands together till the flour from her fingers fell like snow. A half-smile played on her thin, pinched lips.

'But now that you mention it,' she said, 'there was a moment. Yes. A moment . . .'

Her hands grew still. I didn't dare to breathe for fear she would stop.

'It was the first time I'd ever made your father *lokshen* pudding. We were young and the cherry trees bloomed. "Molly, it's delicious," he announced after his second helping. "By far the best *lokshen* pudding I've ever tasted." And then, d'you know what he told me after he'd eaten it all?'

'What?' I asked. This was getting to be disappointing. Trust her. I might have guessed it would.

'He told me I was the first girl he had ever met who managed to cook like his mama without looking like his papa.'

She raised her eyebrows at me, clearly expecting a response. 'Fancy that,' I said flatly.

'Doreen,' she said – and I noticed the pinkness of her cheeks and imagined how she might have looked in the days before she had lost her hope and her home, and, silly me, I wanted to cry. 'Doreen, when your father said that, I knew I had no option. I would carry on making him *lokshen* pudding until the bitter end.'

And that was love? Was Molly's affection for her *lokshen*-eating man the same sort of phenomenon as the bombshell that hit me when I fell for my earnest young doctor with his freckly face and sandy hair and lashless eyes? Goodness, isn't it ridiculous how this emotion, with its attachments so comical, should be glorified and hailed as sublime?

Reminds me of the magic potion that Puck spread on Titania's sleeping eyes to make her dote on the first thing she saw. Remember the story? The lovely fairy queen fell in love with an ass. What an ass . . .

Hilarious. A real hoot – for those on the outside looking in. I'm not sure about the ass but Titania certainly wasn't amused. She was panic-stricken. Gob-smacked. As seriously stunned as I was after hypoglycaemic hallucination or hormonal imbalance or the alignment of the stars had clouded my vision and made me dote on my doc.

Imagine it. There I'd been, minding my own business, having written off the whole idea of romance. Of course I was fully aware that sort of thing went on. But I believed it happened to other people. Thin ones. Handsome ones. I thought all the pathetic mooning about and being in love was a price to be paid for being slim and fair. So I imagined.

Until this mild little five-foot-nothing person cast his grey-green gaze deep into my eyes and uttered my name. Nothing more. 'Doreen.' And my heart flipped over and my skin crawled and the room span and the earth stopped. 'Doreen,' he said. That was all. And the world suddenly seemed a different place.

He wanted to know what I thought. Unlike my father, he really wanted to know. 'What's on your mind?' he asked. 'Is there something else you'd like to tell me?'

Oh, the things that crowded my mind. The confidences I wanted to share.

'Well . . . um . . .'

Brilliantly put. What eloquence. I'd opened and closed my mouth and shifted from foot to foot, looking like a cross between a codfish and an elephant with piles. Get the picture? No, it wasn't elegant. Hardly a sight to launch a thousand ships. God, how I longed for my face to enchant him, my wit to dazzle him, my body to beguile him. My head fizzed and popped with the pyrotechnics of a million reborn jokes. It sparkled with epigrams and glittered with smart repartee.

Yet all I could come up with was a halting '. . . Er – um – no – no, thank you – nothing, Dr Morris . . .' as I beat a hasty retreat through the door.

What was the matter with me? Couldn't I see the absurdity of this? Enormous Doreen Markowitz struck dumb with passion for a sweet-talking, pint-sized junior shrink? It was utterly mad, truly ridiculous. Too, too stupid for words.

But love's no laughing matter, remember. And I was a typical victim despite my atypical stature and quite blind to the comic side of my plight. On legs unbalanced by more than mere cellulite, I wove along white corridors, narrowly avoiding collisions with neurotics of various sizes and shapes.

'Sorry,' I said vaguely. In my head, I was still in Stanley Morris's office and there he was, looking up and mouthing my name. Endlessly. Caressingly.

'Doreen, I know this is going to be hard for you,' he'd said. 'Extremely hard. It's not something we take lightly –

putting a patient on total starvation. You have to believe that it'll be worth while in the end.'

I had nodded obligingly, my attention absorbed by the little lines at the corners of his eyes. Such melting, all-seeing eyes . . .

'Now, the first two or three days are going to be the most difficult. After that, you'll probably find that your hunger will disappear. That's what usually happens. We'll make sure you get enough vitamins, and you can quench your thirst with as much water as you need – but, beyond that, your energy requirements will be met by burning your excess – er – tissue. Do you understand?'

I had nodded again, wanting to say something diverting. To entertain him with my Pickwickian tale of epic over-eating and blissful over-sleeping. To inform him of a definitive series of seismographic studies that had shown how the beds of sleeping fat women moved less than those of their slimmer sisters. To expound on this snippet of useless information with some amusing speculation about the calorific cost of nightmares and the total number of pounds estimated to have been shed by Lord and Lady Macbeth during the course of their restless nights. Instead, I'd asked dully:

'How much – um – weight am I expected to lose?'

He had hesitated, and an endearing frown had crinkled his forehead.

'Let's not think about it. Much better to take it from day to day. We've had patients losing up to 116 pounds in 120 days, if that's any encouragement. But let's see how you go – and, of course, if things get difficult, I'm always here. I'll be seeing you twice a week to start with. But if you should need me at any other time, just give a shout . . .'

'A shout, Dr Morris? Wouldn't that be asking for trouble in a place like this?'

His frown, which had deepened, suddenly changed direction to support the widest grin I had ever seen. Its radiance had turned my knees to jelly. Even now, on my unsteady way back to the Day Room, the recollection of Dr Morris's

118

smile was enough to make me reach for the support of the wall.

'Doreen Markowitz – are you all right?'

It was Staff Nurse Peters, with a clip-board in her hand.

'Yes. Fine, thank you. Just a little – uh – peckish.'

'It'll get worse.' She riffled through her papers. 'I presume Dr Morris has told you about your treatment? Good, good. Now, I'm to be your primary nurse. I'll be the one to weigh you, check your vital signs, write your reports, keep a special eye on you. Understand?'

'Yes. Does that mean . . .?'

'It means you'd better bloody toe the line. No pinching of food. No lying. No fixing of the scales. If you play it straight, I'll play it straight. Got it?'

'Yes. Does that mean . . .?'

'It means that as soon as we understand one another, we'll get along fine. Me and you *and* Dr Morris. I report directly to him. D'you see?'

'I see.'

I saw all right. I saw far beyond the wasp mouth and pinched waist and poised pen of Staff Nurse Peters. I saw how Stanley Morris's face would glow with wonder as his Doreen, glorious conquerer of psychological obesity, finally stepped out of her fatness and into his arms. 'My darling,' he'd say, 'I knew from the moment I set eyes on you . . .'

'Doreen! Are you sure you're OK? You've got a long way to go, you know. Can't afford to collapse at this stage. Oh, dear. I suppose I'd better check your blood pressure. And just when I thought I was getting on top of things . . . Olivia – Olivia, would you be an angel and fetch my black box? And then run off to see Dr Morris. He wants to know how you're doing.'

I had sunk to my knees and was slipping into a fairly pleasant swoon when, at the sound of Olivia's name, I opened an eye. She was watching me. Appraisingly, as though fully aware of the fantasy that filled my head. As though vetting the competition. And as though there was no doubt about who would win.

We'll see about that, I thought.

Had it been only hours before that I'd believed with all my heart that a double-thick malted milk-shake was the height of Cataclysmic Passion? And that Love Triangles should be relegated to geometry classes and left to the devices of Isosceles and Co? Now I knew differently.

'Just you wait,' I vowed silently to Olivia Cook. 'I'll get him in the end.'

And, smitten as I was, I couldn't even smile at the banality of my words.

In her routine report of 4 November, Staff Nurse Peters recorded my weight on admission as an awesome 266 pounds. 'This patient may well prove unco-operative,' she pronounced, and went on to express certain doubts about the likeliness of my adjustment to a 'therapeutic environment'.

'Despite these reservations about the patient's adaptability, our team will do its best to uncover the origins of Doreen's extreme obesity,' declared the Staff Nurse, who was reputed to have a sniffer-dog nose for childhood trauma. 'We shall be paying special attention to parent-child interaction in this case, particularly on visiting days.'

Poor Peters. There wasn't much initial Markowitz interaction for her to observe, apart from the regular arrival of get-well cards, flowers and chocolates for me. She interpreted the cards, watered the flowers, confiscated the chocolates, weighed me diligently and waited. Not until the third Saturday of my incarceration did Molly and Sam finally make it to the hospital to see how I was doing.

'Are they taking proper care of you?' my father asked worriedly. 'This – diet, Dorinke. This starvation . . .' He scratched his head. 'Are you sure it's something that's allowed by law? It couldn't be anything to do with the . . .'

He dropped his voice and leaned closer. I could smell chicken soup and fear on his breath.

'. . . the – er – fact that we're Jewish?'

Before I could answer, Molly broke in. 'Doreen!' she whispered loudly. 'Isn't that . . .?' Her eyes were fixed on the emaciated figure of Olivia Cook at the far end of the Day Room.

'Yes – remember her?'

'Of course. She didn't come here to lose weight as well, did she?'

Molly and Sam both stared at Olivia with horrified fascination.

'Dorinke, is *she* Jewish?'

Sam could hardly utter the words, but I knew immediately what he was thinking and felt a rush of anger. Idiot. Where did he think we were? Didn't he *know* this was the land of plenty? Even *I'd* found out there were no Nazi monsters in car boots. Not even German cars. Why couldn't the man wake up and be crisp and cool like everyone else's father?

'Oh, Dad,' I said with cruel scorn. I couldn't help it. 'This is a nuthouse, you know, not a bloody concentration – '

'Shush!' agitated Molly. 'Doreen, what are you talking about?'

'Heh, heh,' laughed my father uncomfortably and at once my face burnt with shame. He cleared his throat and rubbed his cheek. 'You know what all this reminds me of?' he said.

'What?' I asked reluctantly. He was going to tell a joke. Another damn joke. But if I didn't provide the feeders, who the hell would? I understood how much he – we – needed those silly jokes, you see. Both of us knew. It was something we always understood.

'It's the one about Hymie Schwartz . . .'

'Well?'

'Hymie had to go into a mental hospital and insisted on kosher food. He'd heard it was better than the other kind and made such a fuss, old Hymie, that eventually they gave in.'

121

'And so?' I asked obligingly. My mother was frowning and biting her lip.

'And so, the next Saturday, there's Hymie sitting in a chair and smoking a cigar. "What's this?" the Director wants to know. "Schwartz, you told us you were so religious that we had to bring in special food for you. And now you're smoking on the Sabbath! Surely you know that's forbidden?"

'Schwartz shrugs. "But, doctor," he says, "have you forgotten? I'm mad!"'

Mad. His voice rose with the word. Mad. Mad. Mad. His shoulders shook with helpless mirth and I, after a moment of shock, exploded into hysterical gusts of laughter. Shit, it was funny.

'Doreen! Sam! Honestly, Sam, I'm surprised at you.'

My mother, hoarse with embarrassment, looked round furtively to see the effect of her family's behaviour on the other occupants of the Day Room. Carol was motionless in a corner chair with tear-trails on her cheeks. Mrs Erikson was curled on the sofa, as still as death. Jerry Miller in his silk Paisley gown was sighing and posturing at the window.

Staff Nurse Peters, who had looked up from her clip-board with eyebrows raised, seemed to be the only one who had noticed there was anything amiss. She'd been taking notes furiously. Molly smiled at her primly and straightened her skirt.

'And so, are you at least getting plenty of rest here, Doreen?' she enquired loudly – but didn't dare wait for a reply. 'Mathilda, by the way, sends her best love and hopes you're feeling better.'

'Thanks,' I said through gritted teeth. Mathilda. The cow had sent me a five-pound box of Dairy Milk with de luxe assorted centres. I hated her. 'Tell Mathilda I said thanks. Tell her that I'm getting better and better all the time and that by the time they let me out of here, I'll be completely sane. *Proven* sane, which is more than she – '

'Doreen – sshhh! Keep your voice down. I don't know what's come over you. It's your fault, Sam . . .'

'And thin. I'll be really thin. Even thinner than Lou-Anne. As thin, if possible, as Olivia Cook.'

'Dorinke, calm down. Don't get so excited.'

'And you can also tell Mathilda and Reuven and Ada and anyone else you care to discuss me with that the reason I've decided to go along with all this has nothing to do with the two of you. Or the rest of the family. I'm finished with that.'

'What?'

'What, Dorinke? What are you talking about? Answer me, please?'

'Sam, leave it. Come. We'd better go home. The child's being unreasonable. I don't think she appreciates what it costs for us to cross Cape Town to see her on a busy Saturday afternoon.'

Oh well. If I didn't fully appreciate the visit, at least Staff Nurse Peters did. I caught her eye as she looked up briefly from the spurt of note-taking that followed my parents' departure. She smiled stiffly and I, ever an advocate of job satisfaction, wiggled my fingers and gave her an encouraging nod. She frowned and returned hurriedly to her notes.

Unfortunately for Peters, parental visits were sparse after that. She tried hard to engineer further interaction by suggesting several times that Molly and Sam be summoned for a spot of family therapy. Apart from anything else, she enjoyed family therapy. But Dr Morris – bless him – seemed to think that I was responding perfectly adequately to my individual sessions with him. Although these were as long and as frequent as I could make them, Staff Nurse Peters (she was no fool) still expressed doubts about my therapeutic suitability.

On the other hand, I was losing weight. No one could argue with that. A month after my admission, I had shed 24 pounds.

'A pleasing rate of reduction,' observed Peters hypocritically in her routine report. 'The patient does, however, tend to cling to her assertion that her fatness is simply due to love of food.'

This stubborn insistence was, in her expert opinion, a grave obstacle to my acquisition of insight. And insight, she insisted, was almost more important than weight loss.

'You're going to have to work harder than this, Doreen,' she warned me during one of our mandatory heart-to-heart chats.

'I will,' I promised with crossed fingers. Insight. What a load of crap. When did a chap ever fall for a girl because she had good insight? Huh?

'And another thing,' she continued severely. Her eyes were narrowed, almost as though she were reading my thoughts word for word and disliking them intensely. 'There's a quality that we, in the business, call *altruism*. It means valuing and helping others and helping them to regain hope. Something that the staff has noticed to be particularly absent in your relationship with Olivia Cook. I'd like you to go over and visit her – in the small side ward at the end of the passage. She's a very sick girl.'

I was no Florence Nightingale and I loathed her, but could I refuse succour to a 'very sick girl'? Hardly.

'Olivia – um – Nurse Peters says I should come and see if you need anything. What's the matter? Why are you in bed?'

'Go away.'

'Are you sure I can't bring you something? You seem very . . .'

'Go away, Doreen. Leave me alone. Please. You wouldn't understand about any of this.'

'No. Probably not. But why don't you get yourself up and dressed? Be much better for you. And there's an exciting bit of occupational therapy happening in the Day Room. Japanese paper folding, or something. Cheer you up no end . . .'

'I can't.'

'Why?'

'Not allowed. My weight's – dropped again. They're threatening to force-feed me unless I start eating.'

'So why on earth don't you . . .?'

'Oh, Doreen. You've no idea. It's so complicated. The thing is . . .'

'What?'

'Last night . . . it hit me that I was going to die. It's all been unreal up till now . . . a game . . . an illusion. But I don't *want* to be dead, Doreen. I don't know why I'm telling you this, but I'm scared. Really scared . . .'

'Shall I call someone? A nurse? Dr . . . Morris? Tell you what – why don't I get you something to eat? Go on, Olivia. I'll watch you tuck into it, every single delicious mouthful. Just think how envious I'll feel. Mmmm. Imagine it . . .'

'OK.'

'You mean . . .?'

'Yes. Fetch something. Quickly, before I change my mind . . .'

Everyone said it was amazing. Miraculous. You wouldn't believe the fuss they made about the fasting girl finally agreeing to take nourishment.

'How did you manage it, Doreen?' they wanted to know. 'Why did she eat for you when she's utterly refused for everyone else?'

I'll tell you why. Spite. Sheer spite. I brought her a slice of hot buttered toast and she fixed her eyes firmly on my throat, watching for epiglottal movement as she drew to her lips a fragrant, grease-soaked square. I swallowed. I couldn't help it.

She smiled and chewed and swallowed.

I swallowed again, trying to stop myself inhaling the aroma and almost in tears from the exquisite agony of it all.

'Delicious,' sighed Olivia, watching my face as she reached for another square.

'I'll bet,' I sighed, imagining how one day I, too, would be coaxed to admit a morsel into a parched, reluctant mouth.

125

'Do it for me, my darling,' he would plead. 'Eat something –
you're fading away.' And I would nibble on a crust, peck at
a dainty teacake, sip milky tea, sink my teeth into a few
crackers, wrap my jaws round a couple of toasted buns, gulp
down a milk shake, demolish a creamy wedge of strawberry
pie . . .

No, no, no. I turned away from the butter gleaming
tantalizingly on Olivia's chin and remembered my resolve.

'Want some more?' I asked, keeping my voice as steady as
I could.

'Perhaps – a little later,' said Olivia, resting against her
pillows with a saintly smile. 'Dr Morris will be *so* pleased
with me. He told me yesterday that he'd give *anything* to see
my appetite return . . .'

'Very nice. For both of you.'

I refrained from remarking how much I would give to see
Olivia succumbing to a nasty strain of food poisoning. It
wouldn't seem compassionate, under the circumstances. No
– I decided to bide my time until we were more evenly
matched. Until Olivia, please God, had guzzled her way past
emaciation and slenderness and shot beyond her ideal weight
to plumpness, rotundity and, finally, full-bodied obesity.
Which would be when the new, diminutive me emerged from
my chrysalis of fat – sylph-like and snake-like and poised for
the kill.

Wishful thinking. Olivia continued to eat with loudly
proclaimed enthusiasm while I carried on starving in resolute
silence. Neither of us seemed to change much in shape.
Olivia, infuriatingly, kept bemoaning her extraordinary
metabolism and I developed new variations on my primary
theory about the unfairness of life. The scales taunted me
with their sluggishness.

But they moved. Slowly but undeniably, they moved. And
finally, three months after my admission to hospital, it was
announced that my weight had finally slipped below the 200-
pound mark and that Olivia (good girl!) had reached her
century. It was a singular day.

'Well *done*, Doreen,' Dr Morris enthused. 'We're very pleased with you. Very pleased indeed.'

I smiled graciously, so badly wanting to hear a coded message of adoration beneath carefully chosen words. He loved me. I was sure of it. Well, almost. Surely there was no mistaking those smouldering glances and the longing with which he was touching my arm?

'There's just one thing . . .' He hesitated, after a cough which I put down to sheer sexual frustration. I wanted to fling myself at his feet then and there. 'I don't want you to take this the wrong way, but . . .'

'What?' I asked eagerly. There. He was about to make his declaration. At last. At long last. I held my breath and shut my eyes, rigid with anticipation.

'Well – um – it's Staff Nurse Peters. She seems to think that you don't always have the right attitude to therapy. I can't say I've personally come across the sort of resistance she described. Not in our individual sessions. But Phyl – er – Staff Nurse Peters feels that you're not really *giving* to the group. And I said I'd speak to you.'

'And so?' I couldn't keep the note of anger out of my voice. I looked at him challengingly, daring him, just daring him to . . . but oh, how much I loved him. I'd do anything to make him love me in return. Anything. 'Dr Morris,' I said pathetically, 'tell me what you'd like me to – give . . .'

'Me?' He laughed. 'No – as I said, I'm quite happy with you, Doreen. But maybe, to satisfy the nursing staff, you could try to be more forthcoming in group therapy? More responsive? More *altruistic*? D'you know what I mean?'

'Ah,' I said with a weary nod. 'I know. It's Olivia. You're talking about her, aren't you? Everyone's falling over themselves to be kind to her. And why? That's what I want to know. What's she ever done for another living soul? Starves herself until she looks like an orphan waif and then expects – '

'Doreen. There's no need – '

'No *need*?' I glared at him furiously, blinking away the tears that threatened to rise and rock my composure and redden my nose. Bloody Olivia. Attention-seeking, skinny little cat. 'The trouble with all of you is that you don't know what she's really like.'

'Oh.' He frowned, and I suddenly felt bad. Did I really know what Olivia was really like? Who knew, in the end, what anyone was like?

'Well, I suppose, she's really no worse than most . . .' I began.

'It's such a pity, Doreen,' he was sighing. 'I'd so much hoped that the two of you would get along. Come to an understanding. Complement one another, in a way. You know, like light and shade. Or – for instance – Castor and Pollux, or Damon and Pythias . . . um . . .'

'How about Jack Spratt and his wife?'

'Yes . . . good. D'you see what I mean . . .?'

'I see all right. Mates. Partners. Kissing cousins. Like jelly and custard. Peaches and cream. Eggs and chips. Bread and butter. Gravy and mash . . .'

'OK. OK. That's more or less the idea. But, Doreen, don't you think that perhaps things would be easier for you if you didn't fantasize about food so much? Phyllis – er – Staff Nurse Peters says that when you do participate in group therapy, it's usually to share a recipe or something. Maybe it's time you started to look for some real insight into your problems? It's painful, I know . . .'

'But, Dr Morris, I've lost 66 *pounds*.'

'Excellent. I'm not denying your achievement. You're looking good, Doreen. Really good.'

'Am I?'

'Absolutely. Much, much better . . .'

'Uh-huh?'

'Yes, honestly. A great improvement. That's why we've decided to introduce a few calories into your diet. Just sufficient to give you the energy and strength to face your emotional difficulties.'

'Dr Morris, are you saying that I can start *eating* again?'

'Well – in minute quantities, yes . . .'

'Oh, this is brilliant! Fantastic! I can't wait . . .'

'Steady, steady, Doreen. It's not the end yet. Not by a long way. But will you try and do as I suggested? About taking part? Co-operating? Will you do it – for me?'

'For you?' I gazed at him with such intensity that he had to look away. Suddenly the relaxation of my diet regimen diminished in importance. It didn't matter. Nothing mattered. Nothing mattered but . . .

'Dr Morris, I'd do anything for you.'

I meant it. For Stanley Morris, there were no limits to the sacrifices I was prepared to make, the pain I was ready to suffer, the hunger I would willingly endure. I had long since stopped believing in equality or justice or the ultimate triumph of good over evil, but was utterly convinced that the truth of my love would eventually prevail.

So I stuck it out.

He wanted participation? Boy, did I participate. Group therapy sessions started ringing with my enthusiastic utterances, my empathy, my loud-voiced concern.

'Is this living?' wailed Jerry Miller one day in a fit of despair. 'Sometimes I doubt whether it's worth it all.'

'I know what you mean,' I sympathized and tried to cheer him up with the story about the poor man who had stared with admiration at the large, ornate tombstone of the richest guy in town and muttered, 'Now *that's* what I call living.'

'Very funny, Doreen Markowitz,' said Staff Nurse Peters, her steely voice slicing through the surge of laughter. 'You think life's a big joke, don't you?'

'Don't *you?*'

Staff Nurse Peters sniffed disparagingly and turned away. 'Olivia, perhaps you can tell us *seriously* what you've learnt about life?'

'Me?'

'Yes, dear. What do you think?'

'That life's . . .' Olivia stopped, frowning. I could hardly wait for her answer. Surely the malnourished daughter of an adulterous unfrocked priest (not to mention the poor

129

wronged wife) would have something useful to say about the meaning of existence?

'It's . . . um . . .' faltered Olivia, clearly at a loss.

'Like a fountain?' I suggested. I was only trying to be helpful.

'A what?' asked Olivia, allowing a small puzzled wrinkle to crease her neat *retroussé* nose.

'A fountain. Don't you know what a fountain is?'

'Well – yes.' Olivia looked doubtful.

'Doreen,' said Staff Nurse Peters warningly.

'What?'

'Can you please explain how life can possibly be compared to a fountain?'

'I'm not sure,' I admitted.

'Well then . . .'

'But it wasn't my idea. My father once told me that a famous rabbi had given him the philosophy to guide him through difficult times.'

'Really?' The ease with which Staff Nurse Peters could be taken in by direct reference to the law or the cloth or any Being of passing Supremity amazed me. 'And so?'

'Well, naturally, my father was impressed with the profundity of the rabbi's words and used them whenever he could. Then, one day, he heard that the rabbi was dying and rushed to his side for a final visit. "Rabbi," he said, "I have a question for you. It's about your philosophy – the one you gave me all those years ago, remember? Well, it has helped me through the worst of times. I've quoted it constantly. But, to be perfectly honest, I've never quite understood what it means. Please will you tell me before it's too late – why is life like a fountain?"

'"All right, all right," says the rabbi wearily, "so it's *not* like a fountain!"'

There was a puzzled silence for a moment. Then the staff nurse came to.

'And that's *not* my idea of a worthwhile contribution to group therapy,' she barked. 'Doreen Markowitz, I don't know what we're going to do with you. If it weren't for the fact that you were actually losing weight, I'd have recommended long ago that you be summarily discharged. As it is . . .'

As it was, they could hardly dismiss me as a therapeutic failure. My determination to shed every single excess pound remained as resolute as my passion for Stanley Morris. He, rather clinically, referred to the adoration as 'transference' while I (always particular that words, like prime meat, should never be minced) still insisted on labelling it love.

'Dr Morris,' I dared to ask after I'd weighed in at 165 pounds and a celebratory pint of fresh orange juice had loosened by tongue, 'do you care about me – properly, I mean?'

'Of course, Doreen. We all care about you. Very much.'

'I didn't ask about everyone. Only you. Do *you* care?'

'Oh, Doreen, how can you doubt me? You're very special to me. You and Olivia, both. It's been wonderful – a privilege – to look after the two of you.'

'Oh.'

'And the best thing, the most important thing of all, has been watching the way you've started to take care of *yourselves*.'

'Oh?'

'*Yes*. It's been tremendous. So exciting. You've both come such a long way. In fact – I don't know whether Olivia has told you this yet – we believe that she's now ready to stand on her own feet.'

'Does that mean . . .?'

'Yes, she's leaving. On Saturday. And everyone feels that it won't be long before you'll be discharged too. What d'you think about that?'

I swallowed hard. Freedom suddenly loomed, and a plug of apprehension was blocking my throat. Did he really want to know? What? About my dream that he'd return my love? My fear that he wouldn't? My dread of rejoining the lost souls wandering in the wasteland outside the hospital, the misfits adrift in a desert of unbelonging, all dreaming of home?

Could I tell him about how safe it had felt here in this oasis? Or about the hope that had warmed me and armed me and turned each day into a fascinating contest between me and the scales? Or about how I had won game after game but now was scared shitless that I was losing the match . . .? What the hell did he want me to say?

'You look worried,' he was saying. 'I can understand that. After all, it's been more than six months. A long time. But you just wait, Doreen – once you get home, you'll be fine.'

Great. Wonderful. I could imagine it. I'd be greeted by the growls of Himmler and serenaded by the shrieks of Mrs Venter-next-door yelling at her maid. I'd be given a narrow-eyed welcome by Olive-in-the-kitchen and ushered into the dark, dark dining-room and fed. And as I ate, I would listen to the bitter regretfulness of my mother and the lip-smacking murmurings of my father and see, in the shadows, the ghosts of Nazi monsters and the ever-ripe cherry trees of *Der-Heim*.

'Oh, yes,' I said to Dr Morris, who was watching me eagerly, so keen for his ministrations to have been judged a success. 'It'll be as though I had never been away.'

He heard the bitterness in my voice. Even he.

'No, no. It won't be like that. Look at yourself, Doreen. Come with me and take a good look.'

He gripped my arm and urged me towards the full-length mirror in the corner of his office.

'Now stand up tall and tell me what you see.'

I tugged the other way. He didn't have the right to do this to me. I'd yell. I'd scream.

'Dr Morris,' I said breathlessly, 'mirrors hate me. Honestly they do. If you knew how I've been abused by mirrors. Ballet school mirrors, charm school mirrors, ballroom dancing mirrors. As for the one in the Stuttafords bra department! Oh, no. I couldn't subject myself to another one. I swore I'd never . . .'

'Doreen. Open your eyes. Please.'

Slowly, I unsealed one eyelid then the other. I looked. And

132

looked again. I blinked and shook my head. It was a dazzling sight. A spectacle. I tried to remember what the Ugly Duckling had said when he finally confronted his grown-up reflection in the pond.

'Me? A swan? Oh, *go on* . . .'

Dr Morris gave a little laugh as I placed my hands on my hips and appraised the image that faced me. No. On second sight, it wasn't quite that of a swan. I saw a pale round face with a quizzical frown. Dull brown hair in need of curling or straightening or cutting or all three – if one could be bothered. I noticed a neck . . . a *neck*? Since when had Doreen Markowitz had a neck? And what was that interruption to the once-flowing line from shoulders to hips? Was it – could it possibly be – a *waist*?

I stepped back a couple of paces, speechless with disbelief. Talk about tales of the extraordinary. Talk about bloody miracles. This Ugly Duckling had turned into a – woman.

'So?' asked Stanley Morris eagerly.

'So?' I echoed, shrugging with as much weary nonchalance as I could muster. I turned sideways and struck a languid pose as I eyed my new firm profile.

'Doreen, what d'you think?'

He was watching me expectantly. And it struck me for certain that moment that it wasn't romantic anticipation I saw. No. It was the eagerness of a puppy waiting for his treat. A small, sandy-haired puppy hoping for a succulent scrap of praise. A morsel of gratitude. A titbit of approval.

I swallowed. That damn plug in my throat again. Why did he keep asking what I thought? And what an idiot I'd been to have ever believed that, unlike my father, he really wanted to know the truth. I pictured his disappointment, the way his face would fall if I told him about the struggle inside my new figure-of-eight form. About the pain, the disillusionment and the last, hissing embers of love. So I didn't even try.

Instead, with a small forced chuckle, I tapped my finger against the bridge of my nose.

'If you're asking my opinion, Dr Morris,' I said lightly, 'all I can say is either one likes Picasso or one doesn't . . .'

133

He seemed baffled for a moment. Then, relieved, he saw I was smiling and burst into uncertain laughter. I laughed with him, fascinated by the effervescent tinkling sound I was able to produce, and caught sight of myself again in the mirror. My mouth was open and my head was thrown back and my legs, planted slightly apart, supported a body that went in and out in all the appropriate places and would melt into the human terrain as efficiently as the gear worn by the best-camouflaged ground soldier. I'd acquired the body of an insider. Drawing a deep breath, I sucked in my stomach.

'See?' he asked, watching me proudly. 'Wasn't it worth it all?'

'I suppose so.'

I tried to sound pleased. After all, hadn't this been the aim of the whole exercise? To create Miss Average? To redesign Doreen Markowitz so that she'd end up the sort of shape that mothers were proud of and young men adored and friends liked to be seen with? The sort of girl that junior doctors loved back ... that one particular junior doctor loved back ...

Oh, I'd have one last shot. It would be my final round. My swan song.

'Dr Morris?'

'What's the matter, Doreen?'

'Nothing. Nothing much. I was just wondering whether we could keep – in touch – after I leave . . .?'

'Of *course*. If you have a problem, you're welcome to phone me any time. Any time at all. I'll always find time to see you.'

'Oh.'

It was hardly what I'd hoped for. But what *had* I hoped for? Since when had a down-to-earth person like me set any store by fairy-tale endings? Once again I glanced at my reflection and smiled pertly at the mirror-person and struck a saucy pose. Goodness, how normal I looked. How conventional. How reasonable and well-adjusted. Who would ever guess that beneath that armour of acceptability dwelt such aching confusion?

'I don't imagine I'll have any problems, Dr Morris. I'm almost sure you'll never be troubled by me again.'

'That's my girl,' he said, tapping me fondly on the bottom. I didn't flinch. 'That's the sort of spirit I've always admired in you.'

Yup. He admired my spirit. Never mind the flesh I had flogged into a semblance of sexiness, or the polished wit, or the worldly widsom, or even the carefully cultivated sang-froid. He admired my spirit. Oh dear. What spirit could he have meant? Could he possibly have been referring to the ghost of the late fat Doreen Markowitz?

'Forget it, doc,' I might have said. 'The thing you're talking about has gone. Died. Vamoosed. The spirit has departed but the body lives on. And *what* a body, even though I say so myself.'

But he wouldn't have known what I was talking about. Not our Stan. Not my man. *My* man? He arrived for evening ward-round a few days later with a cuddly little blonde clutching on to his arm.

'Doreen, I'd like you to meet my wife. Doll – Pauline – this is Doreen Markowitz, a patient of mine. And this is Olivia Cook.'

'Hi.'

'How d'you do?'

'So pleased to meet you both. I've heard so much about you . . .'

Had she? What had she heard? About the obese neurotic with an adolescent crush? The skinny anorexic full of post-pubescent crap? Had they chewed on our predicament with their grilled lamb chops and toasted our recovery on best Cape wine and celebrated Stan's cleverness in bed? The prominent bump beneath his sweet wife's pink smocked top affirmed the last. Stanley was patting it proudly.

'Pauline's expecting a little one soon. It'll be our first.'

'Well done,' I said without the slightest hesitation. 'I'm pleased for you.'

135

'Jolly good,' said Olivia. 'Hope it all goes well.'

We looked at one another and smiled and then laughed and knew exactly why we were laughing. Dr and Mrs Morris looked on with matching expressions of incomprehension. They moved closer together in a married sort of way. He fiddled with his tie, which bore an old school crest, and she fiddled with her candy-floss hair. We laughed and laughed. It was wonderful. For the first time ever, Olivia Cook and I were completely in cahoots.

Which didn't mean the beginning of a close, enduring friendship. That would have been as contrary to the course of real life as my finding ever-after happiness with the doctor of my dreams. One delicious swallow doesn't make a double-thick malted milk shake. No, Olivia and I had disliked one another too long and too intensely to pack it in just like that. Still, I couldn't find it in myself to wish her ill on the day she was discharged. She looked scared and still very fragile and seemed to be leaving alone.

'Good luck,' I said.

'Thanks.'

'What will you be – um – doing now?'

'I'm not sure. Try and get a job, I suppose. Save up to go overseas. I'll have to stay with my – mother – in the mean time . . .'

She looked away as she mentioned her mother. Not once in our six-month joint incarceration had any reference been made to the scandal that had rocked the Limelight Academy and set Olivia on her course to starvation. By silent and mutual consent, we had avoided all verbal acknowledgement of our past connection. We had pretended to know nothing because we knew too much.

'And you?' she asked. 'What are you planning to do when you leave?'

'Me?'

I hadn't really thought beyond returning to Gladys Street

and resuming life with Molly and Sam. What else could possibly lie ahead?

'Who knows?' I answered nonchalantly. 'Before I consider anything, I'll have to try myself out for size.'

'Me too,' she smiled wryly. 'Me too.'

That was the measure of it. The long and short of it. The fat and thin of it. The profit and loss account I pondered over on the eve of my departure for home. I sucked the end of an HB pencil (toxic but at least calorie-free) and considered the credits and debits I'd accumulated during my hospital stay.

Despite all my resistance, I had gained a small amount of insight. Enough to teach me that, while love of food had made me fat, renouncing it wouldn't bring me love. Yes, I'd certainly increased on my innate store of cynicism. But in the process I had lost my innocence. Ah well. At least, at the same time, I'd also lost weight. I had gained poise and grace and a normal appearance and surely that was worth a lot? At least a few courses at Arlene Carter's Charm School and a period of grace with Dinkie du Plessis. Molly would be pleased at any rate.

9

Pleased? She was beside herself.

'You look a different person,' she proclaimed. 'Sam – come and see who's home. Far be it for me to say I told you so, but when I'm right, I'm right. And Mathilda too, for all her faults. How long ago was it that she said to me, "Molly, believe me, with a few pounds taken off her, that girl will be something"? I must say I couldn't imagine it at the time. But *now*! All right – so it wasn't quick and it wasn't easy. But, tell me, is anything in life ever . . .'

'Dorinke, you've shrunk.'

'Sam – take a look at her. Hasn't she turned into a real *mensch*?'

A *what*? At last. At long, long last I'd cracked it. I had finally made it to that hallowed inner sanctum and could now take my place with Farella Venter *et al.* as a fully-fledged, Molly-appointed *mensch*. Alongside Marcia Feigenbaum, who had generously parted with her recipe for tongue. And Bubbles Bostok, who had given her drunken maid a second chance. And Hymie Sofer, who was widely known to have secretly sponsored the schooling of his gardener's young son. And Bertha Helman, who chaired more charities than there were days in the week and still managed to achieve perfect grooming. Imagine it. Farella and Marcia and Bubbles and Hymie and Bertha – and me. Somehow I'd managed to shrink into the Hall of Ultimate Achievement. Wasn't it a scream how all those years I'd believed that a *mensch* was a superior sort of being into which someone grew? The thought made me smile.

'And look at her face, Sam. Hasn't she brightened up? Haven't I always maintained that the child would be far happier when she lost the weight? Didn't I say time and again that she'd feel better about herself when she became a normal size?'

He was studying me anxiously, apparently oblivious to the excited jabbering of his wife.

'And so, Dorinke?' he frowned.

'So what?' I asked, frowning back, unwilling to be interrogated. Couldn't he lay off and simply be satisfied to have me home? Well, half of me, anyway. But it was undoubtedly the better half, judging by Molly's enthusiasm.

'So how does it feel to be so thin? You're skin and bone, Dorinke. There's nothing left of you.'

Oh God. Would he never give up? 'How does it feel?' 'What do you think?' Relentlessly asking the questions without wanting to hear the true answers. And anyway, even if I'd wanted to reply, I didn't have words to describe the oddness of my perceptions on leaving the hospital and re-entering the world. I'd felt as though my body had shed much of its weight and most of its substance and yet, strangely, still occupied the same vast amount of space. And I'd been deafened by the city-sounds which had augmented to a roar, while my voice seemed to have been muffled to an inconsequential squeak. In panic, I had wondered where I ended and otherness began and whether I'd finally lost my sense of being Doreen. My sense of being. My sense? I shuddered . . .

'She's shivering, Molly. Dorinke, are you cold? It's that starvation, I tell you. It can ruin a person's health . . .'

. . . And the weirdest thing was that, although I knew in theory that I'd become smaller, it had seemed to me that the world had diminished in size. Drivers had tooted in Matchbox cars and midget workmen had balanced on match-stick ladders and Gladys Street had contracted to the width of a lane. A soundless, lifeless Lilliputian lane. The only observable moving object had been Rex Venter's tiny arm, ceaselessly digging beside his immaculate front path. Even Himmler, comatose at his master's feet, had somehow shrivelled into a miniature breed.

As for our house – it had become a pygmy place. A dark, airless shoe-box hardly large enough to contain an ancient toy-couple called Molly and Sam. And certainly too small to hold someone who was both big and little and heavy and light and hot and cold and confused. Someone like . . .

'Dorinke?'

'Oh, I'm fine, Dad. Honestly. I feel really – good.'

'Maybe you should rest a little, have something to eat. Molly, we wouldn't say no to a bite of supper. Eh, Dorinke? A good idea?'

I nodded, grateful beyond words to be offered the prospect of something familiar. Something entirely predictable. At least there would be the same furniture, the same food and the same table talk. Surely that couldn't have shrunk?

But the table looked smaller and the food less plentiful and the conversation, never exactly known for its sparkle, had taken a definite turn for the worse. We sat in silence over plates of schmaltz herring and even the *shikse*-sounds from the kitchen seemed to have ceased.

'Delicious meal, Molly,' Sam tried at last, wiping his mouth with unconvincing gusto. 'I'm sure it's much better for us that we don't have meat every night any more. What do you think, Dorinke?'

'I'm not sure.'

What could I say? What did I know? I fixed my eyes on my barely touched plate and kept reminding myself this was home.

'Heh, heh.' He chuckled to himself and applied a toothpick to his mouth. 'Thinking about herring reminds me of an old story. It's the one about the rabbi who gets to heaven and for every single meal the angel serves him schmaltz herring. Has anyone heard it?'

'Sam,' said Molly warningly.

'I haven't heard it,' I said, looking up and catching his eye.

140

And for the first time since my return I knew for certain that I'd come home. It was a huge relief.

Molly sighed, rising to her feet and beginning to collect the plates. I suddenly noticed that the dinner bell had disappeared and watched with amazement as my mother, moving with deliberate solemnity, stacked the tray and started moving towards the kitchen.

'Where's . . .?' I began.

But Sam, ignoring both Molly's rebuff and my bewilderment, carried on with his joke.

'Naturally, the rabbi was slightly disappointed with his meals. Not – ' he glanced quickly at Molly's stiff departing back ' – that there's anything exactly *wrong* with schmaltz herring. But you can understand that when a person has been working a lifetime to qualify for heaven he maybe expects something different once in a while.'

He gave a wry shrug and glanced at me mischievously, clearing his throat above the plate-clatter coming from the kitchen.

'To make things worse for our rabbi,' he continued, 'he couldn't help noticing the meals being served Down Below. *Blintzes*, bagels, schnitzel, steak . . . Finally he couldn't stand it any more and called the angel. "I don't want to be difficult," he said, "but I'd like you to explain me why all I ever get to eat is herring while Down Below they eat like kings. Huh? Somehow it doesn't seem fair."

' "You're right, honourable rabbi," said the angel. "It's not as it should be, believe you me. But, to tell you the truth, it just doesn't pay to cook for two people." '

'Oh, Dad,' I laughed, suddenly remembering the rich bounty of jokes I'd been born with and then, as Molly returned from the kitchen with an empty tray and accusing face, the terrible pop pop pop of their demise.

'As you see, Doreen,' she was saying, methodically reloading the tray, 'things have changed here. We don't have help for supper any more.'

'I've noticed. What's happened to Olive?'

'Olive's all right. Please God, everyone should be as all

141

right as Olive. Such a social life she has, you wouldn't believe . . .'

'So why . . .?'

'Why do we have to struggle along in the evenings on our own? I'll tell you why. Because the Government, if you don't mind, has decided to make our area white by night. No consultation. No asking us if we're prepared to go without a live-in maid . . .'

'But Molly – they have to keep order. They're trying to organize things. To keep control . . .'

'Pah! Control. If they're so worried about control, why don't they do something about the pinching in town, for instance? Poor Ada had her bag snatched last week and has been a nervous wreck ever since. Control. I'll teach them control . . .'

She would too, I thought, watching the formidable precision with which she assembled the meal-ends on to the tray and swept, sniffing haughtily, back to the kitchen. Control. Organization. The sort of organized control that Molly and Sam had feared and eluded many years before and still felt safer to see applied to others. Black agitators. Petty pilferers. Lustful maids. Not to mention their formerly fat daughter, whose heritage of repression had proved more enduring than her treasury of jokes and who now clung to self-control with a tenacity that startled her.

I'd become an organizational ace, a dab hand at denial. A po-faced automaton, who established a daily routine as rigid as the patent-leather belts with which I nipped in my new-found waistline. A grapefruit for breakfast, an apple for lunch, a lean, grilled something for supper. Each morning, I checked my weight and studied my form in the full-length bathroom mirror. Like a pilot undertaking a pre-flight inspection, I ticked off my features, one by one. So-so eyes. Interesting nose. Not bad breasts. Remarkably reduced thighs. Nothing to mar my almost-perfection. Nothing to make me feel fat. Nothing to make me feel. That was the aim of the daily ritual. I didn't want to feel.

They suggested a secretarial school.

'Useful,' said Sam.

'Suitable,' said Molly.

'Fine,' said I.

They suggested a social club.

'For the popularity,' said Molly.

'For the investment,' said Sam.

'OK,' said I.

They suggested a catering course.

'The way to a man's heart,' chortled Sam.

'Look where being a good cook got me?' smirked Molly.

'Very well,' said I – proving far more adept at culinary than keyboard and social skills. I clearly had a way with food, which was more than could be said about my proficiency at shorthand and my painful attempts to be part of a crowd. But I tried. We all tried.

Oh, such patience on their part. Such compliance on mine. And, on the face of it, no one had anything of which to complain. After all, didn't I have a good home, no demands made on me, freedom to come and go as I pleased? Educational and social possibilities and, thank the Lord, a fine figure at last? And, for their part, hadn't Mr and Mrs Markowitz finally acquired a daughter of whom they could be proud? A fine-looking girl, as everyone said. Almost – even if they said so themselves – a beauty.

And so why on earth weren't the three of them deliriously happy?

I wasn't *un*happy. I wasn't anything most of the time. I operated on automatic, ingesting measured portions of food and moderated amounts of sensory stimulation. Nothing unsettling. Nothing too evocative of the days when I'd tried to understand things and cried for *Der-Heim* and the fate of Patricia's Robert. The days when I had longed for peanut butter and the richest chocolate thick-shakes ever made. That was over. Finished. Kaput. I was a grown-up now and grown-ups didn't eat or cry or love too much. They were organized and controlled. I was organized and controlled. So were my parents – most of the time.

'I can't understand it,' Molly burst out occasionally. 'Here you are, looking lovely, touch wood. With a typing diploma, a good serve on the tennis court, nice handwriting and not a bad cook. So tell me why it is that you haven't managed to find a serious boyfriend? Not even one? Maybe they think you're too clever, Doreen? Boys don't like that, you know. You're not being too – how can I say? – *smart* with them? Or getting on their nerves – making jokes, like your father . . .'

'Oh no,' I said seriously. 'I'd never do that.'

'Well then, there's nothing to do but to wait. We must all have patience and wait.'

So we waited. And waited. We waited while Lou-Anne broke off her second engagement and Cousin Norman was admitted to a drug-dependency unit and Himmler (the dog) succumbed to terminal tick-fever. And when Arnold Gleeson finished work on his infamous *Confessions of a Diet Doctor*, we were still frozen in expectancy. At least, I was frozen, Molly stayed expectant and Sam, with his usual stoicism, settled down for a long, hard siege.

We hardly noticed the escalating noises being made by the Struggle for Equality, nor the retaliatory responses from Law and Order. Things like police brutality, house arrests, emergency detention and water bombs. Things that scared the stuffing out of Dinkie du Plessis who – still cleverly ahead of the *Zeitgeist* – made sure to slip out of the political arena before it got too hot. Using the names and addresses she had lifted from the Black Sash membership files, she founded a school for transcendental meditation. Naturally, she'd anticipated the arrival of Eastern Mysticism.

Its influence spread like Asian flu. It missed Gladys Street, of course, but managed to reach Prosper Cook who, having failed to sell much life insurance or to satisfy Minerva or to see eye-to-eye with his headstrong Olivia, decided to revert to his original spiritual leanings. And since the Church refused to readmit him, a guru would have to do.

And so he chanted mantras and dreamed of escape to deepest Nepal, while Olivia qualified as a yoga instructor and finally earned enough money for a one-way air ticket to London. By the strangest coincidence, she travelled on the same flight as Cousin Lou-Anne, who was widening her net to catch fiancé number three.

And we were still waiting. I sometimes passed the time practising my cooking skills in Molly's kitchen, which had stoically withstood the advance of technology and the passing of time. Nothing had changed as far as I remembered. Even the half-full bottle of *Native Aperients*, left behind by clumsy Beatrice (or could it have been bibulous Sophie?), still stood on the window-sill, covered in a coat of sticky dust.

'What d'you keep these for?' I once asked my mother.

'You never know . . .' she shrugged.

They were big, brown, powerful-looking pellets and sometimes I considered downing a couple. Just to get things moving. But I didn't dare. It seemed less trouble to sit around and wait.

Which was what the three Markowitzes did. We were unaware of the wave of Liberality which had encouraged Arnold Gleeson to make a fortune from his vices. Nor did we observe the Reactionary Backlash which followed. Gleeson was jailed and *Confessions* was banned. It still enjoyed a measure of popularity with certain readers abroad – among them Geoffrey Bartholomew-Cooper, newly called to the bar. In South Africa, however, Gleeson's *oeuvre* shared the fate of *Black Beauty*, *Das Kapital* and other works of pornography and subversion.

While no hint of Liberality had ever reached Gladys Street, nor the smallest sign of The Struggle nor the faintest stirrings of Feminism nor any hint of Mysticism, somehow the Reactionary Backlash had seeped in through the Venters' back door. Molly, Sam and I still awaited Mr Right. Meanwhile, Rex Venter had embraced the Far Right.

'Time is getting short,' we heard him trumpet to his followers. These included various elderly neighbours, his policeman brother Frikkie, and, of course, Goebbels, the canine successor to Himmler, who shared his predecessor's affable charm.

Molly looked at me meaningfully as Rex's words echoed from next door, for we were still waiting and time, indeed, was getting short. Despite all my compliance, Sam's stoicism and Molly's iron will, it seemed that nobody wanted to share my charm.

Quite frankly, I didn't give a damn. But my mother was in despair. Sunday teas had become a nightmare of duplicity and subterfuge. At first, they had been her weekly show-case, her platform for success. 'Dor-e-en,' she would warble while the family were lip-smacking over the lightness of her pastries. 'Doreen – come and say hello to everyone. Mathilda and Ada want to see you.'

And I'd check myself in the mirror, feeling for the tautness of my stomach and the firmness of my thighs, and then drift absent-mindedly into the room.

'Isn't she looking gorgeous!' everyone would exclaim.

'So who's the lucky man?' Mathilda would enquire.

Molly would be smug and secretive. 'Now *that* would be telling,' she'd say with a smirk.

But Mathilda wasn't fooled for long. Not Mathilda. Her questioning became more specific, more pointed. And Molly soon decided that if a suitor for her daughter didn't exist, it would be necessary to invent him. I went along with it, of course. What did I care?

'He's a lovely boy. A dentist. From such a nice family too. A big business they've got in – Kimberley, isn't it, Doreen? And Joel – that's his name – is starting a practice here in Cape Town.'

'Joel who?'

146

'Freedman. Yes, Joel Freedman. A really lovely . . .'

'And when are we going to meet him?'

'Oh. Well . . .'

It was getting increasingly difficult. Mathilda's interrogations were unremitting and each week more flesh was added to Joel's phantom frame. A sister called Rachel. A fondness for cats. A delicacy of constitution. A passion for music. A sense of humour. A determination to improve on his dental skills by the regular attendance of extramural courses. Courses that frequently took him out of town. I must confess, I was growing rather fond of my imaginary man.

But Molly was growing ever more uncomfortable.

'She knows. She knows all about Joel and she's teasing me. Having us all on,' she muttered bitterly to Sam.

'So, Mollinke, why did you have to . . .?'

'It's Doreen's fault. If she'd made a proper effort to find someone, I wouldn't have been forced to mention Joel. As it was, I only intended it to last for a week or two. Just until Doreen came up with a better proposition. I'd never have believed that, after all we've put into the child, nothing would become of her . . .'

'And so?'

'And *so*? We're going to have to do something about Joel before they absolutely insist on seeing him and I get myself into big trouble. Next Sunday will be his last.'

How unfortunate for Molly that her carefully prepared announcement would coincide with Ada's excited news about her Lou-Anne's latest find.

'A Rothschild, would you believe? A real bona fide Rothschild – brother of the cousin of the great man himself, Lou-Anne says.'

'And what's the boy's name?' asked my mother.

'Kevin Roth. He decided to do away with the "schild". Too pretentious, Lou-Anne says. You know the way children

147

are these days. It's not fashionable any more to boast about one's connections. Now if it were up to me . . .'

'Rothschild, heh heh,' chortled my father into his tea.

'What's the matter, Sam?' asked Molly, far more gently than usual. She didn't mind a distraction from Ada's irritating new-found self-importance. First a doctor, then a lawyer, now a Rothschild. How many times could a person get *naches* from the same daughter?

'Nothing, nothing. I was just thinking of the famous story about when Rothschild was visiting Minsk. Did you hear it, Ada?'

'No – tell me, Sam.' For once, there was a certain eagerness to hear what my father had to say. He beamed. 'I want to learn as much as possible about our new family,' enthused Ada. 'It's so exciting . . .'

'Well,' said my father, drawing out his big moment, 'Rothschild comes to Minsk and he stops in a little Yiddishe restaurant for a light breakfast. Only a couple of eggs he has – but the bill comes to twenty roubles. A ridiculous amount of money. "Why did you charge me so much?" he asks the waiter. "Is it maybe because eggs are so rare in these parts?" The waiter laughs like crazy. "No sir," he says. "But Rothschilds are."

'Heh heh – "Rothschilds are" – do you get it?'

'Oh, how funny, Sam,' simpered Mathilda.

'It's not funny – it's *true*,' said Ada earnestly. 'Has anyone here any *idea* how hard it is to come by a Rothschild? And in London, too, never mind Minsk. To think how many lovely English girls there are there, dreaming of someone like Kevin. And my Lou-Anne manages – '

'Talking about lovely girls,' interrupted Mathilda pointedly, 'how's Doreen keeping? Any news yet about her and the Freedman boy?'

'Actually . . . well . . .'

Molly's moment had arrived but she'd lost her nerve. Her intention had been to launch into a tragic tale of star-crossed love with passing references to her daughter's immense popularity and the abundance of would-be suitors waiting in the wings. Something like that. But Ada's triumph had been disconcerting. To say the least. And Sam's joke, instead of deflating her, had merely enhanced her sense of importance.

'What's that?' yapped Mathilda with the glee of a baby bloodhound getting its teeth into a juicy bit of jugular.

'It's over,' said Molly quickly. 'He wasn't right for her. We told her she should maybe consider someone else.'

'Who?'

'Oh . . . one of many.' Molly rose to her feet and began collecting empty cups. 'Anyway, it's too soon to think of another one. Doreen's still very upset. She's not the type to hop from fellow to fellow just like that.'

She glared at Ada, who – quite missing the allusion to her daughter's promiscuity – rushed over to her and squeezed her arm. Molly stiffened.

'I'm so sorry, Molly,' gushed Ada. 'Poor Doreen. It must be terrible for her. I'll tell you what, though – and this is advice straight from the heart. Send the child to London. Listen to me. You've seen what it did for my Lou-Anne – and no one could have been more upset than she was after the business with that last fiancé of hers. Honestly, Molly – send her to London and she'll never look back.'

'Sam – we have to do it,' Molly announced a few nights later.

'Hmm?' asked Sam, his mouth full of sweet and sour stuffed cabbage. Since Sunday, his wife seemed to have been galvanized into a frenzy of domestic activity. With a new sense of purpose, she had surmounted the crippling conditions imposed by the white-by-night law and produced meals the likes of which Gladys Street had seldom seen. 'Molinke, this is wonderful. I can tell you, it's the best cabbage meat you've ever . . .'

'Can you hear what I'm saying, Sam? I've been thinking things over. There's no other way.'

'What do you mean, Molly? What are you talking about?'

'Doreen. Sending her to London. Mathilda and Ada both agree that it will be her only chance.'

'Oh? And . . .? So what do you think will happen to her in London?'

'Happen to her? Sam, stop eating for a minute and listen to me. Please. You want to know what will happen to her? So tell me, Sam, what's happening to her here in Cape Town? And what happened to Lou-Anne the minute she stepped into London? Answer me that, Sam?'

'Well, these things aren't always . . .'

'And tell me also how long we as her parents should sit around doing nothing and watching time pass. She's not getting younger, Sam. These days, a girl of twenty is not a spring chicken any more. I know it'll cost us to send her overseas – but Mathilda and Ada are right. One can't economize on something like that. You know – it's like specialist doctors, proper fitted shoes, the right schools. Have we ever begrudged her any of those things?'

'No,' Sam said, glancing wistfully at the food on his plate but not daring to resume eating. Not yet.

'So? What do you say?'

'Me?' He looked round the table helplessly, desperate to find another respondent to his wife's interrogation, and settled his bewildered gaze on the only other person present. Me. 'Dorinke – what do *you* say?'

I was busy counting peas. From an enormous distance away, I'd heard their voices discussing the approaching obsolescence and partner-less plight of someone called Doreen. Someone I knew vaguely, but a person of minor concern. Someone not nearly as important or interesting as the calculation that was challenging all the arithmetical knowledge I'd acquired at the Speedy Secretarial College. I was trying to work out whether, if I consumed seventeen peas each containing four calories, I'd thereby employ my entire weekly green vegetable quota. On the other hand, five peas fewer would allow me a large portion of celery or a medium portion of spinach or a large portion of lettuce. Or the tiniest morsel of sweet and sour stuffed cabbage.

And I suddenly longed for the taste of my mother's stuffed cabbage. The smell reminded me of contentment and curiosity and the softness of the cushion on which my once-plump bottom had been perched. It made me hungry and uncomfortable and sad, and I wasn't used to feeling those things any more.

'I wish we wouldn't have such unhealthy meals,' I said crossly. 'Don't you realize by now that I have to control my eating?'

'Dorinke,' he persisted. 'Listen to me. Your mother is saying it would be good for you to go somewhere different. To London, she suggests. I'm not sure . . . it's so far away . . . that's why I wanted to know . . .'

'What?'

'Well, I am wondering what you think about the idea.'

He had dropped his eyes to his plate with its half-eaten meal, and at the sight of him frowning and biting his lip my irritation subsided and the ripple of nostalgia I'd so fiercely repressed swelled into the unpleasant possibility of tears. For I sensed that he really cared and wanted to know if I cared. This time he genuinely wanted to know.

I hesitated. He deserved the truth, if I still knew where to find it. After all, hadn't he already sponsored his disappointing daughter on enough aborted missions? Ballet school, diet doctors, charm school, psychiatrists? One would have imagined that by now – especially after the extended stay in hospital had failed to produce the desired results – he would have been willing, more than willing, to abandon the project entirely. But no, not Sam. Here he was, despite everything, still agreeing to subsidize the biggest journey of all. Surely I should remind him about the *Titanic* and advise him to save his money? Shouldn't I tell him that it didn't matter? That nothing mattered? I opened my mouth to speak.

Then I closed it again. From deep within, from a place I'd believed I had long since starved away, I detected a stirring of something that (if I hadn't known better) I might have called hope. I tried to ignore it as the kind of phantom itch people are said to feel in an amputated foot or the ache in a tooth that's been extracted. But it refused to budge, this disturbing flurry. It pestered me.

Not so fast, Doreen, it whispered. Consider the possibility that something might happen. That something might change. In the hospital, you became a different shape but everything else stayed the same. You returned to the same old street, the same old expectations, the same old life. Surely it could be that if your world became a different shape too, then things might really change . . .?

I took a deep breath. What the hell. What did I have to lose but another wasted trip? And anyway I reckoned that although I'd had many futile journeys, I hadn't yet been on my maiden voyage. The time had come.

I looked at them carefully, each in turn. They were like statues in their places at the table, waiting for my words.

'Perhaps,' I said slowly, watching their faces, 'it's a good idea for me to go to London. I think it would be for the best.'

There was a simultaneous expulsion of breath. They spoke together:

'Didn't I say so?' said my mother.

'Are you sure?' said my father.

'Sam,' she said, turning to him, 'of course she's sure. Why don't you finish your food? I've got stewed apples for dessert.'

'Anyway, Dorinke,' he said, picking up his knife and fork, 'London's not so far away any more. It's not like the old days. If you need to, you can fly home in no time at all.'

I nodded absently, for that flutter of hope had abated and I'd already returned to the counting of peas. If I allowed myself an extra four, say, it would mean that . . .

'Heh heh,' he was chortling with his fork loaded high. 'Modern travel. It reminds me of when the steam train came to Pinsk. Such a miracle it was – a person could leave Pinsk at noon and be in Warsaw at midnight.'

He filled his mouth with stuffed cabbage and smacked his lips ardently. 'Mmm!' he said as he reloaded his fork and, with another small chuckle, returned to his story. 'Can you

152

imagine the excitement in Pinsk? People couldn't get over the speed of the journey. Then a cynic pointed out that there wasn't much doing in Warsaw at midnight, so everyone decided that maybe, after all, it was better to stay put in Pinsk. Eh, Dorinke? What do you say?'

I stopped counting and frowned at him, trying to figure out what he was trying to tell me. Not much, probably. Just another of his old and irrelevant jokes. Anyway, even if there had been anything profound in Sam's anecdote, Molly didn't give me time to dig it out.

'Right,' she said briskly, getting to her feet and gathering dishes. 'Sam – hurry up. Doreen, stop dreaming. Now that we've made up our minds, we'd better get busy. There's a huge amount to do. I think I'd better phone Mathilda immediately. She says she can give me the name of a travel agent. The best.'

Eight weeks later, I'd been parcelled for export. Wrapped and labelled and primped and perfected from the top of my sleek bob-cut head to the tips of my manicured toes.

'I'm exhausted,' said Molly on the eve of my departure. She looked exhilarated. Her eyes had acquired a fanatical gleam and her cheeks glowed vermilion without the slightest artificial aid.

This could hardly be said about the manufactured gloss that suffused her daughter. All the top hairdresser's art and the best cosmetician's guile and the skills of Cape Town's cleverest costumiers had been employed in the beautification of Doreen Markowitz. And the art and the guile and the cleverness had succeeded beyond Molly's wildest dreams. Flawless femininity had been attained at last. At long, long last.

'What do you think, Sam?' she asked, parading her prod-uct along the border of the sitting-room's worn Axminster. I trod along, daintily and obediently, thinking that she might at least have provided a red carpet for the auspicious occasion.

'Mmm?' He looked up from his evening paper. 'Very nice, Molly. Very nice indeed.'

'Look at the cut of her trouser-suit, Sam. Feel the quality of the cloth. It's English. The woman at Garlicks told me it's exactly the sort of thing they're wearing in London at the moment. This year's style. Worth every penny, she assured me. With something like this to fall back on, Doreen will never go wrong.'

I flashed him the kind of smile that I imagined ladies in safe trouser-suits wore. Elegantly arced and gracious, with a touch of daring about the bow and an overall patina of capable confidence. Not my most lovable smile.

'Very nice, Molly,' he said again. 'Dorinke has never looked better.'

'And Sam – the shoes. Have you ever seen such shoes? Italian, the man said. From Milan. Did you ever imagine we'd be dressing our daughter in shoes from Milan? Eh, Sam?'

'Never.'

I adjusted my stance to convey a subtle hint of Continental panache. Then, gazing down my nose in a Latin sort of way, I performed a clockwise twirl that would have brought tears of pride and regret to the eyes of Arlene Carter, Dinke du Plessis and others who'd predicted nothing but failure for poor fat Doreen. I gave an anticlockwise encore for good measure and marvelled at my balance and poise.

'See, Sam? Look how graceful she's suddenly become. And remember how you argued about sending her to the charm school and the dancing lessons? Now you can see for yourself what it's done for her in the long run, huh? Wasn't I right to insist?'

He shrugged and nodded, tiredly conceding defeat. Then he folded the paper and stood up, sighing. 'And so, Dorinke,' he said, 'tomorrow you're off.'

'Yup.'

We looked at one another briefly and he seemed about to say something else, but Molly, in a fever of sorting and packing and weighing and displaying, hurried me out of the room.

'Come, Doreen,' she said breathlessly. 'No time to waste. There's still your blue dress to try on. And your pyjamas to sort. And the new cardigan. And the pleated skirt. And – Sam!' she called over her shoulder. 'Sam!'

'What?'

'Sam – I don't think there'll be time for me to make supper tonight. Will you heat yourself some soup from the fridge?'

Much later, in bed, I heard them talking. Hushed voices floated through the darkness, past the pair of suitcases standing sentry at my door.

'Molly, are you sure she's going to be all right? In London? A Jewish girl on her own?'

'Don't be silly, Sam. She'll be fine. Europe isn't what it used to be in the old days. Things have changed . . .'

'And the weather, Molly. Remember when our ship docked at – what was the place called? – Southampton? How cold it was, and grey and wet . . .'

'That's why I got her such a good coat, Sam. English. Pure wool.'

'. . . and we thought we were so lucky not to be stopping off in England. So fortunate to be coming to South Africa, to the family, the sunshine, the wonderful opportunities . . .'

'Her gloves. I wonder if I remembered to pack in her gloves.'

'. . . but maybe it wasn't really so lucky if things aren't good enough here for Dorinke. Maybe we should have looked for somewhere else . . .'

'Don't be ridiculous, Sam. Did we have any choice, tell me? Where else would you like to have been? In the ovens . . .?'

'Molly! Don't say such a thing. Sometimes you talk nonsense. Real nonsense. God should forgive you. If my sister Rochele could hear you now . . .'

'Your sister. Your lovely sister. Remember, Sam, the way she would watch us ice-skating on the lake in the winter . . .'

'Of course I do. And the trees were white with snow . . .'

'And the air was sweet. So sweet.'

'As sweet as the cherries that my mother had preserved from the summer before. And it was crisp – as crisp as the apples . . .'

'Ah, the apples. Such apples. Where else in the world does a person find apples like that?'

'Only in *Der-Heim*, Molly. Remember the *strudels*?'

'Remember, Sam! Could I ever forget?'

I remembered too. I remembered a time when, perched on my cushion, I had swallowed their nostalgia with the same zeal as I'd devoured all the stuff that was piled on my plate. My curiosity had seemed as insatiable as my appetite for food. And I'd been so sure that if I listened as hard as I ate, then one day I would understand everything.

How naïve I'd been. How callow to have imagined that listening would enlighten me and eating would nourish me. It was almost as dumb as believing in goodness or love or the eventual arrival of a handsome prince to rescue me. Anyway, I soon put a stop to all that. And now, here I was, a perfect shell, emptied of everything and ready to be carried away.

'Are you *sure* she'll be all right, Molly?'

'Sam, will you please stop coming back to it. I told you already she'll be fine.'

Yes, I thought. I'd be fine. Of course I would. How could a superbly groomed creature like me not turn out to be fine? Didn't I have the wardrobe of Molly's dreams and wasn't I looking better – even Ada would admit it – than Lou-Anne? As long as I was vigilant, careful not to feel or to laugh or to question or to eat, I'd be fine. Absolutely fine. I shut my eyes determinedly and counted calories until I fell asleep.

10

The next day I asked my father about God. He had come quietly into my room very early in the morning. 'Dorinke,' he'd whispered, 'I must leave to open the shop. I want to say goodbye . . .'

'Goodbye, Dad,' I said sleepily. I offered him a cheek and he kissed it and then tentatively took my hand. 'Be good. Look after yourself,' he mumbled vaguely and I, equally vaguely, mumbled, 'I will.'

And as he dropped my hand and started moving towards the door, I told myself fiercely that his words were enough. That there wasn't much else he could have said to his departing daughter. That I didn't care anyway one way or another.

I watched his small stooped figure crossing the room and slipping past the pair of suitcases and about to disappear with all the unsaid things I had never dared to ask about and the things I'd given up trying to understand. Suddenly I couldn't bear to let him go.

'Dad.'

He turned round sharply, hearing the urgency in my voice.

'Yes – what is it, Dorinke?'

What was it? Where did I begin? With his lost paradise or the original paradise lost? With Adam and Eve perhaps? Or should I go higher? Should I be daring and start at the top?

'Dad,' I said hesitantly, for I'd never asked him this before. Truly. The Lord's name had been invoked almost daily in prayer and oath and jest and general conversation, but the big question had never been put. Not in our house. Probably not in all of Gladys Street.

'Dad – do you believe in God?'

'God?' He stood still for a moment and then began to return towards my bed. Slowly and thoughtfully. 'Do I believe in God?'

'It doesn't matter if you don't feel like answering,' I said. 'It's a silly question anyway and I suppose it has nothing . . .'

'No, it's not silly. Not at all. It's just maybe not the way I usually put it.'

'What do you mean?' I asked, puzzled. It had been inappropriate, maybe. Ill-timed, perhaps. But the question had been pretty straightforward.

He leaned on my bedpost and kneaded his forehead. 'There's an old story I want to tell you, Dorinke,' he said.

Bloody hell, I thought. Not a joke. Surely it wouldn't be a joke? Not now? But his face was grave as he sat, sighing deeply, at the foot of my bed and looked at me intently.

'It's about a rabbi,' he began. 'A rabbi in a remote part of Poland, who goes to check his synagogue late one night and sees God sitting in a dark corner. "My Lord," says the rabbi, kneeling down in awe, "what are *you* doing here?" And God answers him in a very small voice: "I'm tired, rabbi. Tired unto death . . ."'

Tired unto death. There was silence for a moment as my father's words slid along the dust-flecked light-shafts and out of my window. I saw them fluttering beyond the rising sun and the setting moon and the furthest stars to where a tiny, frail deity was cowering in despair over the transgressions of his people. Tired unto death.

Of all the miserable punchlines, I thought. I wanted to cry and, instead, was about to laugh bitterly, when he spoke:

'Dorinke,' he said, 'you asked if I believed in God . . .'

I nodded wearily.

'. . . and I suppose what I'm trying to explain you is that it's not really a question of me believing in him. You see, the way I'd put it is – does God believe in me?'

158

Not much was said after that. He sat for a while at the foot of the bed, my sad tired father with his sad tired God, and then kissed my cheek again and left the room as quietly as he had entered it.

And I, meanwhile, was furious. Seething. I mean, hadn't it been bad enough having doubts about his existence, this Jewish God who spoke a foreign language and never had his picture drawn or appeared personally in the movies? A voice, maybe, in *The Ten Commandments*. But what was that compared with the Christians and their whole Holy Family – mother, baby, manger? They had a birth and a death. A proper story. The sort of rousing stuff that they could sing carols about while the Jewish kids were sent out of assembly to make toys for the poor. But OK. Who's competing? I could have lived with the idea of old angry, shadowy Yahweh keeping us in line. I hadn't given up on him even after I'd stopped believing in Cousin Norman's theory that he lived in the *mezuzah* nailed to the door jamb and demanded to be kissed each time we passed. I played safe and carried on kissing the thing anyway (what did it cost?) but imagined him up there frowning at me. Stern. Disapproving. Unforgiving. But certainly not tired. *Tired?* What damn right did he have to take off and say he was tired? Faceless was one thing, but how on earth was one supposed to count on a coward?

'Chicken!' I said aloud and looked challengingly out of the window.

But, surprise, surprise, there was no answer. After all, who did I think I was – Moses? Anyway, Moses had probably also disappeared to have a nervous breakdown somewhere. And Sam, my father Sam, had retreated to his tailor shop to sigh.

Molly, on the other hand, was there. All there. No doubt about that. 'Doreen! *Doreen!*' she was screeching. 'You'd better get up. It's late. I've asked the Venters' garden boy to help us with the suitcases, so dress yourself quickly. We have to be at the airport in about two hours.'

Goodness, I'd almost forgotten. Wasn't I about to take off as well? Oh yes – I, too, was quitting town. But I was leaving

159

like a *mensch* in my safe English trouser-suit and soft Italian shoes, with my carefully co-ordinated wardrobe and my neatly plucked brows. And my toothpaste-ad smile and shampoo-ad hair and diet-ad figure and perfume-ad smell. Nothing tired unto death about me. I was perfect. Just perfect. I'd soar into the air and fly as far away as possible from Sam's lily-livered God. Who needed him, anyway?

'Won't be long,' I called as I checked my weight on the bathroom scales to make sure my ascent wouldn't be impeded by a single extra ounce. 'I'll be ready in a minute.'

On the day I left Cape Town, it was reported that some American had landed on the moon. 'A giant leap for mankind,' quoted the awe-struck press, but I shrugged with contempt as I boarded my plane. The moon? A nothing. A mere flea-hop away. Didn't everyone know that the really big leap was mine?

It seemed not. While I was rising like a phoenix above Table Mountain and glancing at the safety precautions I'd extracted from the seat-pocket in front of me, those who weren't straining to see the man in the moon were getting on with their lives. The usual kind of thing. Goebbels Venter was being put to sleep for turning on his master and Arnold Gleeson was being put on parole for good behaviour. Dinkie du Plessis was suffering a hangover induced by a superfluity of brandy and Coke, while Cousin Norman was enduring a drug-related relapse. Arlene Carter, in the mean time, had gone completely off her head. She'd pranced naked along Adderly Street holding a placard that said *Black is Beautiful* and was being charged with disturbing the peace.

Such peace. There was violence in the townships and unrest on the university campus and discord in the tea-room of Stuttafords department store, where Molly Markowitz and her relation, Mathilda, were on the brink of exchanging blows.

'Italian shoes!' expostulated Mathilda. 'Do you mean to tell me, you bought her Italian shoes? I can hardly remember the last time I treated myself to a pair of Italian shoes. And *we* can afford them . . .'

'But Mathilda . . .'

'Next thing Reuven will tell me he had to lend Sam money. For a change. Honestly, Molly, you have no sense of proportion. None at all . . .'

Meanwhile, the shoes in question were killing me. The plane had reached its cruising altitude and my feet had painfully, alarmingly started to swell. 'Don't worry, dear,' said the air hostess, who was even more cosmetically correct than me. 'It happens to everyone. It's to do with the pressure . . .'

What did she know about pressure, with her peachy skin and baby-blue eyes and a cherubic mouth that had never been ravaged by gorging or starvation or the telling of jokes? I scowled at her.

'Why don't you take your shoes off?' she suggested. 'You'll feel much more comfortable that way.'

'No,' I said, more sharply than I'd meant to. 'Thank you.' Poor girl. How could she help her vapid innocence? And how could she possibly know that I didn't dare release my distended feet from their stylish restraints? That I feared that, if freed, they would surely get bigger and bigger, ballooning into infinity . . .

I slept as we crossed the Equator. Dozed fitfully, dreaming about a banquet. I'd had that one before. Food. A glorious fantasy of fattening food and I, throwing off my initial self-control, was feasting with gusto. Cherry pies, apple *strudel*, lashings of cream. Wonderful. Delicious. I was almost able to ignore my unease about the consequence of my binge – until, looking down, I noticed that slits were appearing on my swollen feet. Great gaping fissures on my feet and legs and arms. I was exploding. Rupturing like a giant sausage. Bursting out of my skin . . .

'Please fasten your seat belts. We are entering an area of unstable weather and advise you to keep your belts fastened until the red light in front of you is extinguished.'

I woke with a start. The expensive shoes were cutting deep

into my puffy feet, but I saw with relief that the skin was intact. And, snickering uneasily the way one does after a scary and preposterous dream, I pulled the seat belt tightly round my trim lap and braced myself for bad weather.

There were storms in Cape Town that night. Sam had indigestion after Molly's defiantly extravagant three-course supper and Molly herself was feeling flat. She was missing her daughter – but not nearly as much as Rex Venter, next door, was pining for a long-toothed canine presence at his feet.

'Get a gun,' urged his wife. 'Much more reliable than a bleddy dog. And with the way things are going here, one *needs* something reliable. Did you hear about the dame in Adderly Street? The one with the tits and the banner?'

Who hadn't? Arlene's story, which was judged to have more local interest than a moon landing, had appeared in every paper in the country. It was also, at that very moment, being sub-edited for page two of *The Times* and page three of the *Telegraph*, and was inspiring a left-wing leader for the *Manchester Guardian*. Geoffrey, being Geoffrey, was a meticulous reader of all three.

'Fancy that,' he muttered later, over his prune-based breakfast. He lived in splendid solitude in Kensington, having cultivated regular bowel movements and all the most useful connections that a rising young barrister could need. Everyone said he was destined for big things. Ha ha. 'The tricks people get up to in South Africa. Who knows what will emerge from there next . . .?'

Me, actually. But how could he possibly have predicted that? The only people in London who were aware of the imminent arrival of the new, improved Doreen Markowitz were Cousin Lou-Anne and her Rothschild fiancé, the great and fêted Kevin Roth.

*

162

'Doreen?' she asked, teetering slightly on unstable heels and steadying herself on the arm of the bemused-looking man at her side. 'It's Doreen, isn't it? Gosh, I'd hardly have recognized you. You look stunning. Absolutely *divine*. My mom wrote and told me . . .'

'Lou-Anne.' I would have known her anywhere, from the bleached curls and Hide 'n' Heal-covered vestiges of facial acne to the pawed-at, padded boobs. 'Thanks so much for coming to meet me. Very kind of you. I didn't expect it. And this, of course, must be . . .?'

'Kev.' She nudged him proudly. 'Kevin Roth.'

'Pleased to meet you,' I said, marvelling at the extent of the decline of a rich and noble family. Kev looked as much like old money as I looked like a new-laid egg.

'How d'you do?' He smiled crookedly. His teeth, I noticed, were in urgent need of orthodontic intervention. My mother would have had something to say about that. 'Lou's told me so much about you and, well, I said to her that a cousin of hers is a cousin of mine. That's why I insisted on bringing the motor here to collect you . . .'

'You should have heard him, Doreen. Absolutely adamant. And it's *such* a long way from Finchley Central to Heathrow. Honestly, London's an *enormous* place. As you'll find out for yourself.'

'I'm sure.'

Enormous? It was rapidly shrinking before my eyes. Being reduced to a suburb of Cape Town by the breathy arpeggios of Lou-Anne's flat vowels and the gold Star of David chained to her intended's chest. From the back seat of Kev's Datsun Cherry, I glimpsed endless rows of grey terraced houses and wondered when we'd get to see Metropolitan Life. Where were the Houses of Parliament and Piccadilly Circus and Nelson's Column and Pall Mall? Surely this couldn't be the glamorous hang-out of Prince Philip and the Queen? But Lou-Anne, chattering incessantly, didn't give me a chance to find out.

'You're so *lucky* to have us here, Dor,' she babbled. 'When I arrived, I knew no one. Not a soul. If I hadn't met Sharleen

– that's Kev's sister – I'd've probably given up and gone home. But then Shar – she'd just lost her job and we got chatting in the post office – suggested we team up and start a little catering business. We were both saying how much we liked cooking and – my goodness. It happened so fast. One minute we were talking about it and the next thing . . . a bit like me and you, hey Kev? The two of us deciding to get hitched?'

'They've done brilliantly, Doreen. Amazingly well. In – how long is it now? – oh, less than a year, they've almost cornered the local bar mitzvah market. And it's bit of a closed shop that, I tell you. Not easy breaking in there. Not easy at all.'

'Oh, Kev, you're exaggerating. I'll tell you something, though, Dor – the big thing these days is to get into executive lunches. You know, boardroom meals for the big boys. That's what Shar and me want to do next. Kev thinks it's an amazing idea – don't you, doll? – and so we're busy trying to set it all up . . .'

'Really,' I kept murmuring. 'Very clever.' 'Most interesting.' 'What fun.' Until, at last, when we were slowing down outside a grey house identical to the thousand others we'd passed along the route, Lou-Anne paused for breath and to ask me what I planned to do in London.

'I'm not sure,' I said, my voice sounding hollow and unfamiliar in the sudden silence. 'I've booked into a hotel for a while. I'll have to earn some money if I decide to stay on, I suppose . . .'

'Not to worry. We'll take care of her – won't we, Kev? Why don't you come in and have a wash and a bit of food, Dor? And maybe a little rest. You must be *finished*.'

'I am tired,' I admitted. 'Actually, I feel a bit – strange.'

Talk about understatements. Strange? I felt like an alien. A complete outsider in this grey and grimy city. Foreign to my prattling cousin and her dreary partner and to my empty body and my foggy mind and to the English trouser-suit that had creased horribly during the flight. And those shoes. Those damned Italian shoes. I was a stranger to myself in an unfamiliar world and wondered whether I had landed in hell (or the moon maybe?) and suddenly had a desperate longing for oblivion.

'Perhaps I need to sleep a while before I do anything else,' I said.

'Of *course*,' she agreed. 'She can use our bed, can't she, Kev? I'll get some lunch together meanwhile. Make yourself at home, Dor. Sleep as long as you like.'

The last thing I heard before I drifted off in Lou-Anne's double bed was her interminable voice burbling something about a work permit and how I wouldn't need one if I decided to join forces with her and Shar. I remembered our Sunday family teas and how Lou-Anne would preen herself and sneer at me, and tried to work out why on earth she was suddenly being so effusively nice.

It didn't take me long to find out. There was an element of nostalgia, I suppose. After all, despite her conquest of Kevin and a lucrative corner of the catering market, Cousin Lou-Anne hadn't quite made it here as family favourite and *femme fatale*. Not in London. For her, the memories of those Sunday teas were probably as fond as mine were repugnant, and she must have welcomed the idea of my arrival as a messenger from her glorious past. Her funny, fat cousin. Poor, poor Doreen, to whom she could afford to be very kind indeed.

The fact that I wasn't fat must have maddened her. No longer fat. No longer funny. And what was that the mirror on the wall was saying about the fairer of us two . . .?

I soon learnt that the more disconcerted Lou-Anne was, the more enthusiastically she prattled. And the more she disliked me, the wider she smiled. She offered me a bed. She offered me a job. In a very short time, I saw through the gushing generosity and understood exactly what she was after. Power.

Not a bad second best to supercilious condescension, you must admit.

165

'It's an *awful* situation, Dor,' she sighed a week or so after I'd arrived. I had discovered that London was expensive and, yes, she'd been right, I was not legally entitled to work. 'Permits are impossible to come by. I know. I've tried. Sharleen's managed to organize things for me – until the wedding, of course. That's the answer, isn't it? To marry an Englishman. The thing is . . .'

The thing was that until such an eventuality befell me ('And, being *realistic*, Dor, the odds aren't good with so many absolutely gorgeous girls around and hardly any eligible men'), she would be *delighted* to employ me. Under the counter, so to speak. As a favour to the family. Obviously, since I wasn't what she'd describe as *experienced*, she couldn't offer me exactly top whack. But it would be enough to survive on and, anyway, she'd always be around to help out with this or that. 'What else are cousins for?' she simpered.

What indeed? I resisted for as long as I could. Eked out my dowry in cheaper and cheaper hotels and applied such strict portion control to my increasingly meagre meals that I was in a state of hypoglycaemic stupor most of the time. That didn't prevent me applying my make-up with mechanical precision, but it made my enquiries about various menial jobs half-hearted, to say the least. Like a robot, I walked the streets of London, mouthing the famous names to convince myself I was really there. Oxford Street. Regent Street. Trafalgar Square. I muttered the names but, in truth, could have been anywhere. Or nowhere. I was a mindless, soulless clockwork doll and my motor was running down.

And so, when Lou-Anne telephoned one day in a panic to say that Sharleen was ill and would I please, please save her life and help her with a bar mitzvah lunch for a hundred, I didn't have the strength to refuse.

'You're an angel, Dor,' she sighed. 'An absolute *love*. I'll see you here in half an hour. And don't forget to bring along some rubber gloves and an apron . . .'

*

These were to be the tools of my new trade and latest symbols of my servitude. A sickly yellow pair of medium-sized Marigold gloves and a polyester apron smitten with a rash of jaundiced daisies. I ought to have preserved them for posterity in the Markowitz Museum of Female Fealty, alongside a solitary ballet pump, a worn-out bra of the Stretch 'n' Grow variety, a stale diet biscuit or two and a love-poem composed to a certain gormless young doctor for whom I'd shed my heart and soul and half my weight. Instead, I tied the apron prettily round my waist and pulled the gloves over my manicured hands and presented myself to Cousin Lou-Anne for exploitation.

'Oh, Dor, I'm *so* glad to see you.' She was clearly flustered about her partnerless plight. Anxiety glistened from her unpowdered nose and from the beads of perspiration of her upper lip and forehead while, on the table behind her, gleamed the bodies of about two dozen wet and waiting fish. They weren't looking flustered. On the contrary, they were grinning inanely. 'You don't, by any chance, know anything about – herrings?' asked Cousin Lou-Anne.

'Me? Know about herrings? You're asking *Molly Markowitz's daughter* if she knows about herrings?'

I narrowed my eyes at the scaly line-up, daring them to keep smiling in the face of my familiarity with their fate. They kept smiling, cheeky buggers. I picked up a knife and held it aloft. This was war. 'So how d'you fancy them, Lou? Chopped? Pickled? Danish-style? In mustard sauce, perhaps? How about in sour cream? Or with apples and cucumber? Maybe you'd prefer them with – '

'All right. It's enough, Doreen. I get the picture. What I really meant was – can you fillet the damn things?'

But there was no stopping me. I wasn't looking at twenty-four dead fish. It was my past staring back at me, voices echoing from the distant tiled kitchen and out of a dark, dank dining-room where a fat little girl was perched on a cushion, eating and listening, eating and listening.

167

'Posy, if I've told you once I've told you a hundred times, you must mix Marie biscuits into the chopped herring. It doesn't taste right otherwise . . .'

'Delicious, Molly. Mmm. If I hadn't married you for your *lokshen* pudding, I would've settled for your pickled herring. Which reminds me. Did you hear the story of the two rollmops? Eh Molly? Dorinke . . .?'

'Not *again*, Seraphina. How often must I remind you to use a sharp knife for skinning? You've pulled away all the flesh. I don't know what the master will say . . .'

'Wonderful. Molly, it tastes like a dream . . .'

Like a dream. Like a dream. She ranted and he joked and I ate, and miles away, years away, in Lou-Anne's Formica kitchen in a far corner of Finchley, I could still hear them with the clarity of my mother's finest chicken soup. All the smells and the sounds and the tastes. *Der-Heim*? Was I remembering *Der-Heim*? And – was I imagining the breathy voice of my cousin breaking into my reverie?

'You're brilliant, Dor,' she was saying. 'I didn't know you were such an amazing cook. Gosh – you've dealt with those herrings like a real expert. I never dreamt you had it in you.'

I looked down. While my head had been swimming with sentimentality, my hands had been skinning and boning and paring and slicing with merciless precision. The herrings lay in neat strips on the table. They were no longer smiling. Neither was I. And neither, I noticed, was Lou-Anne.

She had crossed her arms over her perky chest and was surveying me appraisingly. Nostalgia had widened my eyes, but hers had turned into skinny slits. 'I think you'll *have* to come and work for me,' she said, without a trace of her usual gushiness.

I shrugged. I knew what she was after, but it didn't seem to matter. Not then. Not for quite a long while. I resigned myself to my fate as Lou-Anne's skivvy and told myself that it was destiny. Nothing more than my God-given heritage of blood, sweat and tears. Or, to put it gastronomically, it was the way the cookie crumbled and the *latke* browned and the mushroom soufflé rose. If you get what I mean.

The cookies and *latkes* and mushroom soufflés certainly did. There was some mighty crumbling and browning and rising once I'd got into my stride. A genius I turned out to be. A culinary Einstein. The hands and brain behind bar mitzvah lunches across the length and breadth of north-west London.

A modest and retiring brain too. Lou-Anne and Sharleen took the credit and the cash and I, in my rubber gloves and apron, cooked the meals and gave the tips. Like the one about putting a lump of coal in the water to crisp the lettuce. And improving the fluffiness of mashed potatoes with a pinch of bicarb. And adding vinegar to the water to prevent boiled eggs from cracking. Molly Markowitz may have been somewhat grudging with her mother's milk but (fair's fair) she'd been more than generous with her handy household hints.

'You're one in a million, Dor,' Lou-Anne would sigh. 'A complete and utter gem. I only wish that Shar and I could afford to pay you what you're worth. But you know how much we appreciate your efforts, don't you? One day, when we strike it rich . . .'

Oh yeah. When the pigs grew wings and the moon turned green and the birds of the air went to charm school and the beasts of the field danced the foxtrot, then maybe the joint proprietors of Krafty Kooks ('We'll make a meal of your occasion') would dip into their pockets to find Doreen Markowitz a decent, living wage.

'It's OK,' I'd say, glaring at her to show that it wasn't really. But I felt powerless to make an open complaint, for the law was on her side.

Anyway, my needs were simple. Basic accommodation and a food bill that had been pared as close to the bone as the skin on my minimal bum. The English trouser-suit had, admittedly, lost its first fine flush, an Italian shoe had lost its heel and my hair had lost its auburn streaks. But I'd kept my

169

weight constant and, all in all, things could have been worse.
A great deal worse.

'Fry the fish, Doreen,' commanded Lou-Anne.

'The bagels!' screamed Sharleen. 'You've forgotten to
butter the bloody bagels.'

'The potatoes . . .'

'The pudding . . .'

'The dishes . . .'

'The floor . . .'

Orders. Orders. Orders.

'Yes, Lou-Anne. Fine, Sharleen. Can do. Will do.'

I was as sweet as bloody pie. How I managed it, God only
knows. I felt a certain kinship with poor old put-upon
Cinderella, who'd had to endure as much sisterly abuse down
among the embers. More, if possible. And Cinders didn't
even have the compensations that kept me going.

The abundant source of food fantasies, for instance. Oh,
the desserts I concocted. The fillings. The flans. Material for
an endless supply of Technicolor, Vista-vision, mouth-water-
ingly three-dimensional and utterly delicious dreams. Enough
to fill the empty days and arid nights and to pacify (well,
more or less) the rumbling void inside my belly. Lou-Anne
shrieked and Sharleen squealed and I built confectionary
castles in the air. And when I wasn't drooling over things
like Mocca Rousse and chocolate mousse and Italian Cream
Cheese Gâteau, I was gleefully observing the decline of my
cousin's celebrated match.

Yes, Lou-Anne's romance was definitely on the rocks. Kev,
you see, was turning out to have what is discreetly referred
to as 'a roving eye'. He'd even made some rather indecent
suggestions to me. Naturally, I had declined with a tight-
lipped 'thanks, but no thanks'. Taking him up on his offer
would have been sublime revenge, but, frankly, it wasn't
worth it. Not even for that.

'Another time,' I had lied, stirring a pot that bubbled with
sugar and cinnamon and spices and other wicked things.
Kevin had leered down the front of my daisy-print apron and
squeezed my fingers through their layer of yellow latex and

170

I'd watched with amusement as Lou-Anne, looking on with slinky eyes and arms akimbo, had struggled to suppress her fury.

'Doreen,' she had called icily, 'how's that sauce doing? We haven't got all day, you know.'

'It's coming along nicely, Lou,' I'd replied in a voice more syrupy than my sauce. 'Don't you worry about a thing. They'll love it – you wait and see.'

Love it? They adored it. Raved about it. Drooled over it. In fact, the meals emanating from the kitchens of Krafty Kooks were threatening to stimulate so much saliva in north London that there was talk of the Thames overflowing its banks. Swallowing ecstatically, customers made bookings for bar mitzvah lunches up to four-and-a-half years in advance. It seemed that while Lou-Anne's love-life was taking a nosedive, her business was heading for the skies. Thanks to me.

Not that my working conditions improved. Far from it. The gloves had perished, the apron was stained, the second Italian shoe had lost its stylish heel and I was losing patience. The food fantasies had ceased to divert me and Kev's faithlessness no longer amused me and – well, I decided I'd had it. Enough was enough. I was on the brink of demanding a substantial salary increase or else, when Lou-Anne arrived excitedly one morning with an announcement.

'We've done it,' she crowed.

'Hope you took precautions,' I muttered as I rolled out some dough.

'Oh, Dor. You've got a one-track mind. It's us – Krafty Kooks. We've finally broken in.'

'Where?'

'Big business. Executive lunches, remember? The first one's next Friday. In the City. A bank. This could be big, Dor. The meal has to be perfect. And – um – here's twenty quid in advance so that you can smarten yourself up. We have to make a good impression.'

*

171

I suppose a fairy godmother might have been of some assistance here. Not that I'd spent much time on soulful songs about the day a prince would come to rescue Cinderella Markowitz from the Krafty Kooks kitchen. Apart from being tone deaf and too tired, I'd seen enough of Kevin Roth to know the limitations of princely salvation. So why did I go to so much trouble with my appearance for that inaugural executive lunch? Was it a premonition? Female intuition perhaps? Or was it just plain boredom with looking such a mess?

I'll never be sure. All I know was that, *sans* godmother and *sans* magic wand, I miraculously managed to stretch my twenty pounds to finance a comprehensive personal overhaul. My hair was Titian-tinted, my hands were softened, my face glamorized and my legs defuzzed. I acquired a brief black skirt and a tight black top and a frilly little apron and sturdy German shoes.

Yes, I can guess what you're thinking. And, no – we're not talking glass slippers here. I knew perfectly well that the shoes were as suited to my outfit as a bowler hat to a sheep, but there had been something about them. How enticingly comfortable they'd seemed compared with the frivolity of the rest of my get-up. Comfortable and sensible – and, at the same time, irresistibly dangerous. Acquiring the shoes had been as risky as eating imported *Bratwurst* and drinking Black Forest wine and taking a chance on a Volkswagen. All forbidden, strictly taboo in Markowitz circles.

But I'd told myself. I wasn't bound by such strictures any more. Not me. Wasn't I a grown-up? Hadn't times changed? So I had insisted, as I'd surreptitiously checked beneath the 'genuine leather' soles for any lingering traces of Nazi monster. Just to make sure. Then I'd donned the shoes defiantly and, squaring my shoulders, had strode down the street. Who cared what anyone thought? The footwear was an essential part of my outfit. It was my final, subversive touch.

'All set?' asked Lou-Anne on the telephone on the eve of our executive lunch. She was talking about the food.

'Everything's perfect,' I said coolly. I was referring to my appearance.

'Now remember – first the canapés, then the cream of mushroom soup, then the *sole bonne femme*. Followed by strawberries and cream. Then cheese and biscuits. And coffee – oh, *God*, Dor, I'm in such a *state!*'

'Why? Don't be silly, Lou-Anne. This lunch isn't very different to the others we've done. Not really. What are a dozen men, after the hundreds we've catered for? It'll be a cinch, Lou. As easy as . . .'

'And Sharleen says she's not feeling well for a change. And Kevin . . . Kevin . . .'

'What about Kevin?'

'He's . . . oh, I'm sure he's seeing someone else . . .'

'Never,' I lied. 'He's devoted to you, Lou. As faithful as a blind man's dog. As steadfast as – as a knight in arms.'

She didn't believe me. Not as stupid as she looked, was my Cousin Lou-Anne. Mind you, the next day when I bowled up at the bank in my finery, she looked a damn sight more than stupid. Cretinous would have been an apter epithet. Her eyes were glazed, her hair was lank, her skin had erupted and her pale lips were twitching alarmingly. Around her, on tables and shelves and benches and chairs, were strewn the ingredients for our meal in various stages of unpreparedness. The executives were soon to gather for their gourmet lunch and Lou-Anne, it seemed, had fallen apart.

'Doreen,' she was saying limply, 'D'you think you could get things going? I don't know what's the matter with me. I hardly slept all night.'

Placing my hands on my hips, I inspected her with all the languid superiority I could squeeze into my figure-hugging outfit. She started chewing on a thumbnail and I slowly shook my head and sighed, feeling not the slightest twinge of compassion. Mercy may have been the name of the maid who served Molly Markowitz for an indeterminate period between the reign of light-fingered Maggie and haughty

173

Angelina. I, on the other hand, was called Doreen. Deadly Doreen, who was ruthless, revengeful, relentless and ready for the kill.

'You're in a bad way, Lou-Anne,' I murmured, moving methodically from corner to corner as I assembled the raw material and magically transformed it into food. A platter of delectable savouries. Fragrant, steaming soup. Melt-in-the-mouth fish. Steamed vegetables. A sparkling array of summer fruits.

At last, I stepped back.

'There!' I said, untying my apron and removing my gloves. 'All done.'

There were footsteps and guffaws from the adjoining boardroom, where the gentlemen were converging for their meal. I turned to my cousin and was about to advise her sweetly to pull herself together. Then I saw that, wonder of wonders, she had suddenly staged a miraculous recovery from her lassitude. Trust Lou-Anne. Her nose had been powdered and her hair had been combed and, having slipped on her stilettos, she had assumed her usual domineering stance.

'Very good, Doreen,' she singsonged, in the tone teachers tend to use to reward unlovely but co-operative pupils. 'Well done. Now, perhaps you ought to put the final touches to the fish while I go along and titillate the men with this wonderful tray of canapés . . .'

Oh no, I thought, moving neatly into her path. Uh-uh. Not this time, dearest cuz.

'I think that *I'll* take the canapés and *you'll* do the fish,' I said slowly, holding her gaze in a way that brooked not the slightest argument. Lou-Anne hesitated for a moment, then passed me the platter.

'OK,' she said, affecting a carelessness I knew she didn't feel. 'Have it your way then, if that's what pleases you.'

It did indeed. I lowered the tray on to a table and withdrew from my handbag a small mirror and make-up pouch and scrutinized myself carefully, noting with satisfaction the dramatic effect of my blacker-than-black eyes and blazing hair. Good. Excellent. I rehearsed my most enigmatic smile and, almost as an afterthought, outlined it with a lustrous coat of plum-red lipstick. Then I picked up the tray and made my entrance.

What an entrance. Talk about knocking them out. As I appeared at the door, there was a sudden hush. A solitary clearing of a throat and then silence, broken only by the incongruous thumping of my shoes on the shiny parquet floor. A dozen pairs of eyes attached themselves to my sensible footwear and then travelled up my legs to the frivolous skirt and finally settled, comatose, on my cleavage. I breathed in deeply and the eyes, coming alive again, wandered up to my face.

'Afternoon, gentlemen,' I said cheerily. 'Please help yourselves to the hors-d'oeuvre.'

'Jolly good, jolly good,' someone said as, accompanied by several 'ho-ho-ho's' and a general scraping of chairs, their attention migrated from my face to the food. 'Mmm. Delicious. Try the little round one, Charles. Worth sacrificing the waistline for, I'd say . . .'

'Enjoy your meal,' I chirped, beginning my retreat and noting with some disappointment that the men, engrossed in their stomachs, seemed to have forgotten my charms. They were eating voraciously. All of them except one.

I had noticed him as soon as I'd stepped into the room. He was tall and skinny, with dark brown hair that was prematurely greying and thinly pursed lips that seemed to have been shaped for disapproval and discontent. His gaze, when it moved from my legs to my bust, was so intense that it made me uneasy. I had to look away. Even so, I could almost feel him ogling me. His eyes were fixed on my face. My mouth. My glossy, cherry-red lips.

I smiled. He looked down at his plate and blushed. Rather endearingly I thought, for such a suave-looking person. I took a step towards him and was about to tempt him with a titbit from my tray when Cousin Lou-Anne appeared at my shoulder.

'Everything all right, Doreen?' she asked.

I swung round. Lou-Anne, I noticed immediately, had effected an emergency cosmetic overhaul. Her eyes were caked with mascara, her hair was stiff with lacquer and her skirt had been hitched up high above her knees. With a flourish, she extracted the tray from my hands and I didn't react quickly enough to grab it back.

'I'm sure the gentlemen would like some more,' she breathed, swivelling on her stilettos to face the table. But she hadn't counted on the high polish of the floor. Overswinging disastrously, she attempted to steady herself on the bald head of one of the diners. He ducked. She slipped. The tray fell first, followed by Cousin Lou-Anne. I can't tell you how ridiculous she looked, inelegantly splayed in a sea of squashed hors-d'oeuvres.

'Oh dear,' I said. 'Oh dear, what a mess . . .' I know it was mean, but I simply couldn't stop myself giggling uncontrollably.

Several gentlemen made polite moves to restore poor Lou-Anne to an upright position. Others continued eating, trained since birth to put the blandest of bland faces on social embarrassment. The skinny ogler, however, still had his gaze fixed on me. He was staring even more fervently, if possible. His lips were apart and he was breathing irregularly, as though in deep shock. My outburst, I learnt later, had pushed him from a state of moderate adoration to profoundest veneration.

Had I erupted into ordinary laughter of the gentle, joyful kind, it would have had no effect at all on Geoffrey Bartholomew-Cooper. But mine was pure *schadenfreude*. The sort of malicious mirth he had understood from the cradle. For him, the only sort of mirth.

Geoffrey was convinced that he had chanced upon his perfect soul-mate. He had fallen for my figure and glossy red lips and then become hooked, utterly hooked, on my mean-spirited hilarity.

Lou-Anne, meanwhile, was struggling to her feet in a fury. 'Doreen,' she said through clenched teeth, 'get to the kitchen. Immediately.'

'OK, OK,' I said, backing off. Like Cinderella, I could hear the clock striking twelve. Midnight. Back to rags and penury. But I had a strong feeling that my servitude wouldn't last long.

I addressed a final glance at the ogler before turning to the door. Still staring at me, he was slipping into his pocket one of the Krafty Kooks business cards that Lou-Anne had placed on the table. I smiled, nodding almost imperceptibly. He noticed and nodded back, and I was impressed by his astuteness. Later, I would learn – to my cost – that Geoffrey Bartholomew-Cooper never missed a trick.

11

When he hadn't called after six days, I began to wonder whether I had imagined the encounter. I'd arrived back home with both German shoes firmly on my feet, which proved that my prince wasn't being held up (or put off) by protracted investigations into the ownership of a detached and ungainly size seven. And anyway, he'd taken the card. I had seen him. So why the hell didn't he come and rescue me from my plight?

And, boy, did I need rescuing. Things had taken a decided turn for the worse since the fateful Friday of Lou-Anne's fall. Kevin, you see, had finally taken off. His job (selling fancy goods) incurred much travel and, on his regular journeys up and down the Ml, he'd had passing affairs with an assortment of ladies in various positions at self-service restaurants along the way. Several cashiers, three sandwich-cutters, a chip-fryer, innumerable coffee-pourers and a table-wiper or two had, at one time or another, provided Kev with services not depicted with the petrol pump and eating utensils on motorway signs. In the end, a lavatory attendant called Clemmy had enticed him into an overnight stay. And another night. And another. Until, after a frantic week, Lou-Anne had received a brief message (via Sharleen) from the Scratchwood Motel. Her fiancé was not coming back.

Not only that. Sharleen, having confessed to several spells of deep-seated depression and a very nervous disposition, announced to Lou-Anne that the business had become too much for her. The stress. The incipient varicose veins. The indigestion. And, finally, the added tension that would inevitably arise because of the – er – *irreparable* situation between her catering associate and her brother, Kev.

'To cut a long story short, Lou,' she concluded, 'I've decided that, taking everything into consideration, I'm going to have to quit. No choice really. It's what my mum always said: one's health must come first.'

Poor Lou-Anne. She'd been stripped of both marital and business partners in one fell swoop. Her future looked bleak. And there was no one upon whom she could take out her anger and frustration – except me. Poor Lou-Anne, did I say? Poor bloody me.

Gone were the endearments. My cousin, stripped of her honeyed inflections and simpering politenesses, had become a whining tyrant. And I, restrained once more in my apron and gloves and tethered to the kitchen, obeyed her orders sullenly and silently, waiting with diminishing hope for the call that would herald my liberation. At last, when I had almost given up, my patience was rewarded.

'Is that Krafty Kooks?' enquired a deep and educated male voice. I recognized it immediately.

'Yes. Can I help you?' I asked primly, trying not sound too eager.

'Well – er – there was a young lady who was serving lunch at the bank last Friday. A red-haired . . .'

'It's me.'

'Oh? Oh . . . good.'

There was a lengthy pause. He cleared his throat. 'And?' I prompted, struggling to hide my impatience.

'And? What do you mean . . .?'

'What can I do for you? I mean – why did you phone? The meal, perhaps? Was it not to your liking?'

'No. I mean, yes. What I mean is, Miss – er . . .'

'My name's Doreen. Doreen Markowitz.'

'Oh. And I'm Geoffrey Bartholomew-Cooper. When can I see you – Doreen?'

*

That's how it happened. Almost exactly like the plot of a thousand fairy-tales and a million romantic novels. You know – oppressed damsel captures heart of dashing hero, who arrives on his charger and sweeps her off to happiness. In this case, though, there were a few variations on the basic theme. Take him and her, for instance. On minute inspection, they weren't all they appeared. Not quite. Inside her (O lovely creature) there was a funny, fat person struggling to come out. And inside him (O manly one) there raged a cosmic contest between mundane normality and homicidal mania. Not a promising combination, I can tell you. Explosive, to say the least.

As for ever-after happiness – that's as likely a story as the one about the woman whose husband died laughing. Believe that, and you'll believe anything. Or, if not anything, at least a thousand fairy-tales and a million romantic novels.

'You must believe in *something*?' he persisted, leaning earnestly towards me across two feet of starched linen and a pale pink rose in a slender glass vase. 'Surely, at your age, you can't be totally disillusioned about life?'

I considered for a moment. Me? Disillusioned? Not at all. That only happened to people who'd had illusions in the first place. People who had counted on dreams and fantasies and sought goodness on earth and, if all else failed, relied on the ultimate perfection of heaven. People who imagined that, for instance, God would take care of them and Jesus had died for them and that all would be well in the end. Hardly people like Sam and Molly Markowitz. And certainly not their daughter, who'd been born with jokes and a hearty appetite and the clearest of eyes. Eyes that, right from the start, had given her perfect vision of an imperfect world. No room for disillusionment there. But how did one explain this to someone like Geoffrey Bartholomew-Cooper? Even then, I was quite sure that he'd never begin to understand.

Yet he'd asked. He had asked in a manner that made me think he really wanted to know. Stanley Morris, too, had expressed interest convincingly. I had loved Dr Morris and I suppose that in a similar, childish and rather limited sort of way I must have cared for Geoffrey.

'It goes back a long time,' I began.

He straightened his shoulders and placed his hands on his lap and arranged his features to display serious attentiveness. During the previous two hours, his eyes had roamed hungrily and incessantly from my arms to my breasts. They had followed each forkful of food through my cherry-red lips while his had framed questions. Systematic questions. Precisely the sort of questions you'd expect from a barrister. My origins, my criminal record (if any), my parents, my beliefs. Now his lips were tightly pursed as, like a small boy who'd settled down for story-time, he awaited my response.

'I'm not really sure where to start . . .' I hesitated, glancing at him with a shrug. He didn't move. His grey-green eyes were fixed on my face. 'Geoffrey?' I said, frowning. His intensity was unsettling. 'Geoffrey – what is it?'

He didn't answer. Instead, I felt his leg touching mine beneath the table and watched as his lips parted and his gaze grew even more ardent – if possible.

'Geoffrey . . .?' I repeated unsteadily. He reached across the table and took my hand.

And for an instant, I believed. Crazily, I believed in *him*, this man I hardly knew. During that single instant, with our legs pressed together and his hand gripping mine and his eyes unwavering, I felt all the layers of Markowitz cynicism momentarily falling away. I wanted him and I believed he wanted me. I imagined that somehow he would keep me safe. That, in some magical way, his cool reserve, his blatant unJewishness and his grey normality would protect me. That as an insider, he'd shield me and I would feel as though I, too, belonged. Surely no Nazi monster would dare to touch me with someone like Geoffrey Bartholomew-Cooper at my side?

'Doreen, marry me,' he said quickly, almost as if he knew that my scepticism would return before long. 'Say you'll marry me – and then you can take as long as you like to answer my questions. We'll have all the time in the world.'

I nodded. I didn't trust myself to speak.

He smiled.

Trying to ignore the prickle of returning doubt and the fact that no trace of his thin smile was reflected in his eyes, I smiled back. He gave my hand another squeeze, then ordered coffee and the bill. Neither of us exchanged another word. Conversation didn't seem necessary any more. I sipped my coffee, suddenly conscious that my belt felt tight, and occupied my mind calculating how many calories I'd consumed.

'Ready?' he asked, interrupting my sums.

I nodded again, slightly irritated, and was aware, even then, how ridiculous it was for my head to be filled with calories when I'd just accepted an offer of marriage. As I stood up, I caught sight of the single rose on our table and it seemed to have blanched several shades paler than I'd noticed at the start of the meal. I bent towards it, worried that its stem was being strangled by the narrow neck of the vase. I was afraid that it would choke. It would suffocate and die . . .

'Come, Doreen,' Geoffrey was saying, holding out my good English coat. I managed to shake off my inexplicable panic about the flower, and allowed him to fold the coat round me and guide me to the door.

'Mademoiselle!'

The waiter had followed us.

'Mademoiselle – here. This is for you.'

I turned round. He was offering me the rose. The same pale pink rose. I smiled and accepted and ran my fingers carefully along the stem, feeling for the place where the vase had constricted it. There. A slight indentation. But – no. It wasn't as bad as I'd feared. Not imminently life-threatening, at any rate. If I watered the flower and kept it safe, it would survive. At least for a day or two. Three at the most. Surely that was about as much as a pretty flower could reasonably expect?

*

182

Never mind a day or two. The hardy little thing somehow eked out its life for more than a week. And the amazing thing was that once I'd stuck it in a tooth-mug, I didn't add water. Not after the first day. At first I forgot, then I deliberately withdrew sustenance. I'd stare at it callously, challenging it to shed its petals, to give up the ghost. But it defied me, it defied death. It mocked us both and held on and on.

And I suddenly thought of the oil lamp. You know, the miracle of Hannukah. The lamp in the ancient Jerusalem temple that was supposed to have burned for eight days on a single day's supply of oil. 'It was God,' I remembered my father Sam telling me. 'God made it happen. Just like that. He stepped in and changed the course of nature.'

How clever of him. How energetic. That, of course, must have been in the heady days before he'd grown tired and taken refuge in his dark corner. But surely he wasn't rousing himself on behalf of a useless and somewhat insipid pink rose? For some reason, the idea made me angry. I disliked the flower more intensely with each passing day. Weren't there more important matters with which God could be busying himself than this pointless exercise in floral resuscitation?

The rose died on day eight. I was relieved. Somehow, its endurance had paralysed me. Its audacious denial of reasonable expectations had made me most uncomfortable with my limpness, my compliance. Had I really agreed to marry a stranger called Geoffrey Bartholomew-Cooper? Did I truly believe there was no other way? While the flower bloomed, I had disturbing dreams of running free in green fields and plucking apples from laden trees and filling my mouth with the sweetest of cherries. Then it died.

'Good,' I said cruelly, collecting the fallen petals and stuffing them in the bin.

'Good,' said Geoffrey thoughtfully, when I told him that I'd come with him to meet his mother the following Saturday and we'd set the wedding date very soon after that. A small, private ceremony. A registry office affair.

'Good,' said Lou-Anne with patent insincerity when I told her of my plans. 'He *seems* very nice, Dor – a real gentleman. But one never really knows. I mean, what sort of family does he come from?'

'No connection with the Rothschilds,' I replied.

She frowned and became engrossed in her fingernails. I felt mean. That was below the belt – even as a means of getting even with Lou-Anne. 'I'm going back to Cape Town,' she announced.

'Oh.' What was there to say to that? 'Good.'

'Yes, it's probably for the best. It – um – occurred to me that if you wanted to carry on with the business after I've gone, you could take it over. You'll be able to get a work permit now – and I wouldn't charge you much. I'd only want to cover my expenses. After all, you've worked hard enough . . .'

'Oh?' What was the catch? 'I don't know, Lou-Anne. I'll have to think about it.'

'. . . Take your time. There's no rush. And, Dor, if you happen to be writing to your parents or anyone at home, d'you think you can spare the details about – Kevin. You know . . .'

I knew. I knew indeed. I studied her through half-closed lids but made no sign.

'. . . And I'll do the same about Geoffrey. I'll say nothing about his religion or anything like that.'

Now it was her turn to study me beneath hooded lids. I fervently wished I could tell her to go to hell, for I longed not to care about what my parents thought. But I did. I cared. I wasn't aware how much I cared until that moment.

'OK,' I said grudgingly. 'It's a deal.'

'And you'll carry on with Krafty Kooks?'

'I don't know. I think I'd like to. But I'll have to discuss it with Geoffrey.'

The vehemence with which Geoffrey opposed the idea of my continuing with the catering business should have been a

184

warning of things to come. We were on our way to visit his mother when I tentatively raised the subject.

'Never!' he exploded, clutching the steering wheel so that the car swerved alarmingly against the kerb. 'My *wife* serving meals to other men? Do you honestly imagine I could tolerate that?'

'But Geoffrey – it's mainly bar mitzvahs. Family lunches, that sort of thing . . .'

'No. I said *no*! Are you deaf? Can't you hear me? Anyway, there'll be no reason for you to work. My earnings are enough – more than enough – for the two of us to live well. Perfectly well. And if you're so keen on cooking – well, there'll be plenty of opportunity for you to do it for me.'

There was a brooding silence until he stopped the car in a narrow Chelsea street. Then he turned to me and placed a hand on each of my shoulders, forcing me to face him.

'Doreen, I'll take care of you. I promise,' he said, and the anger had disappeared from his voice. It had become kind of shaky and gruff. 'Sorry if I sounded cross. I was frightened – terribly frightened, for a moment – by the thought of us being married and you being away from me, serving – others. I want to keep you close to me so that I can touch you, look at you . . . do you understand?'

I nodded. He was staring at me, devouring me with his eyes. It was frightening, yet tantalizing. Never before had a person been so passionate about keeping me in sight. Never before had anyone seemed to care with such intensity. Part of me wanted to escape, to run for air. But another, stronger part was intrigued. Wouldn't it be wonderful to curl up and stay at his side, to belong to him, to be adored by him? To be kept safe?

'I won't work then – if that's what you want,' I said softly. 'Your mother . . .'

He abruptly withdrew his hands and turned to the window. What had I said to offend him this time?

'Why did you mention my mother?' he asked.

'No particular reason. I was just wondering whether she was expecting us.'

'I think so. I said we were coming.'

He returned his gaze to me. A frown had appeared on his forehead. He extended a hand to my chin, raised it quite sharply and studied my face. 'You could do with a touch more lipstick, Doreen,' he said after a while. 'My mother likes that sort of thing. Her name's Lulu, by the way. Lulu Cooper.'

We took to one another, me and Geoffrey's mum. I can't imagine why. We were as different as two people could possibly be. South African Jewish duckling latterly turned princess and Neo-Knightsbridge tart latterly turned respectable wife. Yes, Lulu had married an elderly stockbroker and finally settled down. And I was supposedly settling down with her son, so we had that in common anyway. But there was something else. Something deeper. Something we recognized in each other immediately Geoffrey ushered me forward in his proprietory way and carried out the formal introductions.

'Pleased to meet you,' she said.

We greeted one another with matching smiles that had been painted an almost identical shade of plum-red. What a coincidence. She noticed it too. I'm sure she did. And I'm almost certain she gave me a knowing look before turning to her son.

'Isn't she lovely, Geoffrey? Pity your new stepfather couldn't be here to meet her. He plays golf on a Saturday, you know.'

'Really.'

Geoffrey was clearly not interested in the habits of said stepfather. He drew me close to his side and made a great play of stroking my neck and tweaking my ear. I fidgeted uneasily. Never before had he openly demonstrated his affection. I'd imagined he wasn't the type. There was something unnatural about the way he was suddenly fondling me in front of his mother. Something exhibitionistic and deeply unpleasant. I tried to edge away.

'Well! How about a nice glass of rum, boys and girls?' said Lulu, who seemed to have observed my discomfort.

'Oh Mother,' said Geoffrey. 'Surely not at this time of day. You're the limit.'

'Same old Geoffrey. Prudish as ever. It's a celebration, isn't it? Your engagement! That calls for a drink, if anything does. You'll join me, won't you, Doreen?' She nudged me encouragingly. 'Come on.'

'All right – I'll have one. Shall we, Geoffrey?'

He shook his head disapprovingly, but I accepted Lulu's offering anyway. I believed I had found an ally and had the naïvety to imagine – how green could I have been? – that, with my mother-in-law on my side, things would turn out, if not perfectly, at least more or less all right. And that, I figured, was about as much as a pretty and dependent wife-to-be could anticipate.

No, I wasn't ambitious. Not clear-eyed Doreen. I believed I was tough and realistic, with no thoughts of exceeding reasonable expectations. After all, hadn't the resilient pink rose – despite its defiance – expired eventually?

As for the bunch of freesias that I carried on my wedding day – they didn't even survive the morning. Maybe the fast-wilting flowers were even more sceptical than I was about the future of our marriage.

'Congratulations,' enthused Lulu, when all had been signed and sealed. 'Now, Doreen, the thing to do is to toss your bouquet to the bridesmaid – and maybe she'll soon be as fortunate as you've been when it comes to finding a groom.'

'OK,' I shrugged, dismissing the note of irony I thought I'd heard in her voice, and aimed the blooms at the lucky lady – who happened (through lack of alternative availability) to be dearest Cousin Lou-Anne. She ducked out of the way.

'Oh – no thanks, Dor,' she said quickly.

I wondered if she shared with the flowers a premonition of

what lay ahead, but didn't have time to ask. Lou-Anne departed soon afterwards to catch her plane to Cape Town and the miserable freesias were dumped in a bin. Then Lulu and Ernst (Geoffrey's new stockbroker stepfather – a silent, dyspeptic man) hurried away to a last-minute yacht-launch in Southampton.

'Bye,' they called. 'Good luck. Good luck.'

We grinned and waved back wildly, a fine-looking couple let me tell you. The bride was statuesque in tailored cream linen that contrasted startlingly with her blazing red hair. The groom, imposing in his pin-striped suit and pukka-club-crested tie, was clearly a man to reckon with. There were a couple of jarring notes, admittedly. But these weren't significant enough to spoil the overall effect. The bride's shoes, for instance. Why on earth did she have to mar the elegance of her outfit with heavy German shoes? And the groom's eyes – why were they so restless, darting perpetually from his wife to the world?

But let's not be pernickety here. Unsuitable shoes, shifty eyes – small details in a picture so promising. Anyone catching sight of Mr and Mrs Geoffrey Bartholomew-Cooper as they made their newly wed way to their freshly decorated Kensington abode, would have been utterly convinced by their apparent compatibility, perfect respectability and general reassuring air of normality.

I was almost taken in myself.

In the beginning it was comforting, the sheer predictability of our existence. Geoffrey led his life as though it had been choreographed by a time-and-motion expert and I slipped into the routine with ease. It suited me well. I, too, was dependent on a carefully structured timetable. No surprises. No jolts to knock me off the tightrope on which I balanced my calorie intake on the one hand and my energy output on the other and kept any unsteadying feelings tightly in check. As far as total lack of spontaneity was concerned, we were an excellent match.

Every day started the same way. The same nutritionally sound breakfast of bran flakes, wholemeal toast and tea. The same maritally acceptable conversation – grumbles about the weather, the disordered condition of the country and the untidy state of the neighbourhood were invariably followed by Geoffrey's enquiry about my programme for the day.

'Where will you be going?' he would ask. 'Who are you planning to see?'

I would answer obligingly, perceiving nothing sinister in his desire to know my movements. Not in the beginning. He was my husband, after all. He was keeping me. He cared about my safety and well-being. That's what I convinced myself – at first. So I outlined projected plans for local shopping trips and forays into far-flung suburbs to find superior ethnic ingredients (the suppers I prepared were superb). And visits to hairdressers and expeditions to art galleries and the odd coach excursion to approved stately homes. He would nod as I named my destinations. 'Fine,' he'd say. 'Good.' He'd be particularly pleased when I announced that the day ahead would be devoted to my appearance. Leg waxing. Clothes shopping. Hair primping. That sort of thing. He would smile in his strange, reflective way. The smile that never extended to his eyes.

'I'll make sure I'm home promptly then, Doreen,' he would say.

Not that he was ever exactly late. Not Geoffrey. Most evenings, after our elegant and punctually served little suppers, we sat in companionable silence. Me watching telly, he watching me. I can't say it was unpleasant. It certainly had the edge on Gladys Street.

But when he said that he'd be home '*promptly*', I knew we were in for fun and games. Those nights, I dressed particularly carefully, well in time for his arrival, putting on – you guessed it – the tight black outfit I'd worn that day at the bank. And the frilly apron, of course. And loads of lipstick, just the way he liked it. And I'd bring him his supper and he'd stare at me in his spooky way and then, sometimes even before he had finished his pudding – well, then we'd do what he liked to call *it*.

God, he worked hard at *it*, did Geoffrey. Such dedication. Such seriousness. On the preordained evenings, he would arrive home with a plain brown bag containing props. Crotchless panties, cupless bras, diaphanous bits and bobs. Useless and, frankly, rather ugly items of apparel to which he had clearly devoted a great deal of time and thought. So, to please him, I'd put them on, take them off, twirl them above my head, pout alluringly, posture unashamedly. Whatever he wanted, whichever way he wanted it. Upside down or inside out, if necessary. What the hell. If it made him happy, I'd oblige. Anything for a peaceful life. It didn't bother me.

But nothing seemed to please my Geoffrey very much. After his huge anticipation and preparations that must have cost him most of the day (and a certain amount of interference with the efficiency of his trained legal mind), he always seemed deeply disappointed after he'd got down – or up, or on, or even in – to *it*. And, what's more, the mean sod didn't like me to be too actively enthusiastic either.

Once he included a box of peppermint creams in his bag of tools and I, in a creative flurry brought on by the proximity of a thousand lush calories and potent memories of the million and one peppermint creams I'd ever known and loved, threw myself into the role of temptress with abandon. I played the seductress, the irresistible vamp. The witch. Yes, the witch who had lured Hansel into her lair. 'Come into my house made of sweets – for soft creamy mints and other sexy treats,' I whispered throatily, striking a rather rude pose. 'If you fancy a taste of this or that . . .'

Suddenly I saw his face. He had backed away from me and was tight-lipped, narrow-eyed, trembling with anger.

'Stop that,' he said in an ominously low voice. A voice I'd never heard before. 'Stop that *immediately*.'

'What?' I asked, frightened and confused. 'But, Geoffrey, I was only . . .'

'Bitch!' He was bearing down on me now, almost foaming

at the mouth with fury. I recoiled, terrified. 'You've done this before, haven't you? You do it all the time. Everywhere. With anyone. You do, don't you? Well – don't you? Answer me. Answer me, bitch!'

'No, Geoffrey. Please . . .'

'Just like her. I knew it. I knew it. You're all the same. All the same . . .'

Then his anger left him as suddenly as it had come and he slumped on the bed in a defeated heap. I watched warily, not daring to approach him lest I fuel again that vicious rage.

'Geoffrey . . .?' I tried, after what I'd judged to be a safe period. He hadn't moved for several minutes and his shoulders heaved now and then. I believed he was weeping and wasn't frightened any more. Just sad for both of us. Sad and full of foreboding. 'Geoffrey – don't cry. I didn't mean to upset you. Truly, I didn't.'

He sat up, frowning. He blinked once or twice. Then he regarded me severely. 'Take those silly things off, Doreen,' he said, almost as though the thing hadn't happened. 'I think we ought to go downstairs and finish our supper.'

After that, I ceased taking any pleasure at all in Geoffrey's games of *it*. I stopped relying on his predictability and no longer felt safe in our ordered existence, our strictly structured daily routine. I remained within its parameters. I had to, for what alternative did I have? I outlined for him my daily programme and submitted to his demands. All of them. Meticulously. But instead of feeling cared for, I'd begun to feel trapped. Imprisoned. I'd started to chafe inside, something like the way my sturdy and comfortable-looking German shoes had revealed their true nature and suddenly began to rub and blister my feet.

But I stuck with my marriage the way I doggedly endured those treacherous shoes. Each morning, I gritted my teeth and squeezed them on, and wore them determinedly till the day had been done. And each evening, the huge relief of removing my shoes almost obliterated the unease that was growing inside me like a cancer. Almost. But I managed to ignore the niggling malignancy, telling myself that it was

191

something I'd have to live with. To endure. For hadn't my father taught me that a person could get used to anything?

He had indeed. It had been his lesson for life. But, as I discovered afterwards, he was proving a dismal failure when it came to adjusting to the absence of his daughter. Molly was beside herself. She had exhausted her culinary repertoire in vain.

'But it's *gefilte* fish, Sam. Your favourite. I made it specially. Hours I spent in the kitchen. Tell me – why aren't you eating? What's the matter?'

'I don't know. I don't seem to be able to taste anything these days. Maybe it's . . .'

'What?'

'Well – Dorinke. She's on my mind all the time. I can't stop thinking about her, worrying about her. Molly – do you think she's all right?'

'All right? *All right?* Sam, wasn't Lou-Anne telling us only on Sunday what a catch that husband of hers was? So – he's not a Rothschild. But, tell me, how many Rothschilds can there be in a single city? Anyway, between us, I still think there's something funny about the sound of that Kevin – even though, all credit to Lou-Anne, if one doesn't truly love a man, his position shouldn't mean a thing.'

She nudged the plate of food towards her husband. He demurred. She persisted.

'Didn't Lou-Anne keep saying, though, what a gentleman Doreen's Geoffrey was?' she continued. 'A proper English lawyer. Never mind a lawyer – a barrister. And didn't Doreen herself write only last week to say she was well and keeping herself busy? Didn't she, Sam? You're worrying for nothing. Always did when it came to that child. About the wrong things too. At least, with me, I did something about her. Took her in hand. You must admit that if not for her mother she'd still be a nothing. A fat little nobody. And just look at her today . . .'

'I miss her, Molly.'

'So? So – you miss her. But that's no reason for a person to go on a hunger strike. Look at you, Sam. Nothing left of you. And such a happy, healthy man you used to be. A pleasure to cook for. I would have thought that at our time of life, with our daughter settled and things not as bad as they could be, one way or another – I'd have imagined that we could do different things together, you and me. Learn to play bridge, maybe. Mathilda mentioned the other day there's a teacher . . .'

Sam put up with his pain as best he could. He'd had plenty of practice, after all. He forced down his food and followed Molly to bridge school and acquired a new set of jokes about bidding and ruffing and finding a fourth. 'Give me a big hand,' he'd say, when the cards were being dealt. But no one was amused. After his Dorinke had left, there was no one around who found him funny any more. Molly warned him time and again to hold back his quips.

'People,' she'd say with a look that left him in no doubt it was Mathilda to whom she was referring, '*people* have said you're a pain in the neck.'

'What can I do?' he would shrug as he counted his points. 'You know the old saying? Man thinks and God laughs. So – I'll get on with the thinking and leave the laughing to the Lord. Eh?'

'Enough thinking, Sam – open the bidding,' ordered Molly. She had taken to bridge like a matzo ball to chicken soup. The discipline suited her. The precision. The rules. 'And this time, watch my signals and listen to what I call. If you'd been more careful with the last hand, we'd have made a slam.'

'I'm trying, Molly,' he said pitifully. 'Can't you see I'm trying?'

Who could fail to see his effort? His strain as he laboured to smile and act normally while a tightening band of misery threatened to choke him to death? Molly saw. Of course she did. She watched him constantly, trying to ignore her fore-

193

boding and the oft-voiced presentiments of the ever-present Mathilda.

'Molly, believe me,' Mathilda would say in her darkest and most confidential voice. 'He doesn't look right, that husband of yours. Something's up. I don't know what it is, but you'd better keep an eye on him. A very close eye.'

So Molly watched Sam, while Geoffrey was watching me. Like a hawk. His breakfast interrogations had become more detailed, more searching. Sometimes he asked me the same question twice, trying to trap me into an error. In the evenings, he'd creep silently into the house and then surprise me in the kitchen, the bathroom, the bedroom. 'Who's here with you?' he'd demand. 'I know someone's here, Doreen. He'd better come out.'

'What do you mean, Geoffrey? Of course there isn't anyone here. I haven't seen a soul for days.'

I hadn't. Not even his mother, whom Geoffrey had decided was a 'bad influence' and not to be consorted with on any account.

'But Geoffrey,' I'd protested, 'I like your mother. Surely there's no harm in that . . .?'

'You don't know her. Haven't I said no, Doreen? No. No, no, *no*!'

'All right, all right. Calm down, Geoffrey. It doesn't matter. I'll never mention her again, if that's what you want.'

I tried to reason with him, but of what use was logic with a madman? Oh, I'd guessed some time before that my husband was insane. Profoundly and dangerously so. His kind of insanity lay hidden deep within a shell of bland normality. It was expressed as an obsessive jealousy that had its roots in something unspoken between him and his mother and had emerged as a mania directed at me. As far as the rest of the world was concerned, he remained an honourable gentleman, a respectable guardian of the law. Nobody else had the slightest clue or would ever have believed me if I'd blurted out what I knew.

'Geoffrey? Never!' they'd exclaim. 'Not Geoffrey Bartholomew-Cooper. Why – he's the sanest man in town.'

But I knew when I was beaten. I never said a word. Not to anyone. Each morning, I crushed my feet into their painful restraints and did all that was asked of me, and endured.

Not that I didn't have a choice in the matter. I wasn't a prisoner, after all. I could have left him, found a job, returned to South Africa. I could have kicked off my shoes and made for somewhere new. I was fit and young and beautiful. But I was mad too. As mad, in my own way, as my poor tormented husband.

I'd lost myself, you see. I'd squeezed Doreen Markowitz so tightly into those glad rags, her armour of glamour, that she'd become smaller and smaller and finally all but disappeared. She'd been snuffed into silence and was as good as dead. And the woman they called Mrs Bartholomew-Cooper, the lovely lady who nodded and smiled as she trod from supermarket to beauty shop and back home again, was an effigy. An empty shell. She was someone who needed to see her reflection in mirrors and her weight registered on scales as confirmation that she was real. She needed the agony of wearing too-tight shoes and the wary jealousy of her husband as proof of her existence.

Watching. Watching. Molly kept her eyes fixed on Sam and Geoffrey observed me. And I found out later that in the dark of each night in Gladys Street someone else was keeping vigil too. Rex Venter was on high alert.

Apparently, he'd heard nocturnal noises which had confirmed that the Mullers, who lived across the road, were illegally harbouring a black live-in maid and she – 'the effing harlot' – was receiving regular male visitors. Rex was outraged.

'I'll catch the buggers,' he swore to his wife. 'Who do they think they are – disturbing the peace of a white-by-night street? Trespassers. Law-breakers. Tramps. If they can't stay where they're meant to be, then they can bleddy-well rot in jail . . .'

'Ag, Rex – why don't you come to bed now? You can't sit at the window all night.'

'Can't I just? I'll stay here all night and every night until I catch them, the slippery bastards. They'd better not think they can mess around with me.'

But despite Rex Venter's watchfulness, regular and joyful episodes of intercourse continued to take place between the Mullers' errant maid and her various consorts. And in spite of Molly's keen eye and assiduous efforts in the kitchen, her husband's worrying restiveness remained.

And, although Geoffrey kept strict tabs on me and was convinced I was cheating, I dutifully (and painfully) toed the line. I answered his questions and obeyed his commands and remained on nodding terms with the elegant image I saw reflected in shop windows and watched the constancy of my weight on the scales.

But deep inside, a tiny germ of small scrunched-up Doreen was stirring and making kicking movements that were becoming increasingly difficult to ignore. Persistent and disturbing signs of life. Unspecific longings that gnawed at the edges of my dreams and eroded the symmetry of the pattern that defined my days. I tried to soldier on, and for a time I managed perfectly. Not even eagle-eyed Geoffrey noticed the inner turmoil that made me pause outside pastry shops and ruminate over the punchlines of half-remembered jokes. For quite a long while, the pressure intensified but nothing happened. I made sure that nothing showed.

Until, one day, on a pilgrimage to Islington in search of a particular variety of organic muesli that Geoffrey had requested, fate brought me face to face with a figure from the past . . .

*

'It's not – it can't be – surely not . . .? Doreen? Doreen Markowitz?'

I'd been rambling round the district in a trance. Dazedly, I had wandered through wholefood shops and antique emporia and woven between market stalls and been tempted, dangerously tempted, by the aroma of baking bread and frying chips and sugar candy. But I'd resisted. Struggled but resisted. And now, laden with parcels, I had been making my wifely way home, when I was startled by the sound of my name.

'What?' I frowned. 'Who . . .?'

Who indeed? It didn't take a moment for me to identify the blonde and beaded flower-child who was pulling excitedly at my sleeve as none other than my old enemy and *alter ego*. It was – who else? – Olivia Cook.

'Olivia!' I exclaimed and felt a violent surge of joy. Joy? At seeing Olivia? Well, yes – strangely enough. It was a rush of affection, a kind of nostalgia that bore little relation to the awful times I had spent in her company. Bloody ballet classes. That miserable hospital. How soppy could a person get? How damn desperate would be more to the point.

While I stood there gawking, she had grabbed my arm and was chattering excitedly. About how marvellous I was looking. Amazingly sophisticated and gloriously svelte and – different. Profoundly different to the Doreen she had known. More serious, in a way. Much more serious.

'Do you still make people laugh?' she asked. 'D'you remember how you used to have us all in stitches – even old Dinkie du Plessis? And as for poor Stanley Morris. Oh, Doreen – you were an absolute scream . . .'

'Was I?'

'Of course you were. You knew it too. I'll never forget your face the day Dinkie allowed you to be the witch. "Play it for the laughs, Doreen darling," she said. You did *that* all right. My God, it was hilarious.'

As she rattled on, we had somehow kept walking. Her hand had remained firmly fixed on my arm and I, saddened beyond words by her reminiscences, trotted meekly along at her side. Finally she stopped and released her grip.

'We're here,' she announced.

'Where? Olivia, it's late. I've got to get . . .'

'Nonsense. Not yet. Look, Doreen.'

With a flourish, she pointed to a sign that said, *The Crown and Goat – Public House. Home-Cooked Meals and Live Entertainment. Late Licence.*

'It's where I work in the evenings. Behind the bar, would you believe? And before you do anything, you're going to come in and join me for a drink. No – no objections. Now that I've bumped into you, I'm not going to let you simply disappear. Come – we *must* have a proper talk. I want to hear everything.'

The Crown and Goat had a peculiar smell. A musty sort of odour that I found oddly familiar and not unpleasant. Olivia and I sat in a corner and – I was going to say chewed the fat but that would have been a bit tactless, given our respective case histories. We talked, anyway. I slipped off my shoes and we talked and drank one lager, then another, until finally I sighed. 'I really *really* have to leave now,' I said. 'As it is, I'll be late. I don't know what I going to do about Geoffrey's supper.'

'Just tell him you got chatting to a very old friend,' she suggested. 'He'll understand.'

'Oh yeah?' I sighed again, inhaling the warm, smoky air with its strange bodily aroma and suddenly, crazily, thinking of blood, sweat and tears. Yes – I recognized the smell. It was my past. It had become my present. And, with the way things were going, it would be the future as well. There seemed little escape. 'Your heritage, Dorinke,' my father had said. How could I argue with that?

Reluctantly, I left the Crown and Goat and it was like being expelled from the warmth of a womb. The first time I'd tumbled into the world with an insatiable appetite and a head full of jokes. Now I stepped into the cold London fog

198

with aching feet and a headache and fear, terrible fear, about the reception I'd receive from Geoffrey. I was deeply unhappy and frightened as hell and sorely tempted to end things then and there. That evening, I was as close as I have ever been to throwing myself under a bus.

But, as it happened, London bus services had been suspended owing to industrial action. While this probably saved me from suicide, it delayed even further my return to our Kensington flat. When I finally arrived it was past ten o'clock and Geoffrey was white-faced and seething.

'And so?' he demanded as I came through the door. 'What do you have to say for yourself?'

I tried my best to placate him. Made contrite excuses. Poured him a drink. Fetched his slippers. Tousled his hair. I'd have done anything. Anything at all. And – hand it to him – after the initial explosion, he didn't mention my lateness again. Not a murmur. But even so, I knew perfectly well that Geoffrey had neither forgotten nor forgiven. That not for a minute had he believed the pathetic story I'd invented to explain my delay.

Which meant he'd be watching me even more closely in the days to come. I was certain about that. And I was equally certain that, despite my husband's vigilance, I would visit the Crown and Goat again. Soon. What did I have to lose?

That night was the first night of autumn in the southern hemisphere and the first night of spring in the north. Quite a chilly night, overall. Especially chilly for those on watch. For Molly, who lay awake and listened for pauses in Sam's breathing and feared the worst. For Rex Venter, who was poised for the sound of black footsteps in Gladys Street and hoped for the best. And for Geoffrey Bartholomew-Cooper, who shivered as he tortured himself with lurid imaginings of where his errant wife had been. He wanted to kill her.

12

My father once told me about the beggar who was employed by the elders of a town to watch for the arrival of the Messiah. He was placed at the top of a tower and told that when things started happening, he should raise the alarm. For years and years, he waited and watched and was paid a regular salary. Hardly big money, that's true. But, as he'd always say when asked about his job, at least it was steady work.

Steady work. Steady watching. Which was all very well as sheltered employment for a beggar, but it must have put a certain amount of pressure on the poor old Messiah. Being watched does that to one, as I'd been finding out. Sam knew about it too. So did the black trespassers in Gladys Street. It was the sort of pressure under which some would bend and some would break, and a few – very few – would slide away from scrutiny and make a dash for freedom. Me and the Messiah were the ones that got away.

At the time, though, I didn't think I would ever be free. And after the encounter with Olivia, I'd become desperate to escape. Something had changed after that meeting. I had briefly touched base again with the Dorinke who had laughed and guzzled her food and loved and suffered and been alive. And all of a sudden my role as the obedient and immaculate Mrs Geoffrey Bartholomew-Cooper had begun to be unbearable.

As soon as I could, I announced another wholefood

expedition to Islington – making sure it was on a day when Geoffrey had planned to work late.

'More muesli?' he asked suspiciously. 'I thought you'd stocked up with enough to last us for the next ten years.'

'Different *varieties*, Geoffrey,' I cooed. 'It's supposed to be very bad for one to stick to the same mixture. The metabolism needs all sorts of things . . .'

'Fine, fine,' he interrupted. He hated me to talk about bodily matters. Very squeamish, was Geoffrey. Which was why I persisted with even more specific references to the state of his internal organs. His heart. His kidneys. His bladder. The movement of his bowels . . .

'Enough,' he said, slamming down *The Times* and rising to his feet. 'Your conversation is quite inappropriate for the breakfast table, Doreen. I don't know what has come over you.'

He grabbed his coat and left, muttering something about the dinner he'd be having that night with the boys from the bank. 'At least the talk will be *civilized*,' he said, and slammed the door.

I smiled. Wasn't I clever – not only to have put paid to his interrogation but to provoke him into revealing his dinner arrangement? Wasn't I a rogue? I chuckled to myself as I tidied the flat and prepared to leave. It was a croaky and rather rusty chuckle, for it had been packed away in storage for quite a long while.

On the way to the Crown and Goat, I bought myself a pair of leather sandals, enormous hooped ear-rings and a double-thick chocolate malted shake. I kicked off my shoes and clipped on the ear-rings and downed the creamy sludge with the sort of gusto I'd repressed for years and years. It tasted heavenly.

'Oi – lady!' called the cafeteria attendant as I was on my way out. 'You've left your lace-ups under the table.'

'Keep them,' I said. 'Give them to charity or something. I don't need them any more.'

He shook his head, muttering something about 'the spoilt rich' as he retrieved the German shoes from the floor. I wasn't bothered. I trod the pavement in my comfortable new sandals and it felt like I was walking on air.

'You seem happier. More yourself, somehow,' observed Olivia later on. She'd been serving at the bar when I arrived and greeted me with the same enthusiasm she'd displayed the time before. Don't think I was entirely taken in by her affection – not cynical me. I knew from the start it was prompted by the same kind of loneliness and nostalgia that I was experiencing – but, what the hell. It suited us both.

'I believe I *am* happier,' I said, drawing up a stool. She handed me a drink.

'Nice ear-rings,' she remarked. 'Much more interesting than the little pearls you wore the other day. A bit big for your face, though . . .'

I nodded in agreement. 'I bought them especially large,' I said, 'I'm planning to grow into them.'

Until I'd said that, I hadn't known I was. The words had been spoken without conscious thought. But their utterance was a commitment and a relief.

'Cheers,' I said to Olivia, raising my glass.

She lifted hers in response.

'Cheers, Doreen. It's great to see you again. You aren't going to rush off so early this evening, I hope?'

'Well – I can't stay too long. Geoffrey will . . .'

'Oh, come on. there's a show later on. Stand-up comedy – tonight's a sort of try-out night. You know, people get up and do their thing, hoping to hit the big time. I must say, most of them tend to be bloody awful. But never mind – we'll have a laugh. Between us, though, Doreen – you could do a million times better than most of the comedians I see here.'

'Me?'

'Easily. I'll never forget the way you entertained us in the hospital – in the beginning. Before you lost all that weight. Remember?'

I was about to make some dismissive response, when

suddenly I pictured a darkened ward and a circle of tense faces. And the way the tension would dissolve into smiles and then laughter. Great tides of laughter, lapping beneath the swing-door into the cold white corridor where po-faced Nurse Peters lurked. And the sense of power that had run through me as, spotlit by the forty-watt bed-lamp, I'd cast a spell over my audience and watched the response. It had been magic. Absolute magic.

'Isn't it strange?' I said to Olivia. 'Until you mentioned it, I'd quite forgotten. It was almost as though I'd expelled it from my mind. I suppose my life's been very different since then . . .'

But now, having retrieved the lost memory, I couldn't let go of it. While Olivia served behind the bar (which she did with the same cool efficiency as she'd once executed *grands jetés* and near-fatal self-starvation), I was lost in a replay of the past. It had suddenly become luminously clear; a bright, moving picture of my growing up – so clear that I could almost smell and touch it. But then, at a point about half-way through the period in hospital, the picture seemed to waver and fade and finally disappeared. And out of the darkness, a small figure emerged. It was the pared-down version of new, improved Doreen. But she seemed so tiny and far away that it was as though I were squinting at her through the wrong end of a telescope. *Me* looking at *her*? Who was she? Wasn't she me?

I took an anxious sip of the lager Olivia had provided and wondered if I were having an identity crisis. But there wasn't time to pursue this disturbing possibility because, just then, someone announced the start of the show.

'Go and find a seat,' urged Olivia. 'I'll come and join you as soon as I can.'

I blinked against the brightness of the lights that beamed on to the small platform wedged into a corner of the pub. A microphone spat and hissed. 'One, two, three,' croaked a man who afterwards introduced himself as Pete MacGraw, the compère. It was hardly the Palladium.

Yet I watched, mesmerized. Not by the performers,

although I clapped enthusiastically and tried to laugh. It was the idea. The idea of me, Doreen, being up there and telling my tale. And it wasn't the faraway, miniature Doreen that I was imagining. Not the charming creature of my mother's dreams, but the original. Yup – fat Dorinke herself, as large as life. At the thought, I experienced a wonderful feeling of fullness. A sense that I was overflowing with stories and jokes and sadness and – I know it hardly sounds likely in a cynic like me – love. Maybe the last was inspired by my consumption that evening of three servings of chips, a triple-decker sandwich, two hot dogs and a wedge of apple pie.

'I don't know how you keep your weight down,' said Olivia admiringly, as I chased the last elusive chunk of apple round the plate and finally shoved it down the hatch.

'Don't worry your little head about it. At this rate, it won't stay down for long.'

'Oh.' She looked at me with a worried frown. 'You're not planning to . . .?'

'What?'

'Well – er – don't you think it would be a pity if you – you know. You're looking so glamorous and all that . . .'

I tweaked one of my huge ear-rings and gave her a wink. Exactly the sort of wink fat Dorinke might have directed at her diet doctor and charm school teacher and ballroom dance instructor. And her father. 'A born beauty,' I said wryly.

She smiled and nodded slowly. 'I think I get it,' she said – and I believed her. Of all the people I knew, who could understand better than Olivia Cook? After all, hadn't the pair of us been like light and shade, Castor and Pollux. Not to mention eggs and chips, bread and butter, gravy and mash, peaches and . . .

It was glorious. It was food. Real, solid food. I tucked into vast meals with the appetite of a football squad – when I wasn't tending my husband and home. It was The Mysterious Double Life of Doreen Bartholomew-Cooper: demure and well-organized wife on the one hand, slovenly glutton on the other. Prissy Mrs B-C and vulgar Miss D. I was probably on the edge of acute schizophrenia. A lesser mortal might have cracked under the strain.

Not me. I loved it. Thrived on it – in every possible way. Within weeks, my waistline had expanded beyond the limits of any elasticized garment I owned. In less than a month, I had gained two stone. After that, I went downhill all the way with the exhilaration of a child on a giant slide.

How I managed, God only knows. Not simply the weight increase – which was quite a triumph considering the budget under which I operated – but the day-to-day operation of this devious existence. The budget, admittedly, imposed a severe restriction on the variety and standard of my secret spreads. It also meant that Geoffrey had to make do with a meatless diet and other little household economies. But I told him it was good for him and presented the nut loaves and carrot casseroles and turnip rissoles with such flair that he didn't argue.

But he watched. And the harder he watched, the more elusive I became. You'd have thought that, instead of ballet and charm and the history of the Great Trek, I'd been schooled in the art of deception. Each penny I spent on food was accounted for in the housekeeping expenses. Talk about cooking the books. As for my absences – they were all carefully, convincingly explained. The muesli excuse was joined by the ethnic rug cover-up and the pineapple pretext. At last, when the purchase of household ornaments and exotic fruits threatened to unbalance the budget, I produced Olivia as my ultimate alibi. The old school friend I'd suddenly met and with whom I wanted to share memories of the past.

'So why don't you invite her here?' asked Geoffrey.

'Oh, I wouldn't want to do that. It'd be boring for you. And disruptive, too. I know how much you rely on the evenings to catch up on your work.'

He returned to his newspaper without another word. How easy, I thought. Why hadn't I told him the simple truth in the first place? Feeling a bit like a cat burglar who scales a twenty-foot building and then discovers that the front door's been open all the time, I poured out more tea. Geoffrey downed his cup silently and then left for work.

But his apparent docility didn't convince me that I was pulling the wool over his eyes. Not for a moment. He knew something was up. He wasn't blind.

'Aren't you becoming – well – slightly *larger* than you were?' he asked one evening. I could tell it had taken much effort to voice the question and suspected that he didn't want to acknowledge my burgeoning size. It probably terrified him.

'Funny – I was just thinking the same myself. Only the other day, I noticed that my skirt wouldn't close. A new skirt, too. D'you imagine it could be something glandular? A malfunctioning thyroid or over-demanding intestine? Actually, I thought I might be pregnant – until I remembered we don't do *it* any more. Haven't for ages. D'you know, the last time you came home with a bag of goodies was . . .'

'All right, Doreen. Shall we not discuss that? I'm not in the mood.'

He was never in the mood. For months now, he hadn't made a single move in that direction – not towards me, anyway. Once, when foraging through his briefcase for an odd fiver, I'd come upon a rather juicy selection of pictures and decided that old Geoff much preferred fantasy females to the real thing. He'd never been one for blood, sweat and tears.

That's most likely why I was failing him so distressingly. I was becoming real. My blood had begun to flow again, sweat was bursting through my pores, and the tears I'd once held back now made frequent and inelegant tracks through my daily application of mascara and paint. Geoffrey had paid a fair price for an obedient dolly-bird with lips just like his mother's and – to put it plainly – the guy had been sold a dud.

And, tell me, who likes to be ripped off? Certainly not Geoffrey. He loathed it. He'd begun to loathe me. I was even worse than his treacherous mother. Not only did I neglect him at night – I'd gone fat on him. And even when I cooked and cleaned entirely to his satisfaction, my size taunted him. He couldn't ignore it. Nor could he ignore my absences, which were becoming increasingly frequent. Only once did he try to talk to me about it.

'Listen, Doreen,' he hesitated, 'I think perhaps we ought to do something.'

'Do what? What about?'

'Your – er – size. People are beginning to talk. Don't you think you should go and see someone? I'm sure it can't be good for you. And, anyway, it *looks* so . . .'

'What? Ugly? Obscene? Geoffrey, I'm sorry. Truly I am. I know this fat person isn't the Doreen you married – but it's me. I don't really expect you to understand, but please accept that I can't do anything about it. This time, I truly can't.'

'You're talking nonsense, Doreen. *Can't*! What does that mean? And what if I insist? What if I say I won't tolerate living with a slob? What if I . . .'

I didn't hear the rest, for I'd left the room. My size was never mentioned again, but Geoffrey's vigilance, if anything, intensified. And it had shed not even the slightest measure of fond protectiveness. I sensed the calculated malice with which he had made up his mind to keep watching and bide his time and finally, when I'd been lulled into complacency, to strike. I ought to have been more frightened.

But I wasn't. Call me short-sighted or deluded or just stupid. I've no idea why I didn't fear the menacing gaze of my husband. Perhaps I was doped by the state of euphoria in which I floated from meal to meal and between my different worlds. My sense of danger could well have been blunted. Or maybe my response to his infuriating possessiveness was a compulsion to tease him to some sort of climax. To a punchline? To an ending? Who knows?

All I remember was that the days now brimmed with purpose and were pregnant with possibilities. Quite ridiculous, really, when all I was doing was stuffing myself with food and slipping out to a pub to indulge in harmless chatter with Olivia Cook and the locals. I hadn't even yet made it to the comedy platform.

I had toyed with the idea, off and on. I had watched countless performances and imagined myself up there and considered how differently I'd do it – how much sharper, wittier and more compelling I would be than almost everyone I'd witnessed. But dreaming about it was one thing – putting it to the test was quite another. And it wasn't until a balmy summer evening a few months later that I finally took the plunge.

I had bought myself a kaftan that day. An emerald and gold creation that glistened in the sunlight and set off to perfection the shade of my hair. I still dyed it red, by the way, because I believed it suited me. In fact, the bottled hair-colour was the sole feature of Designer Doreen that had lasted the course. For the rest, I was Fat Dorinke through and through – but a much more mature and self-assured version. Someone who sailed through the streets of Islington like an African queen.

'Evening all,' I sang out as I entered the Crown and Goat. I'd become a regular by then. Everyone's favourite fellow tippler, sympathetic listener and bon vivant. I was plied with food and drink, and much in demand for my ear and the punchiness of my tales. Nowhere before had I felt so appreciated.

'Doreen – good, you're here. We've been waiting for you,' said Olivia, hurrying from behind the bar to greet me at the door. 'There's a crisis. Pete's not coming. His car's broken down. We've got loads of performers, but no compère and so – well, it was me who suggested that you might . . .'

'What? Take Pete's place? Honestly, Olivia . . .'

'You'd do it perfectly, Doreen. I know you would – haven't I always said so? Just think – this could be a chance. An amazing opportunity. And Jim says he'll pay you a tenner.'

I said I'd think about it. But, in truth, there wasn't much

to consider. Fate had brought me Geoffrey and conjured back Olivia and was now pointing a peremptory finger to the brightly lit stage. It had been hard enough opposing my husband; I sure as hell didn't have the energy to pick a fight with fate. 'OK,' I agreed, with some reluctance. I wasn't being bashful. I was scared.

The pub was fuller than usual that night. The warm weather seemed to have enticed people out of their homes and the Crown and Goat bustled. The babble of *bonhomie* was undisturbed by my ascent on to the stage. It augmented, if anything. 'Good evening,' I tried through the crackling microphone. There was no response. I looked round helplessly. In my fond imaginings, I'd pictured attention and laughter and applause and wild success. Or modest success, at the very worst. I certainly hadn't counted on being totally ignored. This was dreadful. Humiliating. A nightmare. I cast a panic-stricken glance at Olivia, who seemed to be the only person watching me. She nodded and smiled.

And I was suddenly furious. Screw you, Olivia Cook, I thought. Little Goody Two-Shoes, getting me into this. Setting me up to make an idiot of myself, while you nod and smile like a bloody saint. As ever. No – nothing changes. Nothing ever changes.

I took a deep breath. Anger had expelled the panic and embarrassment. I put down the microphone and stepped forward. Then, drawing myself to my full majestic size, I cast a regal and reproving eye over my chattering subjects. There was a lull. 'Good evening,' I said in a voice that surprised me. It resonated commandingly without electronic aid. I hadn't known I could make this powerful sound – this boom that seemed to emanate from the depths of my belly. 'Good evening,' I repeated. There was silence now. I had gained their attention.

They remained silent while I turned round and pulled forward a large, straight-back chair. They watched me as I lowered myself into it, like Cleopatra on to her throne. When I smiled, they relaxed. The collective expulsion of breath was audible.

'That's better,' I said, drawing weary fingers through my hair. 'D'you know something? I'm supposed to warm you up. To tell you a few jokes so that you'll be in a nice receptive mood for the acts we've got lined up this evening. They're — well, I suppose one could say they're the main course. Which makes me the hors-d'oeuvre, so to speak. The savoury titbit. The salmon mousse. The melon surprise. The fresh asparagus . . .

'Now tell me,' I continued, rising to my feet and shaking my head as I surveyed the yards of kaftan that enfolded me, 'tell me if you've ever seen anyone who looks less like an asparagus?'

There was an uneasy pause. Then I winked and they laughed and I heard the sound with wonderment. It was a great wave that rippled through the pub. My first time. My first laugh. It was utterly amazing.

I didn't take the Crown and Goat by storm. They didn't rave and cheer and proclaim me an instant celebrity. Success didn't happen like that. That first night, they listened. They laughed, quite loudly but not too long. I introduced the star turns and they clapped. I prattled on a bit and they laughed again. They clapped a few times more. Then it ended.

'You were brilliant,' enthused Olivia afterwards.

'No I wasn't,' I said. 'But I can tell you something, Olivia — one of these days, I will be.'

It wasn't an idle boast. I knew this to be true. It had come to me, without a shadow of doubt, that I'd been born to entertain. The minute I had stood up and captured an audience's attention and evoked laughter, I'd been utterly certain that this was it. I'd come home.

Yes, home. The Crown and Goat's furnishings weren't what Mathilda would have called *opulent* and the cooking was, at best, somewhat bland. And — most disturbing of all — it was filled with strangers. Dangerous strangers. Strangers who could easily turn into evil monsters and burn and

210

plunder and kill. Hadn't Molly warned me against trusting strangers? Wouldn't she be warning me still?

'Be careful, Doreen,' I could hear her saying. 'Remember what we lost, me and your father. Look after yourself and stick to your own. It's safest that way, believe me.'

I suppose she had a point, if one considered the unfortunate turn my liaison with Geoffrey was taking. On the other hand, I'd taken a risk and gained an experience and he hadn't tried to harm me – yet. And in the mean time, I'd survived and had found a place to share meals and memories and laughter. Now tell me if that wasn't coming home?

'Heard the one about the baby who was born with a head full of jokes?' I asked a hushed, attentive crowd the next time I took the stage. No problem silencing them on this occasion. I took control as though I'd been doing it all my life. Well, I had – in a way. With complete assurance, I sat down and started to tell my story. The tale of small Dorinke, who longed for peanut butter. And fell flat on her butt at ballet classes. And was squeezed into a Stretch 'n' Grow bra. What else did I know? What else could I have talked about? I was perfectly aware that my audience was made up of alien strangers. But we shared something deeper than blood ties or friendship. You know – things like eating, fearing, laughing, getting by. I think they're sometimes lumped together and called the human condition. The punters lapped me up.

'More,' they cried. 'Give us more, Doreen! Go on – more!'

I smiled graciously. 'Another time,' I said.

'This time, you *were* brilliant,' Olivia exclaimed. 'Don't deny it. It's true.'

'Well,' I gave a modest shrug, 'I'm getting better.'

Geoffrey, meanwhile, was getting madder.

'I can't do anything about the way you've decided to stop taking care of your appearance,' he said, his voice fraught with suppressed rage. 'If you want to be – well, frankly, obese – then that's your decision. Although you can't honestly expect me to find you *attractive* like this. However,

211

obese or not, I think you owe it to me to keep me informed of your whereabouts.'

He seethed at me across the entrance hall into which I'd stepped a moment before. It was almost midnight. I had caught the last bus from Islington.

'Sorry, Geoffrey . . .' I began.

'Sorry? You're not sorry. You haven't been sorry for anything almost since our wedding day – since you started your career of lying, cheating on me . . .'

'Geoffrey – I have never, ever – not even once . . .'

But he had turned away and withdrawn abruptly to the sitting-room, muttering something about how I'd discover what being sorry really meant. Soon. Very soon. I followed him and tried to explain. My double life was becoming exhausting and I think I was tired enough to risk his wrath and come clean – to tell him about the pub, the comedy, the wonderful discovery I'd made. But he didn't give me a chance.

'Go away, Doreen,' he said.

I went. There'd been something ominous about the way he had dismissed me. Something final. I couldn't sleep that night. My stomach churned with apprehension.

I think it was probably around this time that Geoffrey acquired a gun.

Yes, my husband was undoubtedly getting madder. So was Rex Venter, who still kept up his nightly vigil in Gladys Street – yet remained unable to trap the trespassers who were supposedly monkeying with the Muller maid. It had become an obsession with him. He couldn't think about anything else. Even Farella (despite the nerve pills which took the edge off her emotions) was concerned about the outcome of her husband's growing fanaticism.

'Hey, Mrs Markowitz,' she called over the fence one morning.

Molly was shaking out a rug she considered too good for the heavy-handed ministrations of the *shikse*.

212

'Oh – good morning, Mrs Venter,' she responded. They'd been neighbours for twenty years, but had never reached first-name terms. Being a *mensch* was one thing, but a stranger remained a stranger. 'Isn't it a lovely day?'

'Lovely. Uh – Mrs Markowitz – have you perhaps heard anything about the goings-on across the road?'

'What goings-on? What do you mean?'

'The Mullers. That servant girl they have. Jennifer or whatever she's called – you must have seen her around. The little plumpish one with the short skirts and lots of make-up. Looks like a real whore, as my husband always says . . .'

'Oh, yes. And . . .?'

'D'you know they let her sleep there?'

'Who?'

'The Mullers. The girl. They keep her there overnight. As though they don't know damn well it's illegal. Hell's bells – the rest of us have to manage without servants for supper, so why can't they? They carry on as if the law had nothing to do with them. But not for long, Mrs Markowitz. Rex is determined to catch the girl. Not only her, but the bleddy boyfriends she has visiting her night after night. They've got it coming to them, I promise you.'

'How, Mrs Venter? What's your husband planning to do?'

'That's the thing, Mrs Markowitz. I must admit, it worries me a bit. You know Rex, when he gets a bee in his bonnet. Stubborn as hell. He's been watching out for weeks. Every night without fail. But he can't seem to spot them – either the girl or her friends. Now he's talking about bringing his brother Frikkie into it. You've met Frikkie, haven't you? The policeman in the family. And Rex says Frikkie will bring along his gun and . . . well, I've tried to persuade him that this is a quiet, respectable street and it would be better maybe for Frikkie to arrest the perpetrators without too much fuss. But, Mrs Markowitz, he won't listen. He's like a real bleddy lunatic.'

*

213

'She says he's like a lunatic,' Molly told Sam over supper that night. It was lamb chops and fried potatoes – a combination which had once set Sam's salivary juices into a frenzy. Now it lay almost untouched on his plate.

'Who?' he asked vaguely. 'What?'

'Sam – please. I'm trying to be patient, but it's not easy for me to sit here every day talking to the wall. If the wall would at least eat something . . .'

'Who's the lunatic, Mollinke?'

'I told you – that Rex Venter. The wife was saying today how he and that brother of his – the policeman – are waiting to catch the boys who come at night to visit the Muller girl. She mentioned that they've got a gun and – well, I think it could end badly, Sam. Even Mrs Venter was frightened.'

'A gun, Molly? Do you mean to say they're going to shoot a man for visiting his girlfriend?'

Sam sat up, all attention now. His eyes had widened and his breathing was short and sharp.

'Sam? Sam! What is it? Look – it's not a pleasant story, but I've heard worse. After all, they're only . . . Sam, it's not necessary to upset yourself over a thing like this. I can't understand you these days. You'd better go and see . . .'

'No, Molly. It's all right.'

He shook his head slowly and gave a mirthless laugh.

'It's just that it – heh heh – reminds me of the one about . . .'

What? What joke had come to Sam's poor troubled mind? Could it, by any chance, have been the old, old story about the black guy in the white suit who'd come whistling along the road to collect his girl for an afternoon of fun? He'd been happy, this fella. The sort of happy that makes some people who witness it – especially those who're feeling put-upon and mean and miserable – want to kill. And if there just happens to be a blood-thirsty mongrel conveniently at hand . . .

Was that the one my father remembered that evening?

214

I believe it was, although I didn't know for sure. I wasn't there, as he was so keenly aware. I was thousands of miles away, remembering my own stories. Sharing with strangers in a dark, smoky pub the things that had made me laugh and cry. Nothing in our family history seemed shameful or secret to me — except the tale of Patricia's Robert, who was felled by a dog called Rommel on his afternoon off.

It wasn't the story itself that stuck in my throat. Worse fates have befallen innocent people. Cruelties and barbarisms that make being chewed by a dog on a sunny Sunday afternoon seem rather pleasurable by comparison. No — it wasn't the actual event, upsetting as it was. It was what my father told me afterwards.

He'd implied that there was nothing, nothing at all, one could do about evil. That truth and goodness were as ephemeral and elusive as luck. That the only certainty in life was terror. My father taught me helplessness. It was a shameful lesson. An obscenity. A lesson I could never bear to repeat.

And so, when he heard about Rex Venter and his gun, did something stir in Sam Markowitz? Had he known all those years that he'd failed me? And when I flew away, so perfectly groomed in my good English suit and smart Italian shoes, did he think he'd lost me for good? He must have seen then how thoroughly I'd been schooled in pessimism and meek conformity, and he probably grieved (oh, how he must have grieved) for the Dorinke who seemed to have disappeared.

'Mollinke,' he said, 'we have to do something. We can't let this happen.'

'Do, Sam? What do you want us to do? Get into trouble? Huh? Is that what you want?'

'I don't know. All I know is that I can't stand around and watch someone . . .'

'And? So what are you suggesting? Don't you know what happens when one starts with people like the Venters? Haven't you always been the one to say we should live and let live? I don't understand what's happening to you these days, Sam. I think I'm going to make an appointment with that specialist Mathilda recommended. Enough's enough.'

'Molly, those animals are going to kill someone – in our street.'

'And you're going to stop them? Sam – come to bed. Don't look for trouble. Phone the police if you want to. Let them look after it.'

'It won't help. That Frikkie *is* the police.'

'So forget about it then. We're two old people. We've suffered enough. Try and put it out of your mind.'

'I wish I could, Molly. I wish I could.'

Fixation upon fixation – Molly on Sam, Sam on Rex, Rex on black trespassers. And Geoffrey on me. Like chains drawing tighter and tighter and tighter.

How strange, how decidedly weird, that fate should have made the links snap on exactly the same August night.

13

Geoffrey had decided to follow me to the pub. Stupidly, I hadn't predicted this possibility. I had watched his brooding anger growing and filling our Kensington flat like a thick black cloud, and known it would eventually have to burst. It was inevitable. But I'd somehow imagined he would challenge me on his own ground, on his own terms, and decided I was big enough to hold my own. After all, I weighed in at fifteen stone and was fighting fit and more than a match for any normal man. And Geoffrey was no Charles Atlas. But I hadn't counted on his trailing me. Nor, in my wildest dreams, had I imagined that my strait-laced husband would have stooped to the illegal acquisition of a gun.

Which shows the level of his desperation. And my blind idiocy. Our collusion in bringing matters to a screaming head. And our madness. Yes – ours. My hubris, my cruel provocation, my striding through the streets of London like an arrogant Colossus, had become a form of insanity almost as virulent as his.

I left a note on the hall table that fateful evening. If I'd been aware it would turn out to be the last message I would ever send to him, I might have scribbled something important and profound. Something about life and death and the hereafter. Something about the meaning of it all. Instead, I wrote: *Geoffrey – your dinner's in the oven.*

I had dug deep into the household budget to produce cottage pie. Cottage pie and *petits pois* with a pot of home-made gravy on the side, and lemon meringue for afterwards.

A jolly nice meal. Pity he never got round to eating it. If only I'd known, I would have scoffed it myself.

But who could have predicted the events in store that night?

Not I. And certainly not my mother.

While I was making my heedless way to the Crown and Goat, Molly, incensed, was berating Sam for his apathy. By sheer coincidence, she, too, had prepared cottage pie for his supper. Sam had picked at it listlessly.

'That's it. I've had it,' Molly pronounced, gathering plates with an angry clatter. 'I'm a very patient person. I don't ask a lot. The things I've put up with, God only knows. But, I'm telling you Sam – I've had enough.'

'Mollinke – calm down . . .'

'No. I've been calm. I've cooked for you till I'm blue in the face. Now it's time to call a spade a spade. You're a sick man, Sam, and tomorrow we're going to see the doctor.'

'All right, all right . . .'

'And in the mean time, since Reuven and Mathilda are coming over any minute for a game of bridge, you can do me one small favour. *Concentrate*. Just keep your mind on the cards. You've got no idea how embarrassing it is for me to keep having to make excuses for you.'

'I'll try, Molly.'

'Try! I hope it's harder than the way you've been trying to eat, trying not to worry about Doreen, trying to forget about the neighbours and their madness . . .'

'Ssh, ssh. You'll see, Molly. Tonight – God help me – I'll succeed.'

'Huh! Is that so? From your mouth to His ear. That's all I can say.'

Which was roughly what Rex Venter was saying next door.

'May God hear our prayers and grant us mercy and receive our thanks for the good things He has given us this day,' he

218

chanted in his pious grace-after-meals voice. The Venters regularly expressed their gratitude for heavenly blessings of one sort or another. These included bodily health and an abundance of food and the Divine Authority which had guided the Venters and their ancestors to their promised land. This Authority extended to the successful subjugation of the heathen masses and necessitated various rules and regulations to keep the savages in check. Separate Development and the Immorality Act and Group Areas and House Arrest were all God's will, swore the Venters. No arguments about it. They'd been ordained by the Lord.

'Amen,' said Rex.

'Amen,' chorused Farella and Frikkie and Babs.

'And so?' said Rex, stretching and yawning and rising to his feet.

'Ja – and so?' said his brother-in-law, patting the holster in which his revolver nestled. The gun was warmly embedded in Frikkie's spreading waist. 'So what time did you say those trespassing kaffirs would come calling?'

'Who knows? I can say one thing for sure, though – they're damn sneaky. We'll have to be on the ball. Tell you what, Frikkie-boy, why don't we take a few beers on to the stoep and watch out from there, hey? Sooner or later . . .'

'Rex, be careful man,' panicked Farella. 'Babs – I've been begging him not to get involved – with the gun and everything. Who knows what those blacks keep up their sleeves? Sometimes it's best to – '

'For Christ's sake, Farella – shut up, won't you? This is man's stuff. Why don't you girls go sit in the kitchen or something? We'll shout when we run out of beers.'

There was no shortage of beers in the well-stocked cellars of the Crown and Goat. Geoffrey ordered one when he'd finally made it into the pub's darkest corner. A pint of best bitter and a bag of dry roasted peanuts, they reported at his inquest. Not his usual sort of fare – but then, the guy must

219

have been worn out after shadowing me through the length of London. He needed sustenance to sharpen his aim.

Not that I'd been hard to follow. In my green and gold kaftan that billowed like an airship, I made my conspicuous way from train to bus and from street to street. My pit stops, admittedly, must have been somewhat erratic – various pastry shops and ice-cream parlours received enthusiastic patronage that day. But otherwise, Geoffrey had it easy.

He did it most capably, though. I have to admit it. Once or twice I felt a shiver. An unpleasant feeling that someone's eyes were upon me. But I dismissed it. Told myself it was August and the first chill of autumn was in the air – and that *naturally* people were watching me. Wasn't it inevitable with someone my size?

I shook off my unease and entered the pub, and people called out my name and I responded. And, in a moment, I'd forgotten entirely my prickle of misgiving and had melted into the dusky warmth.

'Remember – you're on tonight,' said Olivia, handing me a drink.

''Course I do. How long have I got? Gosh – the place seems busy, doesn't it? Looks like we'll get a nice big crowd.'

'It does,' she agreed. 'The show begins in about half an hour. By then, it'll probably be busier still.'

We both glanced round and nodded with satisfaction at the pleasing flurry. Neither of us noticed (why should we have?) the tall thin man sipping beer at a dark side table. Nor did we see (how could we have?) the small but deadly pistol on his lap.

Sam, meanwhile, failed to notice his wife's card signal. For a change.

'Haven't I told you a hundred times,' she raged, 'that when I play high-low it means you should come back a trump? You're impossible. He's impossible, Mathilda. D'you know, he promised – he swore to God – that he would try and concentrate tonight. And instead, what happens . . .'

'Molly!' Sam suddenly started, turning wide-eyed to the window. 'Molly – what's that?'

'What? Oh, Sam. Can you see, Mathilda, what did I say . . .?'

'The noise. I can hear something. Outside – from the Venters'.'

'What do you mean, noise? It's talking, that's all. Mr Venter and his brother-in-law are sitting on the balcony and having a chat.'

'A chat? Outside? But, Molly – it's August. It's rainy and cold – why would someone want to be out there on a night like this? Unless . . .'

'Sam – will you be quiet and deal. Please. Sorry, Mathilda. Sorry, Reuven. It's nothing . . .'

'But, Molly . . .'

'Listen – they're laughing now. Can you hear? Tell me, Sam – aren't two grown men allowed to sit in front of their own house and laugh?'

Of course they were. Men have always been allowed to laugh. Not women, though. Not from cave-dwelling times, when they had to be ever so earnestly admiring of the bison-catching capabilities of their respective partners. Not even in the Bible.

'D'you know something?' I asked in the world-weary conversational tone that would eventually become my comedy benchmark. 'There was only one recorded instance of attempted female laughter in the entire Old Testament. That was Sarah – Abraham's old lady – who was informed at age ninety that she was to have a child. Now was that, or was that not, a sick bloody joke?'

I leaned forward appealingly, palms up, running my eyes along the rows of pleasantly smiling faces. They were enjoying me. I was mellow on their approval.

'But d'you think God thought so, though? Do you? Oh, no – not on your life. Not Our Maker. He didn't think it was amusing at all – roared at Sarah for laughing. Wouldn't relent even after she'd composed herself and fearfully denied ever opening her mouth. "Nay," he thundered, "but thou *didst* laugh" . . .'

I shook my head at them sorrowfully, about to illustrate some further prejudices (both man- and God-made) against female comics, when suddenly, in a far corner, my eyes rested on someone who looked vaguely familiar.

I didn't recognize him for a moment. Never, I thought. Surely not? What would he have been doing here? This was out of context. Unreal. A figment of my imagination. It couldn't be happening. Not here? Surely not here . . .?

Then my attention was caught by the glint of metal. Something in his hand. A thing that seemed to be pointing in my direction. Oh my God. Geoffrey. The man I'd married. My husband. Yes, it was undeniably Geoffrey Bartholomew-Cooper, staring at me dementedly and holding a gun. Once I'd accepted his identity, I didn't doubt for an instant that he had come to assassinate me. That he was about to shoot me dead.

I sprang up, gasping. The audience, bewildered, started tittering, thinking this was part of my act. 'Excuse me,' I muttered, stepping back. Where did I think I was going to run? Who could fail to hit an elephant at point-blank range? I stopped and turned to face him, meeting his gaze as boldly as I could. A direct challenge was my only chance.

'Geoffrey?' I tried. 'Geoffrey, please don't . . .'

That was when I tripped. And fifteen-stone organisms don't simply trip and fall. They trip and crash. And most things beneath them go crashing too. Things like the floor of the Crown and Goat's flimsy wooden stage, into which major portions of my ample anatomy sank and disappeared with a resonant thud.

Everyone gasped. They had ceased giggling. They'd been stunned into silence. Shocked, uneasy silence which was suddenly broken by high-pitched peals of laughter. Hysterical laughter that emanated from a single source – the man with the gun. The only man in the world whose *schadenfreude* was stronger than his desire to kill.

Geoffrey was laughing at my unfortunate tumble. How he laughed. He laughed and laughed and laughed.

Rex and Frikkie had stopped laughing and Sam had noticed the lull.

'Four no trumps,' called Molly.

'No bid,' muttered Reuven.

'Sam,' said Molly in a dangerously low voice, 'Sam, I called four no trumps. What do you say to that?'

'Hmm?' said Sam, his head tilted to one side. He was straining to hear voices through the noise of the driving rain. His heart thudded with foreboding.

'Sam?' repeated his wife. 'Your bid, Sam . . .'

'Sshh!' He suddenly rose to his feet. 'Molly, can't you – can't you all of you – see that I'm listening? Will you please – be – *quiet*!'

Shaking their heads resignedly, Molly, Mathilda and Reuven put down their cards. 'Oh, my. I understand what you mean, Molly,' murmured Mathilda.

'Shush!' ordered Sam.

He strode to the window and pulled it open with more energy than he'd shown for months. An icy gust blew through the room. The rain drummed on to the sill.

'Sam – please,' pleaded Molly.

He ignored her. He remained immobile at the open window, watching and listening. The rain kept falling and the wind sighed and heaved. The street was in darkness, except for a torch that danced and flickered on the Venters' front step. It was the only sign of life.

Then all at once, through the rain-sounds, came the faraway crunch of footsteps on the gravel road. Approaching footsteps. The small light on the Venters' stoep suddenly erupted into a beam that veered drunkenly up and down the street and settled on a lone, dark shape.

'Hey, kaffir!' There was no mistaking Rex Venter's voice. It rose harshly above the splashing and gusting of the weather. 'Hey, kaffir,' he repeated. Sam cringed.

'No,' he said, burying his face in his hands. 'Oh, God – no . . .'

'Hey, kaffir – whatcha doing here, kaffir? Have you ever wanted to know what it feels like to have a bullet in your balls . . .?'

'No. Oh, no,' said Sam again. Then he drew a deep breath, dropped his hands from his face and raised his head. 'No. Not this time, Venter. This time you're not going to get away with it. I'll stop you. I'll show you – all of you – that a person doesn't have to stand by and watch things happen. That there's something that can be done . . .'

And before anyone had time to react, he had made for the door.

'Sam,' Molly called out after him. 'Somebody – stop him. He's crazy. He doesn't know what he's doing.'

'He's out of his mind,' people mumbled when Geoffrey's shrill laughter persisted without respite. 'Potty. Not all there. Completely off the wall . . .'

'He's *armed*,' I gasped from my prone position, with my posterior wedged (permanently, it seemed) into the gap on the stage. Olivia and the others were trying to help me up. 'It's – Geoffrey,' I managed. 'He's got a gun.'

'What?' asked Olivia, horrified. 'You mean . . .'

'Do something. Call the police. He's dangerous.'

His manic hilarity persisted. It was a cruel and terrifying sound, an unbearable mockery of the spontaneous and life-giving laughter that I had inspired night after night. The flip side of humour. I pressed my hands over my ears. 'Stop him,' I cried. 'Won't somebody please – please go and stop him?'

And magically it ceased. There was a sudden hush. Everyone was looking at Geoffrey. He was clutching his throat with one hand. The other had released its hold on the gun, which clattered to the ground. He was gasping and gesticulating wildly.

'He's having a fit,' said someone. 'He's mad, didn't I tell

224

you? Better get hold of the loony-bin men – they'll put him away.'

But although Geoffrey, as we know, was far from sane, it wasn't his madness that proved his ultimate undoing. It was a single dry-roasted peanut that had become lodged in his windpipe. Within seconds, he'd turned bluish. A moment later, he was unconscious. And in a couple of minutes he was dead.

'They'll kill him,' Molly had screamed when her husband had disappeared into the rain. 'Sam – come back. Don't be a fool. Mathilda – Reuven – what are we going to do?'

'Sam,' they had called together. 'Sam – where are you? Come back. Please – come inside . . .'

But there had been no response. The rain had continued and the only sign of life in the street had been the human shape that hovered in the channel of light cast by Frikkie Venter's torch. Molly had watched the dark figure with terrified fascination and had heard again Rex's menacing voice.

'What you doing here, kaffir? D'you think you can come into a white man's street and get away with it, cheeky bugger? D'you think . . .'

Then it had stopped. Another voice had cut in – one which Molly had never heard before.

'Leave him alone.'

Sam? Could that sound of authority have been produced by Sam?

'Let the man be, Rex. He's doing no harm.'

Yes. Sam all right. But how certain he'd sounded. How strong. Perhaps he had been right to intervene.

'Bugger off, Jew. Don't interfere. You'll have it coming to you next. Hey, kaffir – put your hands up . . .'

'Frikkie – quick – he's running away.'

'Who?'

'The bleddy kaffir. Quickly – shoot him in the leg . . .'

'No, you won't.'

225

'Get away, Jew – what did I tell you? Mind! Careful, you fool. You'll get hurt!'

Two gunshots reverberated through Gladys Street. The first bullet narrowly missed the retreating trespasser, who disappeared into the darkness. The second landed inches away from Sam Markowitz's heart. He was lucky to be alive.

Death by misadventure. That was the verdict on the sudden passing of my husband.

Misadventure. Bad luck. A demise due to accident without crime or negligence. No one's fault – so they told me, again and again.

And yet, when I'd finally been freed from the floorboards and made it to Geoffrey's side, I felt a deep wave of guilt and pity and the most terrible sense of waste. It hadn't been me who had made him mad – yet I'd fed off his madness. I'd grown fat at his expense. I'd known almost from the start that it would be him or me – and I'd made damn sure it was me. And now, seeing his thin and lifeless body, I regretted my ruthlessness and asked myself if there mightn't have been another way. A more compassionate way. A way that might have spared us both.

But there wasn't much time to mourn for Geoffrey. Only the couple of hours it took to call an ambulance and clear the pub and have him declared well and truly dead, and for Olivia to accompany me in a taxi to Kensington. As we entered the flat, the telephone was ringing.

It was my mother.

'Doreen?' she said. 'Doreen – something terrible has happened. Oh, Doreen, I have awful news . . .'

14

I laughed when my mother told me what had happened. I
made a horrible noise, gasping in mouthfuls of air and
expelling them with the short spasmodic contractions that
physiologists have dubbed 'inspiration-expiration microcy-
cles'. They sounded like sobs.

Tears fell too. They made a damp patch all down the front
of my green and gold kaftan. I sobbed with laughter over the
comic perversity of fate, and wept mirthfully as I saw how
even the most extravagant and far-fetched jokes failed to
reach the heights of implausibility attained by real life.

'It reminds me,' I said to Molly between paroxysms, 'it
reminds me of the one about the woman whose husband –
died – laughing . . .'

'What?' she asked, her voice crackling along the transcon-
tinental line. 'What are you talking about, Doreen? Surely
it's no time to make jokes?'

'Oh, Mom,' I said, harnessing my hilarity, 'it's the only
time. Daddy would understand. I think he always did.'

Then I told her about Geoffrey.

'I'm sorry,' she said, and she sounded as though she meant
it. 'What a terrible thing. I feel sorry for – both of you.'

No recriminations. No blame. What had happened to my
mother?

'Do you know why he did it?' she asked.

'Who? Geoffrey?'

'No – your father. Sam.'

There was silence for a moment. The line cracked and
hissed.

'Yes,' I said. Of course I did. I had known immediately.
'What do the doctors say? Will he be all right?'

'They don't know. They can't tell yet. He's still in intensive
care. All they say is that it's a real miracle he got away with
his life. Doreen? Doreen – are you there?'

'Yes.' I wanted to laugh again, to rejoice over Sam's
miracle. I wanted to cry, to cry for us all.

'Doreen – he's asking for you. I thought, perhaps . . .'

'I'll come. Tell him I'll be there. I'll get there as soon as I
can.'

But first there was Geoffrey's funeral. The clergyman who
officiated spoke sonorously of the tragic waste of a life that
had been full of promise. He referred in dulcet tones to the
lovely, grieving young widow and everyone stared at me in
voluminous black. Row upon row of grey-suited gentlemen
with wives in large hats and the latest autumn styles. They
hadn't heard about the weapon that had almost made
Geoffrey a murderer nor the manic laughter that had
hastened his end. Only about the peanut. The guilty dry-
roasted peanut that stopped Geoffrey's breath.

'*Media vita in morte sumus,*' pronounced the clergyman.
'In the midst of life we are in death.'

Too true, I thought, thinking of my father's near-miss.
And the bullet that had been meant for me. And the mortal
dangers of everyday existence. Electrocution. Asphyxiation.
Lightning, drowning and dropping off cliffs.

Then I thought of the miracle of survival. That here I was,
alive and well, despite all the efforts of Nazi monsters and a
manic killer and various near-misses with runaway vehicles
and vertical drops.

'We offer you our sincere condolences,' effused the clergyman. If he'd been Jewish, he'd have wished me long life. I
nodded anyway, and glanced across the aisle at Lulu Cooper.
My fellow mourner. My fellow survivor.

'Long life,' I mouthed to her. She nodded, and if it

hadn't been so sombre an occasion, I'm sure she'd have winked.

'I'm leaving for Cape Town this evening to see my father,' I told her after Geoffrey had been settled into his grave. She looked sad. Her lipstick had mostly worn off but, even so, it was the brightest part of her wan face. 'He's been in an accident. Caught in cross-fire or something. They say he's gravely ill.'

'I'm sorry,' she said. 'I'm sorry about – everything.'

I nodded. 'I'll call you when I get back.'

'You're coming back?' she asked.

'Of course. You know what they say – the show must go on.'

When I boarded the Boeing that was to deliver me back to Cape Town, I was convinced it was a much smaller model than the one that had carried me away. But no. The plane was identical. It was I who'd expanded. It struck me then how much larger I had grown.

'We've left the seat adjoining yours vacant, madam – we thought you might need it,' pointed out the air hostess. 'You're lucky the plane isn't full.'

Was this the same primped and painted person who had served me soggy breadrolls and advice about swelling feet on the way out? I remembered hating her for her peachy skin and baby-blue eyes and vapid innocence. Now I pictured her as a plastic princess entombed in her sky-palace, smiling forever above the clouds while, down below, people got older and wiser and fatter. I decided that, on the whole, I preferred being one of the people.

'Yes, I *am* fortunate,' I said, spreading out luxuriously and taking off my shoes. A frown creased her forehead. She clearly thought I was having her on. That someone so enormous had no right to feel lucky. She bared her teeth distrustfully and went mincing down the aisle.

'Hey, miss,' I wanted to call after her. 'Fat and fortunate is nothing. I've just lost my husband and am on my way to

229

the bedside of my gravely ill father, and *still* I feel lucky. How about that?'

She'd have called me mad. Maybe I was. I extracted from the seat pocket in front of me a leaflet labelled *Duty Free* and it suddenly occurred to me that maybe that's what I was. Not especially lucky and not particularly insane, but liberated from the stifling and sacrificial forms and functions that families call duty.

'Would you please try and fasten your seat belt,' said the air hostess, passing me again on her way to the front of the plane, where she was about to mime the emergency procedures. 'It's for your own safety, you know.'

I nodded pleasantly and fumbled with the clasp. I supposed I owed it to myself to take certain bodily precautions. There was the obligation to oneself and one's mother and one's father and . . . oh, drat it. Only things like scent and cigarettes were ever truly 'duty free'.

Molly was waiting to greet me at Cape Town airport. I spotted her as soon as I entered the Arrivals Lounge. She hadn't changed.

'Doreen?' she said, looking rather shocked. I'd certainly changed.

'Mom?' I hesitated.

She stepped back and surveyed me. She hadn't known about my regression to obesity. The daughter she had sent out into the world had been her elegant creation. I had sabotaged her life's work. I'd ruined her dream. As she silently took this in, I stood there remembering the tight-lipped disapproval that had shadowed my childhood. And, despite my resolve to be strong and calm, I felt my stomach knotting and sweat breaking out through every pore. I watched for the stiffening of her mouth and was nauseous with fear.

'And so?' I asked. I couldn't help it. I desperately wanted to know. 'What do you think?'

'What do I think?' she repeated, shrugging. Then she

230

looked up at my face and I saw there was a resigned smile on hers. A smile tinged with – I'm almost sure I detected it – a hint of relief. I nodded, quite dizzy with my own relief. 'Well, Doreen,' she said, 'I wouldn't choose it for myself. But if this is the way you want to look, then who am I to argue? There are more important things in life . . .'

She told me about my father.

'He'll be very glad you've come, Doreen.'

'But – how is he? Have the doctors said anything more?'

'He's out of danger, thank God. But it's going to be a long business. A long and painful business. They say he'll get better, though. Eventually.'

We didn't say much after that. I collected my luggage and we took a taxi home. On the way, she asked me about Geoffrey. I tried to explain what had happened but it was clear she didn't understand. I knew she never would. Somehow, it didn't seem to matter.

Gladys Street had changed even less than my mother. At least she'd acquired a new hair-colour (flintstone with a hint of amber) and a certain acceptance of the vagaries of fate. The street, however, looked as unfriendly as ever. It was still and silent under a leaden sky.

'What happened to the Venters?' I asked, as the taxi slowed down.

'The Venters? What should happen to the Venters?'

I paid the driver and extracted my suitcases and looked vengefully at the house next door to ours. Its front lawn had been crew-cut and flowers bloomed up the path. A net curtain rustled.

'Do you really want to know what I think should happen to the Venters?' I asked, following my mother to the door. But before I could begin to enumerate the catalogue of disasters that I wished for our neighbours, she had preceded me inside. The telephone was ringing.

'Oh – hel*lo*, Mathilda,' I heard her say. 'Yes – she's here. Looking – well – not too bad, under the circumstances. You know – tired and a bit – er – heavier, but very cheerful, considering. Sam? Oh, yes – he'll be thrilled to see her. It will

231

give him a tremendous boost – you know how he's been going on about his Dorinke . . .'

I smiled to myself as I wandered into the kitchen. Yes, I'd come home.

'Morning, madam.'

'Oh – hi. How do you do? I'm Doreen. I've just – arrived.'

It was a new occupant. A new face, who announced herself as Theresa. She was wearing the same threadbare pink overall and was surrounded by the familiar cupboards and appliances and tiled walls. They were shabbier and smaller than I remembered them, but they'd remained unchanged. On the window-sill stood a dusty brown bottle that I thought I recognized from the past. Even that seemed not to have altered. I reached out to examine it.

'That's mine, madam,' said Theresa.

'Oh – I'm sorry.'

'It's for my stomach. The chemist gave it to me.'

'I see,' I said, glancing at the label. It said *Extra-Strong Laxatives*. Ah, well. The tablets looked the same, but they weren't known as Native Aperients any more. Was that progress? Could it be that merely calling something by a different name was a significant sign of change? I didn't have time to pursue the insight, for Molly was calling me.

'Doreen,' she was saying, 'Theresa's prepared some fish for our lunch. Come and sit down. Afterwards, we'll go and see your father.'

It was strange sharing a meal with my mother. We'd never done that before, just me and her. We both looked at Sam's empty chair and then glanced at one another and couldn't think what to say. If I'd been able to, I'd have told one of his jokes as a mark of respect. But my mind was a blank.

'So, the Venters aren't sorry?' I said at last.

'Sorry? What do you mean, sorry? Sorry for what?'

'Oh, Mom. For you. For Dad. For the whole damn thing . . .'

'Don't be silly, Doreen. People like that aren't sorry. They

232

blame your father – for getting in the way. For interfering with the course of justice, I think they call it. Do you know, they're thinking of charging him. After he's recovered, of course.'

'*Charging* him? I don't understand . . .'

'There's a lot one doesn't understand about people . . . about the law. I've learnt that in my life. But, I must say, she's different. Mrs Venter.'

'Oh? Really?'

'Yes – she was here the very next day with a cake for me. One couldn't eat it, of course. Her baking is terrible. I had to give the cake to Theresa. But it was nice of her. Didn't I always tell you – '

'Of course, of course – that Mrs Venter was a *mensch*,' I interrupted. 'You did indeed, Mom. I've never forgotten it.' She didn't seem to notice the irony in my voice.

'Ah, well,' I said after I'd finished my fish. 'I think it would be only right for us to reciprocate Mrs Venter's friendliness. Don't you?'

'How? What do you mean?'

'I don't know. Perhaps take them a little something as well, just to show there are no hard feelings. Something they'd all enjoy – and maybe even share with the brother and sister-in-law. Haven't they always said how they just love Jewish food?'

'Oh, yes. Everyone says *that*. But – well – I don't really know, Doreen. With your father in hospital, who's got time for cooking at the moment? I was telling Theresa only today how exhausted . . .'

'Don't worry about a thing. I'll do it. Lou-Anne must have told you what a good cook I am. I'd like to share my skill with the Venters. Tonight, I'll prepare them something they'll never forget.'

'Doreen, I don't understand you . . .'

She never had. My father, on the other hand, understood immediately.

233

'Dorinke,' he said, his eyes moistening. 'Dorinke – you look like your old self. I'm so glad you came.'

'Oh, Dad.' I knelt beside the bed to which he was tethered by at least twenty tubes attached to various parts of his body. A heart monitor bleeped behind him. 'I believe you're going to be all right.'

'So they say.' His voice was weak. My mother had told me how defiantly it had rung the night he'd been shot. I wondered if it would ever resound that way again.

'Come, Doreen,' said my mother. 'We mustn't tire him. We'll be back tomorrow, Sam. Have a good rest.'

I squeezed his hand.

'You saved a life, Dad,' I said. 'Wasn't it written somewhere that if anyone saves a single soul, it's as if he had saved the whole world?'

He smiled. 'That's a good one,' he said.

That evening, I made chicken soup. Chicken soup and kneidlach, stuffed with a filling made of egg yolk, chicken fat, cinnamon, sugar and the crushed contents of Theresa's stomach pills. I promised to replace the bottle the following day.

'The Venters will *adore* this,' I said to Molly, after I'd put the final touches to the soup. A dash of salt. A sprinkle of pepper. A hint of parsley. A touch of rogue garlic to disguise any untoward smell.

'I hope so,' she said, slightly doubtfully. 'If I'd been you, though, I'd have saved my energy to cook for your father. He's going to need a lot of building up when he gets out of hospital.'

'Never mind about that now. We'll feed him plenty. In the mean time, though, we must sort things out with the neighbours.'

'If you say so. But I don't think you'd better go in tonight. It's past ten – they're usually asleep by now.'

'Fine. I'll take it over tomorrow. All the more time for it to mature.'

*

The aroma of chicken soup had seeped to my room when I drifted off to sleep a few hours later. I dreamt of a great vat of the stuff, bubbling and boiling like witch's brew. I was stirring the mixture, watching it thicken and increase satisfyingly in potency, when suddenly I smelt burning.

In my dream, I heard a crackling sound coming from outside and went to the window and saw that the Venters were having a braai. Rex, Farella, Frikkie, Babs and Bee were barbecuing long coils of boerewors. Rommel was panting and wagging his tail.

'Hey – Doreen,' called Mrs Venter, noticing me at the window. 'Come and join us, man. Look at all this boerewors we've got. Come and have some.'

As she talked, I noticed that flames had leapt out of the barbecue and were spreading along the grass. They were getting bigger and bigger. Clouds of black smoke were drifting upwards. I was choking on it, yet the Venters continued eating in blissful oblivion.

'Come on, Doreen,' Mrs Venter called again. 'Don't be unfriendly. Come and eat with your neighbours.'

'Watch out,' I shouted. The Venters would soon be engulfed by flames. 'Watch out . . .'

I started coughing and woke with a start. My room was filled with smoke.

'Mom – *Mom!*' I called, almost falling out of bed. I rushed to the window and saw flames flickering next door.

'The Venters' house,' I screamed, running down the passage. 'I think it's on fire.'

It wasn't a big fire. Enough, though, to destroy the garage and its contents, to ruin the immaculate garden, and to inflict a fair amount of damage on the furnishings and Mrs Venter's fragile nerves.

No one ever discovered the cause of the conflagration, but the Venters ended up blaming the garden boy, who tended to throw his fag-ends into the compost heap. I knew better, though. I put it firmly down to the Lord.

After all, hadn't floods and flames always been his traditional, tried and tested means of showing his presence and wreaking his revenge? This time, it probably had an additional purpose: it was a sign to tell me that the doctored kneidel soup would not be necessary. And, most importantly of all, I saw it as a message to my father.

I destroyed the soup and went to visit Sam and told him what had happened.

'Do you remember, Dad, that I asked you once if you believed in God?'

He nodded.

'Well, I think we can safely take it that whatever happened between the two of you is in the past. He now believes in you.'

A few days later, I was in the air again. Strapped into my double seat, I soared high above the Peninsula and toasted the miracle of flight with a miniature Scotch. Wasn't it amazing that a person my size could be carried so high?

I deliberately ignored the safety precautions. Who needed to be reminded that the system could fail? Instead, I glanced at my complimentary copy of the *Cape Times* and decided that there was nothing like being up in the clouds for feeling removed from the strife and struggle and miseries of the world. Up in the clouds or dead.

I read about violence in the streets and starvation in the tropics and the sudden appearance of a new disease called Aids. There were pieces about tidal waves and terrorist attacks, cyclones and soccer hooligans – and a twice-born millionaire called Arnold Gleeson, who claimed to have discovered the secret of eternal youth.

'Arnold Gleeson?' I exclaimed aloud. My fellow passengers looked at me curiously. The last I'd heard of my erstwhile diet doctor was his conviction on charges of public indecency. Whatever his shortcomings in the sphere of ever-after

236

juvenility, I had to hand it to him – he knew a thing or two about human resilience.

So did Arlene Carter, Minerva Watson and Dinkie du Plessis. I discovered over the next few months that Arlene, having been discharged with a warning after her naked revels along Adderly Street, had taken to nudity with a passion. She had founded a select naturalist club at Clifton Beach and had applied for a permit to make it multi-racial.

Minerva hadn't waited for a permit to legalize her position – which remained, by and large, horizontal. She had abandoned poor Prosper, after years of dissatisfaction, and taken up residence with a trumpeter of mixed parentage. They said they were ecstatic.

Prosper, on the other hand, hadn't quite reached that level of bliss. But he remained optimistic. All he needed were another few decades in deep meditation and daily communion with his maharishi, and he was sure he would attain enlightenment.

Enlightenment had somehow bypassed Dinkie du Plessis. Instead, New Ageism had arrived to enhance her old age. Dinkie wasn't quite sure what that entailed, since her mind was often befuddled with the effects of too much brandy and creeping senility. As she sniffed around in increasing bemusement, she sometimes wondered whether her nose for the *Zeitgeist* was destined to outlast all her other senses. Could it be that the spirit of the times would precede her to her grave?

If so, it would leave something of a gap in the world.

Cousin Norman, for instance, was already finding himself in dire need of a cause. Politics had landed him in jail, mysticism had led to drug addiction and New Age asceticism confused him. Finally, he'd engaged himself to a nice girl called Gwenda and was disturbingly relieved to be sinking into suburbia. His capitulation terrified him.

Lou-Anne, on the other hand, would have given anything for a Kev in the suburbs to call her own. She wasn't wearing well, though, and her various foiled marital attempts had wrought havoc to her sex appeal. She had almost decided to abandon the search for a mate in favour of feminism, but wasn't sure how to go about it.

As for me – I returned to London and picked up the threads of my life. Perhaps it was fitting that Lulu Cooper became the instrument of my success. It was she who brought the theatrical agent to see me perform at the Crown and Goat, and it was he who proposed me for the comedy series that made my name.

You probably know the rest – including all the trivia, true and false, that the Sunday supplements like to print about the lives of the famous. What I eat for breakfast, how I do my hair, where I buy my clothes, whom I go to bed with. In these days of political correctness, they don't call me fat. Instead, they say I'm 'nutritionally challenged'. I like that. It makes me sound less greedy and far more interesting.

But who cares what they say? It's the comedy that counts, in the end. The jokes. The punchlines. The . . .

By the way, have you heard about Stein, the tailor, who went to Italy and managed an audience with the Pope?

'And so?' asked his partner when he got back. 'What did you think?'

'Thirty-nine short.'

I must remember to tell that one to my father.